Edward Miner Gallaudet

Life of Thomas Hopkins Gallaudet

Edward Miner Gallaudet

Life of Thomas Hopkins Gallaudet

ISBN/EAN: 9783337333393

Printed in Europe, USA, Canada, Australia, Japan

Cover: Foto ©Raphael Reischuk / pixelio.de

More available books at **www.hansebooks.com**

LIFE OF

Thomas Hopkins Gallaudet

FOUNDER OF DEAF-MUTE INSTRUCTION IN AMERICA.

BY HIS SON
EDWARD MINER GALLAUDET

NEW YORK
HENRY HOLT AND COMPANY
1888.

PREFACE.

On the one hundredth anniversary of Dr. Gallau-det's birth, this record of his life is completed and offered to the deaf of America, and their friends, with an assurance of their friendly interest in its publication.

The writer ventures to hope, also, that to pro-moters of education and benevolent effort, gener-ally, the volume will be welcome.

A word of explanation is due for an omission which may be noticed by certain readers.

The Hartford School for the Deaf has in its cor-porate and popular name the word "asylum."

Whatever may be said in justification of the use of this term in earlier years, it is now generally condemned as altogether out of place when applied to establishments designed solely for educational purposes. Many institutions for the deaf have dropped it from their official titles as inappropriate and misleading. No schools organized within the last thirty years make use of it. It has been thought best, therefore, in the interest of a most reasonable reform, to omit it from the following pages.

The portrait which serves as a frontispiece is

taken from an oil painting made by the late George F. Wright, of Hartford, a short time after Dr. Gallaudet's death.

Mr. Wright's intimacy with Dr. Gallaudet had been so close and so long extended that he was able to produce a likeness much more characteristic and satisfactory; in the estimation of the family, than any other; not excepting the daguerreotype from which all of the existing prints and photographs have been copied.

NATIONAL DEAF-MUTE COLLEGE,

KENDALL GREEN, NEAR WASHINGTON, D. C.

December 10th, 1887.

CONTENTS.

LIFE OF

THOMAS HOPKINS GALLAUDET.

CHAPTER I.

1556—1685—1787—1805.

Ancestry — Parentage — Childhood — Family Environment —
School and College Life.

IN Thomas Hopkins Gallaudet were combined, by inheritance, more or less of the
canny Scot, the persistent Briton, the vivacious Frank and the graceful Italian. These
elements were harmonized and unified by the
fire of that devoted and self-sacrificing spirit
which has made the term Huguenot noble in
history.

Tracing the ancestry of the subject of this
biography, we go back, first, to Joshua Gallaudet, who lived at Mauzé, a village about
twenty miles east of La Rochelle, France, at
the time of the Revocation of the Edict of
Nantes, 1685.

Very little can be said, on authority, as to the origin of the Gallaudet family. The name, in the spelling of which no change has taken place, seems to be rather Latin than French in its composition. A coat of arms, brought by the family from France, has as its motto :—

UT QUIESCAS LABORA.

The wife of Joshua Gallaudet was Margaret Prioleau. Their son, Peter Elisha, spoken of as a physician, fled from France, not long after the Revocation, and settled very early in the last century at New Rochelle, N. Y., where some of his descendants now reside. Thomas, a son of the emigrant, born in 1724, was married about 1750 to Catharine Edgar, a daughter of Thomas Edgar, of Edinburgh, Scotland, who belonged to the Edgar family of Keithock and Wedderlie. This Thomas Edgar, known in his day as "the squire," married Janet Knox of Edinburgh, and settled in Rahway, N. J., about 1718, building a house which has remained uninterruptedly in the possession of his descendants.

Second of the six children of Thomas and Catharine Edgar Gallaudet, was Peter Wallace, who married Jane Hopkins of Hartford,

Rev'd Thomas Hooker,
from England, first
Minister in Hartford,

His son, Rev'd Sam'l
Hooker, Farmington,

His son, Nath'l Hooker,
Merchant, Hartford

His daughter Alice
married Sam'l Howard,
Hartford,

Their daughter,
Alice Howard,
married Thomas Hopkins,
Hartford,

Their daughter, Jane,
married P. W. Gallaudet

T. H. Gallaudet,
their son,

So T. H. G. is the
great grandson
of the great grand
daughter of Rev'd
Thomas Hooker

Conn., a descendant of John Hopkins, one of the Puritan settlers of Hartford, as also of the Reverend Thomas Hooker, founder of that town, and first pastor of its first church. An interesting memorandum in the handwriting of Thomas Hopkins Gallaudet gives the direct line of his descent from the Hartford divine as follows.

" Rev. Thomas Hooker, from England, first minister in Hartford. His son, Rev. Samuel Hooker, Farmington. His son, Nathl. Hooker, merchant, Hartford. His daughter Alice married Saml. Howard, Hartford. Their daughter Alice Howard married Thomas Hopkins, Hartford. Their daughter Jane married P. W. Gallaudet. T. H. Gallaudet their son. So T. H. G. is the great-grandson of the great-grand-daughter of Rev. Thomas Hooker."

Margaret Prioleau, the mother of the first Gallaudet in America, was the grand-daughter of Elizée Prioleau, a distinguished Huguenot, pastor at Niort, near La Rochelle, from 1639 to 1650. The Prioleau family furnished many devoted and eminent clergymen to the Huguenot church, among them a son of Elizée named Samuel, pastor at La Rochelle, 1660, and later at Pons in Saintonge, where he died

in 1683; and Elie, a son of Samuel, who succeeded his father at Pons, fled from France
after the Revocation and became the first
pastor of the Huguenot Church in Charleston,
S. C., where some of his descendants are still
to be found.

Elizée Prioleau, of Niort, had the title
of "Sieur de La Viennerie," and is on good
authority stated to have been a son of Antonio
Priuli, Doge of Venice, 1618–1623.

The Priuli family was prominent in Venice
during the sixteenth and seventeenth centuries,
furnishing the Doge Lorenzo, 1556–1559, and
his brother the Doge Jerome, 1559–1567; also
the Cardinal and Patriarch Lorenzo in 1592 —,
besides several ambassadors and other nota-
bles.

There are writers who deny that Elizée
Prioleau was the son of the Doge Antonio
Priuli, and derive his lineage from an ancestry of clergymen resident in the district of
Saintonge. If these writers are correct,
the connection between the Prioleaus of
France and the Priulis of Venice still remains,
for it is recorded in the history of Venetian
diplomacy that in 1554 a young nephew of the
Doges Lorenzo and Jerome, named Antonio,
going with a maternal uncle on an embassy to

France, fell in love with and married a daughter of a gentleman of Saintonge. A law of Venice forbidding the nobility of the Republic to marry foreigners, young Antonio was banished, and took up his residence in Saintonge among his wife's relations. Here he became the father of a numerous family, which embraced the Huguenot faith during the reign of Henry IV. Among his descendants was Benjamin Priolo, born at St. Jean d'Angely in Saintonge in 1602, who became a distinguished author and diplomat. Benjamin Priolo's claim of descent from the Priulis having been disputed, he submitted evidences to the Venetian government on the strength of which he received a patent under the seal of the Republic in 1660, recognizing and substantiating his right to consider himself a member of the noble Venetian family.

Mr. Gallaudet's mother possessed many of the qualities of her Puritan great-grandparents. Her father, Captain Thomas Hopkins, was for some years the commander of a vessel engaged in foreign trade, and built the first brick house in Hartford, bringing the shingles and bricks for the same from Holland.

The letters of Mrs. Gallaudet to her son

show her to have been a woman of clear
intellect and deep piety, her most cherished
object in life being to make it certain that
her children should be active, earnest Christians.

Peter Wallace Gallaudet was born in New
York City, April 21, 1756.

He settled in Philadelphia early in life, and
was engaged in business as a commission
merchant in that city at the time of his marriage in 1787.

In the year 1800 he removed with his family to Hartford, Connecticut, where he lived,
a merchant, for nearly fifteen years. During
this residence in Hartford, he was honored
with several positions of trust by his fellow-
townsmen, among which may be mentioned
the treasurership of the " First Church" (Congregational), in which he was a prominent
member. It was during his incumbency of
this office that the last church erection took
place, and a carefully kept account book in
his handwriting is in existence, showing all
the receipts and disbursements for this
object.

He lived in New York for a few years after
1815, for a short time in Philadelphia about
1820, and in 1824 took up his residence in

Washington, D. C., occupying a position in
the Register's office in the United States
Treasury until the time of his death, which
occurred in May, 1843, a few weeks after he
had entered upon his eighty-eighth year.
Although nearly seventy years of age when
his Washington life began, he was more
actively engaged than many of his juniors.
He was made an elder in the Fourth Presbyterian Church in 1830, filling this position to
the time of his death.

Early in 1835, then in his eightieth year, he
became the founder of "Washington's
Manual Labor School and Male Orphan
Asylum," associating with himself Michael
Nourse, James L. Edwards, John Coyle,
Peter Force, and other prominent citizens.

To raise funds for the support of this institution, he and his friend, Michael Nourse, at
the time chief clerk of the Register of the
Treasury, secured the publication of "A fac-
simile copy of the Accounts of General Washington's expenses during the Revolutionary
War, also a copy of a line of march proposed
by him for the British army in the expedition
of 1758 against Fort Du Quesne."

An examination of the records of the society shows Peter W. Gallaudet to have been

not only the founder but the moving spirit in the organization.

From the sale of the fac-similes of Washington's accounts some two thousand dollars were realized, and in 1842, when he had been made president of the society, the institution was incorporated by Act of Congress.

Following the passage of the Act of incorporation steps were taken to secure the establishment of the school, but with Mr. Gallaudet's death, the life seems to have gone out of the society, and nothing was ever done except to increase the small endowment already secured, by the addition of accruing interest to the principal.

In 1860, the officers of the association, seeing no prospect of being able to raise a sufficient sum of money to provide for the establishment of the proposed school, asked and received the permission of Congress to dissolve the corporation, and make over its assets, amounting in value to some $5,000, to the Columbia Institution for the Deaf and Dumb, in which the income of the fund has been used to promote industrial training among the deaf.

Peter W. Gallaudet is remembered by a few now living in Washington. In manners

he was a gentleman of the old school; in disposition retiring and charitable, at the same
time progressive and public-spirited, having
clear convictions of duty, with the courage to
express and live up to them. He was a veg-
etarian for the last twenty-five years of his
life.

His frequent letters to his son Thomas show
him to have been in full sympathy with all his
benevolent works, and ready to encourage him
to spend his strength in them, rather than in
labors calculated to win applause or wealth.

The subject of this memoir was born in
Philadelphia, on the 10th of December, 1787.
He was the eldest of a family of twelve children. Little can be said of his childhood, except
that he was of studious habit, precocious in
mental development and of delicate physique.
During his infancy an event occurred which
could not have failed to exert an important influence on the family life. His father, when thirty-
seven years of age, having up to that time lived
without acknowledging any personal obligations in matters of a religious nature, passed
through a season of great thoughtfulness,
which resulted in his making a public profession of his faith.

A few paragraphs from a letter written to an

intimate friend on the fifteenth of May, 1793, will disclose something of the character of the man, giving, at the same time, an idea of the experience through which he had passed :—

"During my life, like all the human race, I have been in pursuit of happiness. I have sought it in the paths of what the world calls pleasure, amusements and gratification of the passions. I have pursued it by my endeavors in acquiring wealth and reputation. Still as it eluded my grasp I changed my grounds or added to those that of domestic enjoyment ; but even here I found something wanting, though I could not tell what. I had frequent periods of leisure, which were often filled up with anxious thought. When busily engaged, not having time for reflection, I had the most happiness, if it could be called such ; but at best it was only of the negative kind. . . . I have reason to be thankful I have been arrested in my way and made to see and feel that the pursuit of religion, only, can give and secure happiness. . . . I have less anxious thoughts and find myself more patient and equal to all the various duties connected with my situation, and to what but the blessed influence of religion can I attribute this change. . . . I believe whoever will read the Scriptures dispassionately, with a desire to receive instruction therefrom, earnestly seeking the truth, and if these things be true that their minds may receive them as such, will assuredly find a disposition within them leading them to assent to and embrace the precepts therein contained. . . . Religion, like all other acquirements, seems to me to be progressive. What can we learn that is useful without diligence and perseverance ? No science unfolds itself all at once ; and shall we reject a system because we can not on slight reading or thinking comprehend all its parts ? After a long life spent in arduous study in any science how many things remain in mystery ! and is it surprising that in the most important of all, mysteries should also be found ? . . . How are they who reject religion deceived ! They conclude it to be a continued scene of self-denial and mortification, calculated to sink the mind in gloom and inaction, preventing every useful or ornamental improvement. Allow me to assure you, my friend, so far is this from being the case, that it is a life of true rational pleasure and enjoyment, and will lead to all useful improvement. . . . I have with truth and candor related my sentiments, and as your well-wisher do seriously recommend the sub-

ject to your dispassionate reflection, believing
that our present happiness and eternal felicity
depend on our embracing the truth as revealed
in the Scriptures, and for our encouragement
we have an assurance that *they that seek shall
find.* That you may be led thereto is the
earnest prayer of

"Your sincere friend,

"P. W. GALLAUDET."

During a life prolonged for fifty years, to a
day, from the writing of this letter, its author
proved the sincerity of the sentiments and
purposes so clearly expressed to his friend.
The rules he laid down for the government
of his family would, probably, be now called
austere. There was more Bible reading and
prayer and churchgoing and exhortation than
is common in our day. And while it is true
that some of the sons grew up to reject
religion, for a time, if not to scoff at it, it can
be said that a majority of this large family
became men and women of singular purity
of life.

In the letters found among Mr. Gallaudet's
papers from his brothers and sisters, much
may be gathered of the spirit and manner of
the family life. And were this to be a larger
book, many extracts of interest might be

inserted from this correspondence. Room for but very few can, however, be taken.

Charles, who was later a partner in business of William H. Imlay, well known as the first millionaire in Hartford, Conn., writes to his brother Thomas :

"The pursuit I have in contemplation is to become an engraver. I think it is a profession more suited to my taste and genius than a mercantile life. . . . In activity of enterprise, in shrewd sagacity, in jostling through the crowd and being on my guard against the cunning of men I am deficient—I want decision of character."

The seventh child of the family was William Edgar, a boy of unusual intelligence and vivacity. When fourteen years of age he naïvely informs his brother Thomas that his "studies go on as usual, but under a different guidance. I have left the Grammar School *through request of the master* and am pursuing my classical studies at home in the forenoon."

A few weeks later he writes: "I do think it is my duty to disappoint your anticipations of my misapplication. I shall endeavor to gain as much knowledge of Greek as possible from Homer, but in my humble opinion I should be more acquainted with it, if I followed it, not as a classical study, but a familiar language. The same, I think, holds true in other studies. A child in his first attempts at speaking and language is not presented with the sublime diction, but the vulgar conversation. The rules and principles of language are the necessary followers, not precursors, of his attainment."

On leaving Yale College at eighteen, William writes his brother as follows : " It is after much deliberation that I have decided to take the profession of physic, and I assure you, entirely of my own choice, unless it be the company of Legaré, an intimate friend of mine from Charleston, S. C., who contemplates the study of medicine in New York. I struck the balance between literary errantry, merchandise, law, and physic. The first had too little respectability and wealth ; the second too little science and reflection, and the third not enough either of science, literature or wealth ; so that I decided in favor of the last, which unites in itself science, literature, wealth and honor. You see I have not taken ease into consideration ; and I have not, because I do not think myself made for a gentleman at large. I want some employment that will give scope to all the vigor I can·bring

into the field, and yet I am so much a votary
of sense as to wish for wealth to gratify my
passions."

William, however, for reasons which do not
now fully appear, gave up the study of medicine and made his way to a south-western
state, where, after meeting with some disappointments, he secured a position as a teacher.
He writes of his first experiences as follows:
"To be as I have been in the midst of
strangers without money; to meet with the
impertinence and often the insults of those
whom in my heart I despise ; to be obliged to
muffle my pride lest it should injure my fortunes; to make a thousand pretenses to gain
the respect of people and then to bear my
own contempt for the meanness of dissimula-
tion ; these are things which come home to
that proud spirit which I know all our family
possess.   After pawning various articles. I
have at length found a temporary resource in
a little copy of poems which have been collecting since I left home.   These are transla-
tions from the Spanish which I made on Captain B.'s plantation, under Mrs. P.'s instruction, and a few short pieces, such as a version
of Solomon's Song and some parts of Job.
The rascally publisher has, however, cheated

me through my necessities, and has boasted since of getting for fifteen dollars what I might have disposed of for fifty."

Returning to New York in June, 1817, he lived in that city for four years, doing some literary work both in prose and poetry, having plans for publishing a periodical, and finally entered the office of the city clerk. While in this position he was taken suddenly ill and died at the age of twenty-four.

The tenth child was Theodore, who became a Presbyterian clergyman. His pastorates were in Virginia and Maryland, and the last twenty-five years of his life were spent as an itinerant missionary and Bible distributor. He was a man of some eccentricities, but of great earnestness in the performance of whatever he believed to be his duty. He died near Westminster, Md., in the summer of 1885, in his eighty-first year.

Three years younger than Theodore came Edward. This brother developed in a marked degree the artistic talent possessed two generations earlier by his great-uncle Elisha, who engraved a portrait of George Whitefield in New York as early as 1774.

Two miniatures of Edward, painted when he was in his twentieth year, show him to have been a youth of uncommon beauty. His success as an engraver was brilliant, and specimens of his work give evidence of a marvelously fine and sympathetic touch. But his life, which opened with the most flattering promise, was overshadowed by a grievous disappointment, from the effects of which he never recovered.

While practicing his art in Boston, side by side with his intimate friend and fellow artist, John Cheney, he became engaged to a young lady who was his equal in personal beauty, and in other ways most attractive. Her parents looked with disfavor on Edward Gallaudet, only because he was not then a professing Christian. Their opposition was so pronounced that the match was broken off.

The effect on Edward was disastrous, and although he could, and did when he exerted himself, execute engravings of a high order of merit, he worked irregularly, and with a broken spirit.

A portrait taken of him at thirty-five, not long before his death, shows him to be what he was, a disappointed and shattered man.

Not many years ago one of his nieces met quite accidentally an elderly lady, who on learning her name inquired with eagerness if she were a relative of Edward Gallaudet. On receiving an affirmative answer, the old lady, with eyes full of tears, said : " My parents broke off my engagement to your uncle and I married another, but my heart has always belonged to Edward Gallaudet."

The family letters, from which the incidents just narrated have been gleaned, give frequent evidence of mutual devotion and tenderness of feeling, as beautiful as they are rare. But the especial interest attaching to them, as affecting the subject of this memoir, grows out of the fact that they show him to have been the actual center of the family. Leaned upon and often sought in counsel and otherwise by his parents in their laborious and not always successful struggles for the maintenance of their many children ; looked up to and confided in by his brothers and sisters as, perhaps, their most able adviser, this faithful and helpful elder brother foreshadows in the earlier third of his life those qualities that marked his dealings with the world at a later period.

Thomas was thirteen years of age when his father removed from Philadelphia to Hartford in 1800.

He completed his preparation for college at the Hartford Grammar School in the summer of 1802, and entered the Sophomore class at Yale the following autumn.

In writing, a few years later, of his boyhood he says :

I can remember that when I was a boy I used to steal away from my companions, and find out a lonely spot in the fields or woods where we were sporting, and, seating myself under the shade of some venerable tree, and drawing a thousand strange figures in the sand before me, and ever and anon whistling a simple air of the nursery, give up my youthful fancy to any dreams of future happiness or greatness which it might choose to form. And as I grew older, I used to delight to dwell upon what *might* be, and to conjure up such scenes of prosperity for myself and friends and all mankind, as would more than realize, could they have an existence, the warmest expectations of the most enthusiastic philanthropist.

These were no idle dreams—they were the "stuff" his future was "made on"; and that he was no mere dreamer even in the days of his youth, his career in college gave abundant proof. His classmate, Heman Humphrey, writes thus of him as a collegian :*

---

* "The Life and Labors of the Rev. T. H. Gallaudet, LL. D." by Rev. Heman Humphrey, D. D., pp. 22, 23. New York : Robert Carter & Brothers, 1857.

More youthful in appearance than even in age; modest, unobtrusive, and strictly correct in all his habits, Gallaudet was a universal favorite in his class. We all loved him and anticipated much from him, in whatever profession he might choose to enter. In his studies he was remarkably systematic, and was scrupulously punctual in his attendance upon all college exercises. Rarely, if ever, had he a mark upon the monitor's bill, and whoever else might boggle over the lesson, Gallaudet was sure to have mastered it. He had a talent and a taste for mathematics, which would have given him very high distinction as a professor in that department had he chosen to devote his life to it. In English composition he had no superior, and no equal in his class. Indeed there was no branch, except declamation, in which he did not excel; and in that he always acquitted himself handsomely, though his voice was not strong, and he was too modest to do himself full justice on the college stage. He graduated in 1805, with the highest honors of his class, and left our Alma Mater with the confident prediction of those who knew him best, that should his life and health be spared he would become one of our brightest ornaments.

Although, as his classmate states, he did not excel in declamation, he was a frequent debater in the meetings of his literary society, the Brothers in Unity. The notes of his speeches on such questions as :—" Ought the

dictates of conscience invariably to be followed?" "Would it be just and politic for
the nations of the earth to combine and extir-
pate the Barbary powers?" and "Would it be
politic in the United States to emancipate
the slaves?" give evidence of maturity of
judgment, depth of thought, and ability to
keep close to the subject not common in a
boy of sixteen. In the debate on the question of emancipation it is particularly interesting to note that while the writer is
strongly opposed to slavery, his arguments
are full and conclusive as to the *impolicy* of
the immediate and wholesale manumission
of the slaves.

Manuscripts are in existence of two
addresses delivered by Mr. Gallaudet at the
close of his college career, one to the members of the Brothers in Unity, the other his
commencement oration.

The former is evidently the only copy he
made of the address, being full of corrections
and interlineations. It conveys an earnest
and thoughtful appeal to his juniors in the
society to maintain the organization, and
presents an array of advantages to be gained
from such a society by those who avail themselves of their privileges and discharge their

duties as members.   He ends with a short
original poem, the closing lines of which are as
follows :

> May the bright lamp of science guide your way,
> Your minds illumine with perpetual day,
> Teach you to aim at truth and truth alone,
> Error forsake and virtue call your own.
> To these be added all the heartfelt joys
> Of sweet domestic life, far from the noise
> Of proud Ambition's bustle and alarm,
> Kindling with frenzy, raging like the storm.
> And when the busy cares of life are o'er,
> When sounds the trembling silver cord no more,
> When bursts, at length, in twain the golden bowl,
> And when the cistern wheel no more is whole,
> May purer joys than blest the Elysian field
> To your rapt senses kindly be revealed.

The subject of the commencement oration
will doubtless provoke a smile, for we of this
day find it difficult to realize that in 1805
there was warrant for raising a note of warn-
ing " On the increase of luxury in Connecticut, and its destructive consequences."

The cry of this youthful Jeremiah must
have exerted a greater influence than is commonly traceable to the oratory of college
commencements, for it is certain that the ruin
predicted for the then young commonwealth

has not as yet overtaken it, and the relative standard of morality and religion is known to be higher now than it was in the early days of the century.

A word as to the appearance of the manuscript of this commencement essay of eighty years ago will be interesting as indicating some of the personal traits of the writer.

It is written on unruled paper, with a most careful regard for lines and margins, suggesting the use of underlines, in a clear, well rounded but unclerkly hand, the essential character of which belonged to Mr. Gallaudet's penmanship through the whole course of his life; and the signature differs little from many that were made forty years later.

Carefully enveloped in a cover of marbled paper, secured with a bit of pink and white silk ribbon, it speaks of habits of neatness and order in the boy, which were maintained through life.

Gallaudet was one of six, in a class of forty-two, to graduate with the honor of an oration. Rev. Gardiner Spring, D. D., the eminent divine of New York, was the valedictorian.

The story is told on good authority that
the marks for scholarship of Spring and Gallaudet reached the same aggregate ; but that
the former being some inches taller than the
latter was considered to have a *higher standing* in the class, and therefore received the
greater distinction.

Gallaudet was accorded the additional
honor on Commencement day of speaking,
with five of his classmates, in a dialogue
entitled Timophanes, or the tyrant of
Corinth. On the "Scheme of Exercises," as
it was then called, appear the names of
Heman Humphrey, Samuel Farmar Jarvis,
Salmon Wheaton, Jeremiah Evarts and
William Maxwell, well known in later
years as eminent in the scholarly walks of
life.

Mr. Gallaudet's college course was pursued
under the presidency of Timothy Dwight.
Among his instructors may be named Jeremiah
Day, Benjamin Silliman, then youthful professors, Moses Stuart and David A. Sherman,
then acting as tutors. In the latter portion of
his life, he was afterward heard to speak of his
college days with unmixed satisfaction.
Many friendships then formed he maintained
until his death. His devotion to study was

not carried so far as to stand in the way of his mingling a good deal in social life; and in this the maturity of his mind gained him the companionship of many much older than himself.

CHAPTER II.

1805—1815.

Study of Law—Tutorship in Yale College—Serious Ill-health—
Religious Despondency and Doubts—Active Business and
Travel—Theological Study at Andover—A Call to the Minis-
try at Portsmouth, New Hampshire.

IN the autumn of 1805 Mr. Gallaudet entered
upon the study of law in the office of
Hon. Chauncey Goodrich of Hartford, having
the benefit at the same time of instruction
from the Hon. Thomas S. Williams, late chief-
justice of Connecticut. "Here, as in every
thing he undertook, he was punctual and
methodical, and his recitations were remarkable for their accuracy. He gave every assurance of becoming in time a thorough and successful lawyer. The state of his health, however, compelled him at the close of the first
year to suspend his legal studies."* During
the year which followed he devoted himself to
the study of English literature and the prac-

---

* Barnard's tribute.

tice of English composition. Evidences
appear among his papers that he did some
editorial work, or at least contributed to the
periodicals and newspapers of the day. In
September, 1808, he delivered an oration in
Hartford on :" Ambition as a motive in Education," a single quotation from which will sufficiently disclose the lofty train of thought and
illustrate the style of the young orator.

" The love of praise, say they, was given for
wise purposes. It softens and ennobles the
heart. It is the nurse of great and noble
enterprise. It is the just meed of labor. It
creates a mutual dependence among mankind,
knitting them together by the nicest and most
refined of all ties, a sensibility to esteem and
reputation. Would bards have sung so sweetly,
would patriots have bled so nobly, would kings
have reigned so justly, if their hopes had not
brightened at the prospect of a glorious immortality of renown ? Who then shall censure
what has so long been felt by the greatest and
the best of men !

. " But to this oppose the genius of Christianity. Take its prominent characteristic, humility. Behold it in the living example of its
great Author. Where was His love of praise ?
Did He show it in his parentage ? His reputed

father was a carpenter. In His birth? It was
in a manger. In His life? He conversed with
publicans and sinners. In His followers? They
were poor fishermen. In His death? He bled
with malefactors. It was His Father, and not
Himself He came to honor. Who will propose
to Christians, and it is a Christian audience
the speaker is addressing, any other example?
But if in this great personage the love of
praise was never seen, how can it be justified in
those who are bound to imitate Him. Men
ought to consider and weigh every subject
relating to human conduct, not only as men,
and as moralists, but as Christians. False and
ruinous are those theories, that would form
an economy of human life, or conjure up a
system of ethics different from those which
have been given to mankind by their divine
though incarnate legislator."

Shortly after the delivery of this oration
Mr. Gallaudet accepted a position as tutor in
Yale College, thus renewing with great satisfaction his connection with his Alma Mater.
Of his life during the two years of his tutorship
few incidents are recorded. But a little manuscript book of twenty-six pages entitled
" Prayers, Meditations and Reflections," cover-
ing a period somewhat longer than that of his

second residence at New Haven, gives interesting and sometimes even tragic glimpses of
his spiritual experiences. These records make
it evident that from his twentieth to his twenty-
fourth year his mind was constantly and
deeply exercised on the subject of personal
religion; that he passed through seasons of
skepticism; that he fell under the stress of
temptation; and that it was only after a severe
struggle with contending elements that he
came at length to a final and practical acceptance of the Christian faith.

Under date of January 1, 1808, after some
reflections natural to the New Year, the following appears :

I intend to mark what I think are my *standing*
defects of character, both in great and small things.
. . . Generally I am too forgetful of futurity,
too much occupied by the world, too negligent of
cultivating a Christian temper. But more particularly :

First.—I am languid, and cold, and slothful, and
irregular in the performance of my more immediate
duties to God. I resolve with divine assistance, in
future to pray morning, noon and night in secret.
At noon I will repeat the Lord's Prayer. I will
read in the Scriptures thrice a day. . . On the
Sabbath I will read five chapters in the Old and the

same number in the New Testament. . . . I will always attend divine worship if there be any, unless prevented by some necessary cause.

Secondly.—I am too often disrespectful and unkind to my parents, and unkind to my brothers and sisters.

Thirdly.—I am too irritable.

Fourthly.—I am too much addicted to the indulgence of loose and impure and trifling thoughts and words; I have not that scrupulous regard to *exact* truth in what many, even moralists, think are things of no importance, such as the recital of stories, pleasantries of conversation, the forms of civility.

Fifthly.—I am much, very much, too indolent.

Sixthly.—I indulge, too much, my appetite for food and drink.

Following this enumeration of faults an earnest prayer is recorded for God's help to overcome them. Under date of January 6, after allusion to Psalm cxvi., this prayer is recorded :

Heavenly Father! I have been baptized with the baptism of thy Son. Oh! shed forth thy grace more abundantly in my heart that I may soon also drink of His cup. Remove, I entreat thee, those timorous doubts, and perplexing scruples, and indeed criminal thoughtlessness which yet keep me from the table of my Lord. I ask this for Christ's sake. Amen.

Some weeks later he writes despondingly :

God has taken His' Holy Spirit from me, and left me to the influence of surrounding temptations and to the infidelity of my own mind. For in infidelity, either more complete or partial, do I at such seasons take refuge. Man's free agency, his natural depravity, the impracticability of his effecting a radical change of character, the immediate and exclusive and supernatural agency of the Holy Spirit in regeneration, the necessity of publicly professing one's belief in Christ, and of partaking of the Lord's Supper, and the eternity of future punishment, have been the subjects on which I have thought with no little distraction of mind.

Then, after self-reproaches and a prayer for help from above, he continues :

I will here note down some of my conjectures on those subjects which have lately occupied my mind, that I may be able at some future period, when my opinions are more settled, to review them and judge of their correctness or the reverse.

The soul, I have thought, comes into existence with no positive qualities, but merely a capability of receiving impressions from surrounding objects by means of the body. As this body, and indeed the whole economy of the natural world, by which the body is constantly influenced, are polluted by sin, some, and indeed most of the impressions that the mind at first receives, being physical, tend to make it participate of that general depravity with which

it is surrounded. This, together with the influence
of bad example and improper education, I have
thought sufficient to account for the depravity of
human nature. In short, man's mind is depraved,
because its receptacle is a depraved body, its dwell-
ing a depraved world, and its associates depraved
beings. Or, to present these ideas a little differ-
ently, there is no necessary tendency to sin in the
original organization of the mind; so that if any
mind, human I mean, were introduced into a holy
state of existence, with a receptacle perfectly pure,
and among beings perfectly holy, it would itself be
without sin.

I have thought that God's influence upon the
mind in effecting regeneration was no greater than
that which He exercises upon the natural world ; that
His providence in this change always operates by
what *we term* secondary causes; and that man's
agency in effecting this grand transformation of
character is as much concerned as in bringing about
any effect in the natural world, and can be calculated
upon as likely to be efficient, if *proper means are
used*, with as much certainty in the one case as in
the other. My reasons for this have been founded
in considering that all possible events are parts of a
general system, and are nearer and more remotely
connected with each other : so that no single event
exists without a dependence upon an infinite chain
of prior events,—that God exercises a particular
providence, and acts equally in and upon the whole
material and moral world ; so that the bringing about
of *every* event is to be attributed to His imme-

diate agency; and that when we use the terms
"natural" and "supernatural" we can mean nothing
more than that in natural events we can trace the
uniformity of God's operations through a greater
succession of what we call causes and effects, than
in those events which we term supernatural.

It does not speak well for the religious teachings of his day that this young theologian,
whose own views were so clear and reasonable,
should have been plunged into the depths of
mental misery by the exigeant and extreme
doctrines given forth from the pulpits of his
time.

A month or two later, writing more hope-
fully, and believing himself nearly, if not quite
ready, to make a public profession of his faith,
he thus shadows forth the broad charity which
beautified the whole course of his later life.

I think it of little consequence which sect I join,
provided its church exhibits in its doctrine and the
lives of its members evidence of evangelical Christianity.

And yet not long after he writes in the
depths of despondency and doubt because
some one has been stirring up his mind on
"the necessity of a mysterious regeneration,"

"eternal torments," "the guilt of man," and the like.

That towards the close of this year of 1808 other influences than embarrassing speculations in theology seem to have been working against him, appears in the following record:

Sunday, December 25, 1808, Yale College.

I know now that I am walking in the way that leads to eternal perdition. Dreadful infatuation; deplorable rashness! I am fully convinced of the truth of Christianity, of the insignificancy of the world, of the certainty of death, of the awful realities of heaven and hell. I see my own woful depravity; my ingratitude to God, my indulgence in sensual gratifications in food, the impurities of my imagination, my hypocrisy, insincerity, pride and vanity, and the improper and selfish motives of my conduct. I know the safety, and happiness, and real nobleness of a Christian, and yet day by day, I live without God in the world. I even seem to deceive myself when I wish (in a lifeless manner) for another character.

An incident in his life while a tutor in Yale College, related a short time since by an aged friend of his still living in Hartford, should be told, if at all, in this volume, in connection with the quotation just made from his diary.

On a certain social occasion, he was carried away by the hilarity in the midst of which he found himself, and led to take wine to such an extent as to be plainly overcome by its intoxicating influence.

His mortification and distress were so great that he could have no peace of mind until he had repaired to Hartford and made public confession to the officers of the church with which his parents were connected, and which he himself expected sooner or later to join. And it is a fact that long before the "temperance movement" began in this country Mr. Gallaudet was a strict abstainer from every thing that could intoxicate.

The same friend who related the foregoing incident furnished another belonging to the same period, the recording of which can do no harm, while it will illustrate several peculiarities of temperament.

The young people of Hartford, early in the present century, were in the habit of enjoying themselves at so-called "Assemblies," held in a public hall, the entertainment consisting mainly of dancing. These gayeties were fascinating to young Gallaudet, and he was often a leader in them.

On one occasion, in winter, when an "As-

sembly" was in its full tide, word was
brought in that a young man known to all
had just been drowned while skating on the
river, and that at the moment his body was
being carried by. Gallaudet appealed to those
who bore the news " not to tell the ladies," for,
added he, " it would break up the dance."
But the words had hardly passed his lips
before his conscience smote him for his heart-
lessness, and he presently hurried away from
the " Assembly " never to attend such a gathering again.

It seems not improbable that this incident
of his early days had much to do in leading
him to oppose most strenuously the amusement of dancing, as he did to the end of his
life.

During the winter of 1808-9 the enfeebled
state of Mr. Gallaudet's health occasioned him
much depression of spirits, inducing an evidently morbid condition of his feelings as to
religious matters. After several entries in
his diary that give proof of this, the following record is made :

Thursday morning, April 6, 1809, Yale College,
in my chamber. In prayer this morning I made
two solemn vows to Almighty God ; one that if He

would afford me rational conviction of my having
passed from death unto life I would (as soon as I
had obtained this) make a profession of religion;
the other that if in His providence He should see fit
to restore me to health and strength of body, and a
capability of studying, I would devote myself to the
ministry of the Gospel. I here record them for my
future benefit.

Next succeeding the following entry is the
following, made after an interval of ten
months :

1810, February 4.   *Hoc opus, hic labor est.*

Then a few days later :

1810, February 17.—*Rursus.*

Of what fruitless struggles after peace of
mind this single word " backward " pathetic-
ally speaks !

Mr. Gallaudet's labors as a tutor in Yale
College closed in the summer of 1810 without
that improvement in health for which he had
so earnestly prayed. He therefore thought
it prudent to seek some pursuit that might
keep him much in the open air, and accepted
a commission from a large commercial house

in New York to travel through the states of
Kentucky and Ohio. This journey, made
mostly on horseback, greatly improved his
physical condition, and he found the attractions
of a business life sufficiently strong to induce
him to enter into a permanent engagement,
on his return to New York, with the firm for
which he had been traveling.

It is certain that for a time he dismissed all
idea of entering upon a professional life of any
sort, and that he possessed excellent capacities
for business. But he was, in spirit, more of a
scholar than a man of business, and his convictions of duty, though overborne for a time,
soon reasserted themselves. When it is considered what the man afterward became, no
surprise is occasioned by the discovery that in
his private diary immediately succeeding the
despondent *Rursus* of 1810, comes the following entry after the lapse of two years.

"Andover, Massachusetts, Sunday morning, January 12, 1812. I joined the day
before yesterday (Jan. 10) the divinity college
in this place, and this morning took up my
residence within its walls. O! Thou God of
all truth, if my purpose in devoting myself to
the ministry be any but the right one, I
humbly beseech thee for Christ's sake to dis-

cover unto me the deceitfulness of my own heart in cherishing it, and to lead me, by thy good spirit, to engage in my intended pursuits with a single eye to the promotion of thy glory and the extension of the Redeemer's kingdom on earth. I desire solemnly to dedicate myself, soul, body and spirit, with all my powers and capacities of action, to thy service. Oh ! accept this offering, I beseech thee, which indeed is justly thy due, and prepare me by thy grace affecting my heart, thy wisdom illuminating my mind, and thy strength invigorating my present weak and sickly body, to work with diligence and success in thy vineyard."

Mr. Gallaudet reached his decision to study for the ministry before he had ever made any public profession of his faith, and in the early part of his course at Andover seems to have been harassed, as when a tutor in New Haven, with doubts and disposed to self-condemnation.

Having been in Andover several months, he takes occasion, when noting in his diary the fact of a day of prayer in behalf of some graduates who had gone into the foreign mission field, to make the following record :

I would seize this occasion to mourn before the
searcher of hearts my own deplorable sinfulness,
and particularly one event of my past life in which
I grossly sinned against God, and which ought to
fill me with shame and confusion of face in His presence, and also to lament my present coldness and
stupidity.

The next and last entry in the little diary
of Prayers, Meditations, and Reflections is in
these words :

I made a public profession of my faith in Christ
on the 11th of October, 1812, and was admitted a
member of the first ecclesiastical Congregational
Church in Hartford, Rev. Nathan Strong being pastor thereof.   The vows of God are upon me.

Small record remains in any form of Mr.
Gallaudet's life at Andover.   Letters from his
father disclose the facts that an accident occurred to one of his eyes which threatened serious results, and that at the end of the first
year the state of his health was so unsatisfactory as to raise a question as to his continuing
study.   But in spite of all drawbacks he completed the full course of study and was licensed
to preach by the " Association of Salem and
vicinity, meeting at the house of the Rev. Mr.

Walker, in Danvers, June 14, 1814." His diploma of graduation from the seminary bears the date of September 23, 1814, and the signatures of Ebenezer Porter, Leonard Woods and Moses Stuart, professors.

Mr. Gallaudet's reputation as a scholar at Andover was so high, and the faith of his instructors in his success as a preacher so strong, that before the completion of his theological studies he received several flattering invitations to take charge of vacant pulpits.

Among them was a very earnest call from the " North Parish" of Portsmouth, N. H., of which Rev. Dr. Buckminster had long been the pastor, signed by John Langdon, Ammi R. Cutter, Daniel Webster (then just commencing his career in Congress), and Henry Ladd.

Mr. Gallaudet's reply to these gentlemen reveals much of the spirit of the man, and shows at the same time against how great odds he was struggling in the matter of his health.

ANDOVER, July 7, 1814.

GENTLEMEN:—

Permit me to thank you for the very kind manner in which you are pleased to invite me to labor among you as a candidate for settlement in the Gospel ministry. Whatever opinion my friends may be good enough to entertain of me I feel myself, at present, very incompetent to perform the arduous duties and undertake the high responsibility of such a station as he who may become your pastor will occupy. But this is not my only, nor indeed principal, reason for declining entirely a compliance with your solicitations. I have been very much of an invalid for these nine or ten years and still labor under the pressure of considerable bodily infirmity. My eyes and lungs are both weak and my general health is such that I can devote but little time to study. My purpose is, for some time to come, to preach only occasionally as my strength will permit, to journey at frequent intervals, and to decline being settled, unless indeed some situation should offer which would involve cares and duties far less numerous than must be attached to the ministry among so large a congregation as yours. Indeed with my present state of health, I should deem it not only an ungenerous imposition on your good will, but a rash exposure to the entire loss of future usefulness, and of course an unwarranted reliance upon unexpected aid from Providence, to attempt the supply of your pulpit. So grateful do I feel to you, gentlemen, for the very delicate and obliging nature of your communication, and so strong is my impression, as I trust, that an invitation like yours is to be considered most seriously and prayerfully by one who ought to hold himself ready to go wherever the great Master of the vineyard shall direct,—that I hope this my refusal will, on the one hand, appear perfectly reasonable and satisfactory to yourselves, and, on the other, be no breach of that solemn obligation which is imposed upon me of entire devotedness to the interests of Zion.

Wishing you, gentlemen, and the society to whom you stand related, the continual protection and blessing of almighty God,

I am very respectfully yours,

THOMAS H. GALLAUDET.

During the following autumn and winter Mr. Gallaudet carried out his purpose of preaching occasionally and traveling considerably. That some of his friends thought him disposed to live rather easily and postpone the assumption of serious duties is evident from a caution in a letter of a fellow student at Andover, written in April, 1815: "What have you been about this winter? Do not love your liberty too well. Pledge yourself to some constant, arduous efforts. '*Labora ut quiescas.*'"

What indeed had Mr. Gallaudet been about during this winter of 1814–15! The sequel will prove that he had been no idler, nor mere lover of his liberty ; it will also show that this undersized invalid, who with " eyes and lungs both weak," " could devote but little time to study," was ready to spring joyfully to his life work when plainly called to it ; that in his delicate frame dwelt a spirit large enough and strong enough to make him the practical pioneer if not the father of all systematic philanthropic work in America ; that the culture of New England had fitted him to meet, on a level, the scholars and philosophers of the mother country ; that in the capitals of Europe this fledgling from a humble provincial school of theology could win the admiration of the ablest critics as a preacher.

CHAPTER III.

1815—1816.

Interest in Deaf-Mutes—Alice Cogswell—An Invitation From Citizens of Hartford to Undertake the Education of the Deaf in America—A Tour to England, Scotland and France to Gain Information—Difficulties and Hindrances in Great Britain—Success in France—Temporary Pastorate in Paris.

DURING the winter of 1814–1815 Mr. Gallaudet remained mostly at his father's home in Hartford; preaching occasionally, and waiting for some decided indication of Providence as to the path of duty. There was no marked improvement in the state of his health.

Among his papers, one, entitled " A Reverie," bears internal evidence of having been written about this period, and closes as follows, after a reference to the importance of the then novel work of preaching the gospel to heathen nations:

Before the millennium arrives will *one* language prevail and swallow up the rest, or will mankind agree to form a universal language? Would not such a project be pregnant with incalculable advantages? How shall it be accomplished? What shall this universal language be? Is there already one, provided by Nature herself, easy of acquisition, universal in its application, and which demands neither types nor paper? Has such a language yet eluded the research of the profoundest philosophers, and is it left for some happy genius yet to find it? As is often the case, just when the mind is ready to light upon some most wonderful discovery, the capricious fancy disdains the dull process of beating out truth upon the anvil of experiment—and my reverie ended.

Again can it be said in telling the story of this life that "we are such stuff as dreams are made on," for the fulfillment of his "reverie" came to Mr. Gallaudet when this possible "universal language" demanding "neither types nor paper" was realized in the language of signs which played so important a part in his work of teaching the deaf.

One of Peter Wallace Gallaudet's nearest neighbors in Hartford was Dr. Mason Fitch Cogswell—a physician of high professional and social standing. Among Dr. Cogswell's children was a lovely daughter nine years of age, on whom the blight of total deafness had fallen some years before, the result of a severe

ALICE COGSWELL.

attack of spotted fever. As is not uncommon in such cases a loss of speech followed the loss of hearing, and before she had completed her fourth year this child was practically dumb as well as deaf. Her parents and family friends did what they could, in a very imperfect way, to develop her intelligence. But while their efforts were by no means fruitless, they did not succeed, as time went on, in establishing any clear and effective means of communicating thought. The child gained nothing of verbal language from the teachings of her zealous and loving friends.

It was during one of Mr. Gallaudet's vacations, while a student at Andover, that his attention was directed to the deaf child of his neighbor. His first interview with her was in his father's garden, where she was at play with his younger brothers and sisters.

One* who married, a few years later, a sister of Alice Cogswell, writes thus of this meeting :

His compassionate interest in her situation, with a strong desire to alleviate it, was immediate and deep. He at once attempted to converse with and

---

* Lewis Weld, who was Mr. Gallaudet's successor as principal of the institution for deaf-mutes at Hartford.

instruct her, and actually succeeded in teaching her the word *hat* before she left the garden where the interview took place.

Another,* writing of this memorable incident, says :

Following up this first step in such methods as his own ingenuity could suggest, and with such lights as he could gather from a publication of the Abbé Sicard which Dr. Cogswell had procured from Paris, Mr. Gallaudet, from time to time, succeeded in imparting to her a knowledge of many simple words and sentences, which were much enlarged by members of her own family, and especially by her first teacher, Miss Lydia Huntley [afterwards well-known as the poetess Lydia H. Sigourney]. This success encouraged her father in the hope, that instead of sending his child, made more dear to him by her privations, away from home, to Edinburgh, or London, for instruction in the schools of Rev. R. Kinniburgh, or Dr. Watson, that a school might be opened in Hartford.

As Mr. Gallaudet's acquaintance with Alice Cogswell continued, there grew up, to quote Mr. Weld again, "a very intimate intercourse with the child and her father's family, during intervals of relaxation from professional studies, extending through several years,

---

* Henry Barnard, LL.D. Tribute to Gallaudet. Hartford : 1852.

which resulted in her acquiring, chiefly through his agency, so much knowledge of very simple words and sentences, as satisfied her friends that she might learn to write and read, and that Mr. Gallaudet, of all the circle of their acquaintance, was the person best qualified to undertake her instruction."

It was during Mr. Gallaudet's winter in Hartford, after his graduation at Andover, that his interest in Alice Cogswell began to take practical shape, and that he induced her parents to place her under the direct instruction of Miss Huntley.

Nothing was more natural than that the mind of Dr. Cogswell, made thus painfully alive to the importance of establishing schools for the deaf in America, should turn to the young clergyman who had shown such enthusiastic interest in his child, as the man of destiny for the deaf of his country.

At the invitation of Dr. Cogswell the following friends and neighbors met at his house on the 13th of April, 1815, to confer with him as to the practicability of establishing a school for deaf-mute children in Hartford : Ward Woodbridge, Daniel Wadsworth, Henry Hudson, Hon. Nathaniel Terry, John Caldwell, Daniel Buck, Rev. Nathan Strong, D. D.,

Rev. Thomas H. Gallaudet (all of Hartford),
and Joseph Battel, of Norfolk, Ct.

The blessing of God was invoked on the
enterprise by Dr. Strong, and after an evening
spent in discussing various means for attaining
the desired object, it was determined to make
an effort to send a suitable person to Europe
for the purpose of acquiring the art of teaching
the deaf in some one of the schools then
existing in the old world.   Dr. Cogswell and
Mr. Woodbridge were appointed a committee
to ascertain the name of a competent man
who would consent to go, and to raise funds
to meet the expense of sending such person.
So great was the interest taken by the benevolent of Hartford in the novel undertaking,
that Mr. Woodbridge was able to secure the
promise of ample funds in a single day.

Mr. Gallaudet was the first choice of all
interested in the enterprise.   His modesty and
distrust of his ability to undertake so important a work led him to defer accepting the
mission for a number of days, and to urge
that some other man should be named.   His
friends, however, were so convinced of *his*
peculiar and eminent qualifications that they
were hardly willing to seek for any other man.
So at the end of a week Mr. Gallaudet felt

himself compelled to respond favorably to what seemed to be a plain call of duty.

The following entry heads the first page of "A Journal of some Occurrences in my Life which have a Relation to the Instruction of the Deaf and Dumb."

Hartford, Conn., Thursday evening, April 20, 1815. I informed Dr. Mason F. Cogswell and Mr. Ward Woodbridge of my willingness to undertake the employment of instructing the deaf and dumb in my own country.

And now must be noticed one of those strange coincidences that occasionally mark the lives of men, especially of such as seem to be called by Providence to do some particular work in the world.

Events in Mr. Gallaudet's life had led naturally up to his selection by those who knew him best in the home of his youth, to undertake an enterprise the success of which demanded a rare combination of qualifications.

But in no way connected with this chain of circumstances was the following letter which undoubtedly reached his hand on the very day he decided to accept the proposal of Dr. Cogswell and his friends:

ANDOVER, April 18, 1815.

MY DEAR FRIEND:—Three days ago I met in
Boston your old friend Mr. George Hall. He told
me he should sail the next day for Savannah.
Thence he should go to England, thence to the continent. The next winter he will spend in Paris, with
the intent of acquiring information in regard to the
instruction of the *deaf and dumb*. He does not mean
to become a teacher, but to perfect his old system
and gratify curiosity is his design.

He wishes *earnestly* for a companion, and for *you*
to be that companion. Having but lately determined upon this voyage, and ignorant of your abid-
ing place, he had no opportunity of communicating
his wishes to you. His first question when I met
him : "Where is Gallaudet?" His second " Will you
write him this very day?" He will be five or six
weeks in Savannah. There he wishes you to join
him ; visit England and then France. Or find him
in England in the summer, etc., etc., etc. He will
stay here or there as long as you please, do what
you please, and be as agreeable as all the world. He
believes that his old system of instruction will afford
great facilities in acquiring information on the subject of the mission, that your acquaintance with
deaf and dumb persons will be also of essential
service, and that of course you will be mutually
serviceable to each other, and be of all the rest
of the world the most suitable for such an undertaking.—He is sorry he could not have seen you, but
nevertheless wishes you to pack up, and be off with
all convenient expedition. He wished me to write

without delay, and urge every motive that might induce you to engage in this benevolent undertaking. I make no comments. May Providence direct and bless you always.

Yours truly,

LORD.

[Nathan Lord, later President of Dartmouth College.]

A letter received on the same day, from Ebenezer Kellogg, who had been with Nathan Lord a fellow student of Mr. Gallaudet's at Andover, and who was for many years a professor in Williams College, says :

I had a letter from home yesterday:—the deaf and dumb girl I carried you to see makes very considerable progress.

From both these letters evidence is afforded that Mr. Gallaudet had been led by his interest in Alice Cogswell to seek out other deaf children, while he was still a student at Andover, and that he was known by his friends to have considered, at least, the subject of general deaf-mute education.

Of course the suggestion of Mr. George Hall, through Nathan Lord, can not be said to have produced any result. And yet the object he aimed at was attained through the very man he had named as fitted, better than any other, to the work.

Mr. Gallaudet was now in the twenty-eighth year of his age. Precocious in his early development as a scholar, he had added to his college course of study a decade of varied and valuable training. A year's study of law; two of teaching; three given to active business, including extended travel; three of theological study, and one spent in general reading, with practice in writing and public speaking, had combined to give him an experience, every element of which was of importance, as will appear in the sequel, in preparing him for the work that now opened before him. His social surroundings had been such as to make it easy for him to meet, on a level, persons of the highest rank in society. His sacred profession gave him a standing in the community second to none. His personal character secured him the confidence of every one who knew him, while his manners were so engaging as to inspire almost equal trust in the minds of strangers. In spite of his delicate health he exercised great personal magnetism. Although small in stature, his bearing was so dignified, and the evidences of his intellectual and moral strength so marked that many persons have been known to say, after meeting him, that they remembered him as a person of imposing presence.

All these elements of strength and influence would have proved as valuable in the profession of his choice, as they did in the career to which he was chosen. Few men have ever stood on the threshold of the Christian ministry with greater promise of success than was Mr. Gallaudet's at this time. The esteem in which he was held at Yale College and Andover Seminary was such as would have insured him an eligible position whenever he should signify his disposition to begin work. It was after many mental struggles that he had decided to devote himself to the preaching of the gospel, and he felt "the vows of God" to be upon him. He had completed his preparations in spite of great difficulties and discouragements and was now ready to preach. He was not without ambition, and in 1815 the position of a clergyman in New England carried enough of weight and influence to make it attractive to a young man.

It is not difficult to perceive, therefore, that while Mr. Gallaudet accepted cheerfully the responsibility now laid on his young shoulders, and did not hesitate to respond to the call of duty, so soon as he perceived it to be such, this decision involved no small personal sacrifice.

But the decision once made there was no looking back, and the second entry in his journal (May 10th) shows that in less than three weeks he was on his way to Europe. In the mean time (May 5th) he went with Dr. Cogswell to Glastonbury, ten miles from Hartford, where he had a memorable interview with the blind deaf-mute Julia Brace, then eight years of age, whose education at a later period attracted a degree of attention second only to that excited by the development of the more brilliant Laura Bridgman.

Spending a few days' in New York, where his father's family were then residing, Mr. Gallaudet embarked on May 25th, in the *Mexico*, burden three hundred tons, S. Weeks, Master, for Liverpool. Among the passengers was Washington Irving; also a number of English army officers, of one of whom Mr. Gallaudet related the following incident :

One of my military friends who was commonly lively and cheerful in his manner came to the table one morning with a very long face. I took occasion to ask him, later, if any thing unusual had occurred to dampen his spirits ; when he told me that during the night he was suddenly awakened by what seemed to be the pressure of a heavy weight lying across him. Rousing up he perceived by the light of the moon, the body of a man in naval uniform stretched out on him in his berth. For some seconds after he was fully awake the apparition remained, and then gradually faded from his sight. He rose, dressed and walked the deck until morning. The chief cause of his depression of spirits lay in the fact that he had a brother in the navy. A note was made of the day and hour, and on our arrival at Liverpool my friend told me before we parted on the wharf that news had met him of his brother's death at sea on the night when his wraith appeared.

Mr. Gallaudet landed at Liverpool on Sunday, June 25th. During the few days he remained in Liverpool he made the acquaintance of Rev. Thos. Raffles and Rev. Robt. Philip, and visited the school for the blind several times. The following Sunday he spent in Leicester, preaching for Rev. Robert Hall in the afternoon, spending the evening, until a late hour, with the noted divine.

. Of this visit he writes as follows to a friend in Hartford :

I called at his house just before the morning service, and went with him to his chapel, which is quite a small building in an obscure part of the town. Mr. Hall's discourse was from these words: " There shall be no more curse there." His subject was set forth in a very plain, perspicuous and affectionate manner, with considerable feeling. There was nothing in his style, or expression, or turn of thought, very remarkable or eloquent. Yet there was a charm cast over the whole, a delicacy, a tenderness, a simplicity, in short, an accommodation of a great and lofty spirit to the weak comprehension of even the lambs of his flock, which raised my admiration more than the grandest display of his decidedly powerful talents would have done. . . . I witnessed his family devotions in the evening, and there was something in his prayer which said, what he well knew and felt, that the real saint has always in remembrance the injunction of our Saviour, which requires of His followers to become like little children. Mr. Hall, though a Baptist, is most liberal in his feelings toward other Christian sects. His congregation are in part Independents, who, of course, have their children baptized by some other clergyman. Oh! that the spirit of Catholicism would pervade all the Christian world!

On Monday, July 3d, he visited a small school for the deaf in Birmingham, on Tuesday he had a glimpse of Oxford, and on Wednesday, the 5th, he reached London, where he expected to achieve the object of his mission to Europe. He was aware that schools for

the deaf had been in operation for more than
fifty years in Great Britain, and that in London the largest and presumably the best of
them was to be found.

To the managers of this institution he presented himself with suitable letters of recom-
mendation, expecting to find open doors, cordial hearts and ready hands to aid him in his
work of benevolence. A very different reception awaited him. For he was soon to learn
the astounding fact that in Great Britain the
benevolent and Christ-like work of teaching the
deaf had been for two generations a monopoly in the hands of a certain family; a
monopoly so heartless that it refused to allow
schools to be established in Ireland, and so
grasping that at the moment of his visit to
England a member of this family, of doubtful
reputation and unsteady habits, was in America
seeking to establish the monopoly in the New
World.

The following letter from Mr. Gallaudet to
Dr. Cogswell gives so full an account of the
difficulties encountered by the former in London, that it may be inserted entire without
further comment than to remind the reader
that all the persons mentioned have long
since passed away: in view of which it can

not be thought indelicate to permit Mr. Gallaudet's expressions concerning them, never before published, to be made public.

LONDON, August 15, 1815.

MY DEAR SIR:—I have not yet received a single letter from America. Surely my friends have not been waiting to hear from me before they wrote. I expected to have been made acquainted, before this time, with the progress of the concern in which we are mutually and so deeply interested. And such information I have really needed in order to conduct my negotiations with the school here in the best manner. For my application for admission into it has been attended with delays and obstacles that I did not expect. I will find no fault at present with those who compose the committee of the school, for I believe they have really wished to gratify me in what I requested of them, nor with Dr. Watson, its instructor, till I know a little more of his true character and learn whether his conduct toward me has proceeded from a wise and prudent caution or a cold and selfish heart.

Premising that since my arrival in England I have written yourself and Mr. Woodbridge five times, giving you an account of what I had then done with regard to our project and the circumstances in which I stood—I will now lay before you a succinct narrative of my proceedings till the present day.

I arrived at Liverpool on the 25th of June last and in this city on the 5th of July. On the 7th I

delivered my letter of introduction to the Rev. John
Townsend, accompanied by Mr. Barlow (Mr. Woodbridge's friend). I made Mr. T. acquainted with my
object in visiting this country. He wished me to
call at the City of London Tavern on the 10th,
where he would converse with me further on the
subject.

July 8th, I formed an acquaintance with the Abbé
Sicard, who has since returned to Paris. He promised me every attention and facility at his school
there, and his secretary invited me to attend the
lectures which he was then delivering in this city.

10th, I called at the City of London Tavern, and in
a note sent my credentials to the Rev. Mr. Townsend,
who was in the committee room. After some time
I saw him. He told me that he had laid my application before the committee and that a sub-committee
had been chosen to confer with Dr. Watson on the
subject. The same day, in the afternoon, I attended
the Abbé Sicard's lecture.

14th, I called on Mr. Michael Gibbs, one of the
sub-committee. Nothing had yet been done respecting my application.

21st, After waiting a week, in hopes that I should
hear from the sub-committee, I called again on Mr.
Gibbs. He was not within. I left a note for him.
I called again and found a note from him, in which
he informed me that Mr. Townsend had two days
before sent him my papers (meaning my credentials,
such as Gov. Smith's, Gov. Goodrich's, Dr. Strong's,
Dr. Green's of Princeton, certificates, which, by the
way, so great is English caution towards foreigners,

I have found absolutely necessary and almost indispensable)—which he had sent to Dr. Watson. He
also advised me to go with Mr. Townsend, who
could attend to it in a day or two, to Dr. Watson's.
I had been advised before by Mr. T. not to visit the
school for the present. I immediately rode to Mr.
Townsend's, who lives some distance from town, but
did not find him at home. 24th, I received a note
from Mr. Townsend, in which he said that on the
26th he would accompany me to Dr. Watson's.

So on this day I had my first interview with the
doctor. He started certain fears and difficulties on
the subject of my admission, and I explained the nature of my object and views. I observed, at parting,
that I wished for an answer to my application as soon
as convenient, as my expenses were considerable and
their increase was diminishing the fund in America
for the relief of our unfortunate deaf and dumb.
Dr. W. said he wished for a little time to consider
the subject, and that after conferring with Mr. Gibbs,
he would acquaint me with the result. On my
return I called on Mr. Gibbs and was informed that
he had left town and would not return till the ensuing week. 28th, I visited the school and had a
short conversation with Dr. W., but nothing decisive
transpired. 29th, I went to Mr. Townsend's and had
some conversation with him on my business. He
said he would do every thing in his power to serve
me, that he would endeavor to see Mr. Gibbs
immediately on his return and urge the importance
of a speedy meeting of the sub-committee.

31st, I again visited the school, and had some

conversation with Dr. W. In the course of it, I inferred from what he said, that it would have been more correct for me (in his opinion), to have originally made my application to himself rather than to the committee, inasmuch as his engagement with them was simply to instruct the pupils of the school. But I acted by the advice of Mr. Townsend, the original founder of the institution and now one of the committee, and indeed, would it not have been indecorous in me to have gained an introduction to a public and charitable institution without first applying to those who have the management of it? Aug. 1st, I visited Mr. Townsend and also Mr. Gibbs, who said he would endeavor to have a meeting of the sub-committee held in two or three days. 3d, I called again on Mr. Gibbs, who said the sub-committee would meet the ensuing week. 5th, I had some conversation with Mr. Piper, one of the sub-committee. He expressed his wish to promote my views, but alluded to some difficulties that Dr. Watson had suggested, with fears that they might not be obviated. 7th, I had another interview of considerable length with Dr. W. I asked him if he could propose any plan by which he could give me the benefit of becoming acquainted with the theory and practice of his art. He replied, that he should rather wait to see the decision of the sub-committee. He again observed that the committee had no control over him any further than that he had engaged with them to instruct the deaf pupils who might be introduced into the school.

10th, I left with Mr. Piper a paper of some length

to be laid before the sub-committee, who were to meet this day at the City of London Tavern, accompanied with my credentials for their examination. In this paper I gave a succinct account of what had transpired before I left home with regard to the proposed institution at Hartford, and also stated my reasons for not being willing to assent to any proposal of carrying to America with me an instructor of the deaf and dumb from this country, or of pledging myself, at present, to continue with Dr. W. for a definite period of time, without first making trial of my capacities for improvement in his art. I concluded with respectfully asking the sub-committee, whether they could in any way assist me in the accomplishment of my object.

11th, I received a note from Mr. Stephen Hough, chairman of the sub-committee, inclosing a copy of the report which they had concluded to make to the committee. It was as follows—

"Resolved, That after mature deliberation, taking into view the due discipline of the institution and the proper time requisite to qualify an effective instructor of the deaf and dumb: The auditors, in conjunction with Dr. Watson, beg to recommend the committee to allow Mr. Gallaudet to be received into the school for one month upon liking, with the view that on the expiration of that period he shall be engaged as an assistant for three years on the usual terms, with power to Dr. Watson to release him from his engagement sooner, if it should appear that Mr. G. is qualified before the end of that time."

12th, I called on Mr. Parnell, one of the sub-

committee, to inquire whether the "liking" mentioned in the report was to be reciprocal. He said
that that was the intention of the sub-committee.

15th, I visited Dr. Watson at the school in order
to inquire into the duties of his assistants. He
informed me that it is expected of them, and would be
of me, to be in the school from seven o'clock in the
morning till eight in the evening and also with the
pupils in their hours of recreation. He observed
that the first employment of an assistant is to teach
the pupils *penmanship*. This I remarked would be
a part of the principal difficulty that I had anticipated and would serve to illustrate it. For it showed
that I might be familiar both with the theory and
practice of certain stages of his pupils' improvement
and yet be detained from advancing until they also
should become familiar with them. This I observed
would be a useless sacrifice of time on my part. I
suggested again the plan of my having intercourse
with his private pupils, but he declined saying any
thing on that point, till I had made up my mind
with regard to the proposal of the committee.

I called also on Mr. Parnell. He informed me
that the committee had accepted the report of the
sub-committee.

Thus you see, my dear sir, the dilemma in which
I am placed. The committee throughout all this
affair have been obliged to act with the greatest
caution toward Dr. Watson. They have not been
willing to offend him. I think I do not use too
strong language. And I do believe had my business
rested solely on the feelings of the committee I

should have had every facility granted me that I could wish. But Dr. Watson, I must say, from the very first has conducted toward me with a cautious reserve that I did not expect, and suggested certain plans which I thought interfered a little with my right of private judgment, not to say with my feelings of delicacy and honor. For instance, he alluded to the Mr. Braidwood, who is now in America, and suggested the expediency of his being associated with me in the school at Hartford. On this I need make no remarks. He also urged quite strongly the scheme of my carrying one of his assistants to America with me. How could I do this? How could I at present (not having heard a word from you) pledge myself to bear the expenses of an assistant across the water, and also that he should be supported when he arrived there. Besides, I knew not the character or talents of his assistants, and a more formidable objection still was the fear, lest my plans of instruction and government might clash with this assistant's. He would be wedded to Dr. Watson's mode. I should wish, and I yet hope, to combine the peculiar advantages of both the French and English modes of instruction. For there are considerable differences between them. Well, Dr. Watson saw that I was bent upon acquiring the art myself and of pursuing my own plans of conduct. He now began to talk of difficulties in the way of my admission into the institution, always taking care to let me know that I ought originally to have applied to him and that the committee had no control over him in reference to this affair. He invited me, to be sure, to visit the school and look among the pupils. He promised to give me any information in his power and to solve if possible any difficulties I had found in his art. But although I feel thankful to him for these civilities yet he must have known that I never could think of visiting his school, day after day, in the character of a mere visitor. I should soon have rendered myself obnoxious to him and to his assistants by the ardor of my curiosity and the frequency of my intercourse with his pupils. No, I wanted a definite arrangement with him of some kind or other that would have enabled me for several months, perhaps more than a year, to have become familiar with the theory and practice of his art. I offered him a remuneration for any services of this kind, but he declined it. He always talked of the length of time that would be necessary to acquire his art and generally spoke of four or five years. He alluded also to the difficulty of introducing me into the school in any other character than that of an assistant and for any short period of time ; *inasmuch* as doing otherwise would create disaffection among his assistants, who engage to stay with him five years. I doubt not his views and feelings had great influence upon the sub-committee in making their report. And you see what this report is. If I comply with it I must *bind* myself to *labor for Dr. Watson* three whole years, be subject to his complete disposal of me during that time, have no hope of freedom unless he please (and all his feelings of interest would lead him to detain me in order to make his art appear as difficult and impor-

tant as possible), and what is worse than all, be continually retarded and cramped in my progress,
because I should be obliged to wait for the progress
of the pupils whom I might instruct.   Besides, when
am I to avail myself of the Abbé Sicard's kindness?
During these three years ?   No ; Dr. Watson would
not consent to this.   Afterwards ?   Then four or
five years must elapse from the time when I left you
to my return.   This is too monstrous a sacrifice of
time and patience and money.   Again, is it generous
to place me thus absolutely at Dr. Watson's disposal
to say when I am qualified ?   Shall I be treated like
a mere apprentice, whom his master must chain by
indentures lest he make his escape ?   Is no confidence to be placed in my own judgment and integ-
rity?   The more I think of this proposed arrangement the more I dislike it, and I already begin to
look for some other way in which Providence may
guide me to the accomplishment of my wishes.   I
do hope my perplexities here have taught me more
sensibly my dependence on Him.   To Him do I look
for direction and I ask your prayers and the prayers
of my friends, that I may be enabled by His grace
to conduct with all due wisdom, discretion and prudence in my arduous undertaking.   I ought to have
observed that a salary of £35 per annum (with my
board), for the first year and something more for the
next is offered me, if I become Dr. Watson's assistant.   This would be well earned in toiling for him
from morning till night with only one-half day's
recreation in the week allowed me!!!   Think, my
dear sir, what a wound my feelings have received in

all this business. Think how we used to speak before I left you of the ready welcome and the cheerful assistance that I should receive here. Compare this with what has happened. You can easily fill up the picture. Well, it has all been ordered right *and I have not despaired. I do not.* Edinburgh and Paris are yet open to me. At the former is a very respectable school under *noble* patronage, of which a Mr. Kinniburgh is the teacher. My friends here (many of them) advise me to go there. *I can not* get worse terms than are offered me here. *I may get better.* The Scotch are hospitable. No rivalry exists between Mr. Kinniburgh and the Abbé Sicard. Living may be somewhat cheaper. The voyage thither occupies at this season of the year only three or four days and costs only as many guineas. The Rev. David Bogue, of Gosport, of whom you have doubtless heard, is now in London. I have often consulted with him on my business. He advises me strongly to go to Edinburgh. He has been there and is intimately acquainted with several eminent characters. He does not doubt my success. He will give me the best letters of introduction, among others, one to his particular friend, J. F. Gordon, Esq., one of the secretaries of the deaf and dumb institution. If I go to Edinburgh, I shall hope for more openness and cordiality, and for some arrangement with Mr. Kinniburgh which will enable me to become acquainted with the English mode of instruction at the same time that I may be revising my French in order to go to Paris, as soon as the state of France and my own preparation for

such a visit will permit. As to revising my French
here or having any leisure, it would be out of the
question under the arrangement which the committee propose to me. I can not write you any thing
yet respecting the internal economy and arrangement of the school here, for I have not had the
opportunity of becoming acquainted with them. I
hope you are advancing in the affair at home. Whatever arrangements can be made with regard to the
collection of money, for the erection of buildings
and the support of *charity scholars* ought, I think,
to be done. With regard to the structure of such
buildings, and the mode in which the pupils are
received, and supported and taught, I shall give you
the earliest information in my power. *My funds*
also will require an increase. My expenses are considerable already, although I conscientiously study
the strictest economy. They were much increased
by my journey from Liverpool hither. Besides, I
wish to purchase all the valuable books that I can
procure which have a reference to my future profession—the instruction of deaf-mutes. I have already
been to almost every bookshop in London for this
purpose and have procured a few, both in French
and English. The school in Hartford must have
such a library. It is a pleasure to me to think that I
have the confidence of my friends at home, so that
when I ask for funds they will, I know, feel satisfied
that they will be applied with prudence to the furtherance of my object. I sometimes feel, however,
that as I have devoted myself to the deaf and dumb
in the early part of my life, with no stipulation with

regard to my future support, trusting for this to the
ordering of events by a kind Providence, that I
might now be indulged with something more than
the mere paying of my expenses. A trifling sum
which I might use while in Europe for the procur-
ing of a small library of my own would be a favor
to me, and this I desire only because I have now
so good an opportunity of collecting a few books,
and have no resources of my own to do it with.
And, in fact, rather than be deprived of the advan-
tage of this opportunity, I should even seek for a
loan of a small sum of money from some of my
friends, hoping to be able to refund it after the
establishment of our school. But on this point I
merely disclose my feelings to yourself and Mr.
Woodbridge, and I should *never wish to have it
mentioned* if it would be at all unfriendly to the
nicest honor of my own character as a man and a
Christian, or unfriendly *in the least* to the welfare of
the projected undertaking in which we have
embarked.

I ought to have mentioned that there are various
school-books and ingenious modes of instructing
youth in the different branches of knowledge, which
I ought to purchase while abroad for the use of our
school, and this also will make an increase to the
fund necessary. Perhaps in the course of the fall,
if it is practicable, you had better remit some money
to Peter Barlow, Esq., 8 Tokenhouse Yard, London,
by the way of a bill drawn in his favor on some
house here for my use. This would be better than
to draw in my favor directly, as I may be in Edin-

burgh. In the meanwhile I shall hope to get permanently settled and to write you more explicitly than I now can respecting the probable extent of my expenses and the length of my absence. I have already expended since I concluded to embark in this enterprise a little more than £130 sterling. But you will observe this sum went to pay for the necessary preparations for my voyage before I left America; my expenses from Hartford to New York and same at New York; my passage to Liverpool and expenses there; my journey from Liverpool hither; a month's residence here and some clothes and books. What my expenses will in future be I can not tell. I fear, however, that with the strictest economy my personal expenses when settled (not including necessary traveling or voyages, nor books, etc., for the school), will not be less than 1000 dollars a year. And this in London just enables a single man to live comfortably if he means to preserve an intercourse with a few respectable people. August 17th. This morning I breakfasted with Mr. Bogue and laid before him all my views with regard to the arrangement proposed to me at the school here. He thought it best for me immediately to go to Edinburgh, so that you must not be surprised if I conclude to shape my course thither within a few days.

The mother of Mr. Braidwood, who is in America, will be much obliged by any information you can give me respecting him. Do take some pains to do this. I wish to oblige her, and write all you know of him, be it good, bad or indifferent.

If, after all, I should judge it expedient to carry

back with me an assistant from this side of the
water for the benefit of the school in Hartford,
when I have qualified *myself,*—or should this
become the more necessary, in case I should continue to be met with obstacles in becoming familiar
with the English mode of instruction, and have easy
access only to the French school, what would the
patrons of our school say to such a plan? Should
we *commence* with a considerable number of pupils,
such an assistant might be quite necessary; for I
said that *one person* can not successfully devote his
whole attention to a great many. I only suggest
this for consideration and I wish to hear from you
and the other gentlemen on this point.

BE PARTICULAR also to send me by *the earliest*
opportunity an exact account of what has been done
with regard to the proposed school. And also something in the shape of a document to show these *two
things :* that the school is to be a public and charitable institution, and that I am the proposed teacher
of it and sent abroad for that purpose. Let this be
signed by some persons in their official capacity. I
have wanted already such a document very much.

August 19th. Yesterday I saw Dr. Watson and
informed him that I had concluded not to accept of
the arrangement proposed to me by the committee.
I asked him whether he could propose any plan for
the accomplishment of my wishes. He rather
waived the subject and soon observed that I might
perhaps as well make experiments upon deaf and
dumb pupils in the United States as here. And yet
he often speaks of the long time in which, under

Mr. Braidwood, he was acquiring a familiarity with the theory and practice of his art. I did not press the subject. He again alluded to the difficulty there would be in introducing me into his school in an *unknown* character, meaning, no doubt, that I had not brought with me any *official* document to show that I was designated as the instructor of a public and charitable institution.

But with regard to what I have said of Dr. Watson's character and motives, it is my most earnest and particular request, that no publicity be given, in any shape. I have a right to form my own opinion of the treatment which I have met with here and to communicate it in confidence to my friends. But it is the part of prudence and of Christian forbearance, too, in what we say openly of others, not to impeach their motives of conduct unless they avow them. It will be enough, therefore, to say, that the committee have proposed terms to me, that I could not feel myself justified in accepting, when I considered the importance of accomplishing my object as speedily as its final success would permit.

I hope to leave London for Edinburgh next week. I shall have the best letters of introduction, and I hope Providence will see fit to smile upon my visit there. You shall hear from me very soon again. Yesterday I wrote Mr. Woodbridge by the *Criteria* for New York, giving him a sort of epitome of this letter. This I did that you might be sure to hear from me.

What has become of Julia Brace? I hope she will not be forgotten. You may think it chimerical, but I do believe she might be taught many words and perhaps to read, by having raised letters, in relief, as it were, which she might feel. This is the way the blind are taught at Amsterdam. I have a specimen of their type. They are now learning to *read the Bible* with their fingers.

I long to see Hartford once more and to be in the midst of my deaf and dumb children. I feel more than ever devoted to the object. Be assured I shall not be deterred from prosecuting it by *any obstacles.* It's a good cause, and Providence, we have every reason to think, will crown it with final success. But we must feel our dependence on Him. Mere human wisdom and strength are broken reeds on which to lean. How much I want to hear of your welfare and that of your dear family—may I say, of your spiritual welfare. How often while I was with you, did I wish to ask the question, but my heart failed me, whether you did indulge the hope of being born of God. Even now, perhaps, I am taking a liberty which it is sometimes thought even the closest friendship will not justify. Pardon me. You will not object, however, to my saying that it is often my most earnest prayer that all that dwell beneath your roof may receive the richest of spiritual blessings in Christ Jesus, and that God may enter into *covenant* with each of your souls. Let me ask, also, your prayers for me, that I may be preserved in safety till my return, and above all, that I may be enabled continually to act with a reference to the glory of God and to the best good of my fellow-men.

I have once written Alice, and I again write her.

I shall hope to hear from her. Remember me
affectionately to Mrs. C. and all your family and
to other friends who may think of me.

Yours sincerely,

T. H. GALLAUDET.

A few days after writing this letter, Mr.
Gallaudet repaired to Edinburgh, with strong
hopes of attaining the object he had so much
at heart. But in Edinburgh, as in London,
he was to encounter the Braidwood monopoly,
and to find men of naturally benevolent dis-
positions and generous impulses, willing to
recognize its binding force as against such an
appeal from a distant foreign land as he most
eloquently urged. Mr. Gallaudet's experience
in Edinburgh is fully given in the following
letters, the first being to Dr. Cogswell:

EDINBURGH, Sept. 22, 1815.

MY DEAR SIR:—Not a syllable has yet reached
me from Hartford. Indeed I am much grieved at
this. I want to know your movements with regard
to our project. I can not account for your silence.
So many opportunities by which to write me, and
yet four months now have elapsed since I left you,
and I am wholly ignorant of what you are doing.
I have written you and Mr. Woodbridge again and
again, giving you a circumstantial detail of my proceedings. My last letters were sent by Mr. Junius

Smith, who sailed in the *Venus*, bound for New York, the latter part of the last month. By him I gave you a journal of my proceedings at London. Strange that I should meet with any disappointment at the institution in that metropolis for the deaf and dumb! But so it was. Although I had frequent access to the school and several conferences with. Dr. Watson, yet when I proposed any thing like an effectual arrangement for the accomplishment of my object, terms were offered me by the committee to which I could not accede. But of all this transaction, I have given both yourself and Mr. Woodbridge, by different vessels, a particular account. And here also I am surrounded with unexpected embarrassments. Mr. Kinniburgh, the instructor of the school in this place for the deaf and dumb, received his first instructions in his art from Mr. Thomas Braidwood, the grandson of the original Mr. Braidwood, to whom he bound himself not to communicate any information respecting the subject to any individual for seven years. Four years of this period have expired. I have been corresponding with Mr. Thomas Braidwood on this subject, in hopes that I might prevail on him to release Mr. Kinniburgh so far as his bond might refer to America. But Mr. Braidwood is not to be moved. This morning I received a positive refusal to my application. The reason for this which Mr. B. assigned is, that his brother, Mr. Jno. B., is in our country,—the same gentleman of whom we heard as being in Virginia. The truth is, he left this place a few years since in disgrace. · He was solicited to undertake the super-

intendence of a public school for the deaf and dumb.
He conducted so badly and contracted so many
debts, that he was obliged to abscond. What dependence can be placed on such a character! Still
I do not despair. I hope yet to persuade the committee of the school here either that the bond
under which Mr. Kinniburgh is laid is an illegal one,
or at least that it has no reference to one from a
foreign country. Still my success in this is prob-
lematical. I shall make all the efforts in my power.
If I fail I shall resort to one or two private instructors in this neighborhood and in London, and if the
state of France will permit, I shall visit the Abbé
Sicard. I shall want more money to be remitted
to Mr. Barlow. My expenses have been considerably increased by my unexpected delays and disappointments. Indeed I am confounded almost by
this scene of trial which I have to pass through.
But I do not despair. You must trust me that I
will gain all the advantages I can for the promotion
of our common object. I feel devoted to it. I long
to see it accomplished. If you mean to have this
business carried through, it will be necessary speedily
to remit more money. Not that I am yet in want
of it, but it is better to be beforehand in affairs of
this kind. Perhaps I may yet have to expend some
money in accomplishing my arrangements with the
instructor here or with some private instructor in
the way of a fee. Possibly an offer of this kind may
yet move Mr. Braidwood. Mr. Kinniburgh wants
no such reward. He is a most benevolent man.
Should such an arrangement be necessary, how large

a sum can you devote to this purpose? How much
have you already raised? Rest assured I shall study
economy in all my personal expenses; but if, after
having devoted myself to this object simply on the
condition at present of having my expenses defrayed,
I am left in the lurch for the sake of a little money
which I know could be raised in a short time in
Boston and New York, I shall be extremely disappointed with regard to the generosity of my
countrymen. For some days past I have been
laboring to procure acquaintance among persons of
influence here who may be able to assist me in any
plans which I may finally think it expedient to
adopt. Among these I feel a peculiar satisfaction
in naming Dugald Stewart, Esq. And how do you
think I found access to him? It was by means of
Julia Brace, the little deaf, dumb, and blind girl, the
importance of visiting whom I so strongly urged
upon you, as you, no doubt, recollect. I mentioned
her case to Dr. Buchanan, one of the clergymen of
this place, observing that I should much like to
communicate the facts respecting her to Mr. Stewart.
Mr. S. happened soon to be in town. Dr. B. introduced me to him. I was invited to spend a day and
night in his family at Kinneil house, about eighteen
miles distant. I did this a few days since and left
with him an account of Julia Brace with which he
appeared to be much interested. I shall hope to
see him in town before long. In the meanwhile
Mrs. Stewart gave me a letter of introduction to
Dr. John Gordon, the writer of the article "Deaf
and Dumb" in the Encyclopedia, one of the com-

mittee of the institution here, on whom I have called,
and I have no doubt that he will do every thing in
his power to promote my object. He feels a deep
interest in the general subject. But you can hardly
conceive how slow a business it is to get at large
bodies of men in this country. Several weeks, you
recollect, elapsed in London before their committee
could give me their ultimatum. And it will be some
time before I can make my final arrangements here.
I rejoice, however, that I came to Edinburgh. Here
men of science have taken an interest in the instruction of the deaf and dumb. Here there are several
pupils, men of respectability, of the former Mr.
Braidwood's, with whom I can have an acquaintance.
There is also one gentleman in town, and another
thirty or forty miles distant, who have practiced
this art; so that I shall procure a great deal of
general information on the subject, even if I should
not be able finally to get access to Mr. Kinniburgh's
school. As soon as I make any definite arrangement
I shall be careful to inform you by the first opportunity. I have been in Mr. Kinniburgh's school.
Several of his pupils have made great progress;
Turner, especially, whose letters are published in the
Edinburgh Encyclopedia. I am now reading the
Abbé Sicard's system in French, by way of prepara-
tion, in case I should visit him in Paris. He expects
to publish a new work on the subject in the course
of a few months. It will appear in London. Could
I get all the necessary instruction in Scotland or
England, and have a complete set of the Abbé
Sicard's works, I should think it of less importance

to visit Paris. But time alone can determine this. In the meanwhile, I hope my friends in Hartford will continue to remember me in their prayers, that I may be carried through this arduous undertaking successfully. Indeed I long to return. I feel more and more satisfied that the simple, quiet, retired path of duty, in which we can in some way or other serve God and do good to the bodies and souls of men, is the only path of peace. Oh, that we may all be enabled to walk in it! During the short time that I have been in Edinburgh I have seen objects and formed acquaintances which, on the other side of the water, would, in prospect, have filled my soul with the most splendid visions of delight. To tread this classic ground, to be in the Athens of the world, and even to have intercourse with some of its greatest philosophers and literati, all this would promise much. But it has all served to convince me that nothing can satisfy the immortal mind but God Himself, and that so long as we *divide* our hearts between Him and *any* other object, so long there must be a tumult of wretchedness in our breasts.

How do you all do? What advances is Alice making? My best regards to Mrs. C., to Mary, Elizabeth, and Mason. Nor would I forget your domestics, to whom I wish to be remembered. May Almighty God continue to bless you all with every needful temporal and spiritual good.

Yours truly,

T. H. GALLAUDET.

In a letter bearing date Edinburgh, December 6, 1815, to Mr. Ward Woodbridge, of Hartford, Mr. Gallaudet, after rehearsing his futile efforts to induce Mr. Braidwood to release the authorities of the Edinburgh school from their bond of £1,000 to him, writes as follows:

Notwithstanding Mr. B's refusal, I still had hopes that the committee of the institution, might, upon reflection, consider the bond as an illegal one, or, at least, as not applicable to my case. I was encouraged in this by several of my friends. I resolved, of course, to apply to the committee. Many of them, and Mr. Gordon among the rest, were in the country. I had to wait some time for their return. They at last met and were unanimously of opinion that good faith required of them a strict observance of the bond even in the case of a foreigner. I wish, however, that you should understand that in all the intercourse which I have had with the committee and with Mr. Kinniburgh, the worthy and able teacher of the institution, I have met with the most kind and liberal treatment; and I have not the smallest doubt, that had it been possible, I should have received from the institution, gratuitously and cordially, every assistance which it could afford me. These events occupied some time. The season had advanced considerably and several reasons determined me to spend a few months longer in Edinburgh. The state of France was at the time very unsettled. A few months would probably determine whether the Bourbons could maintain their place. The libraries here contain several rare and valuable works on the instruction of the deaf and dumb, which I could not probably have any other opportunity of examining. From these, especially from a treatise by Dalgarno, belonging to Dugald Stewart, Esq., I have made extracts that I hope will be of service to me. Dr. Gordon also, the author of the article "Dumb and Deaf" in the Edinburgh Encyclopedia, and Dr. Thos. Brown, Professor of Moral Philosophy, have been kind enough from time to time to lend me books which treat directly on the subject of my intended pursuit. I have also been attending Dr. Brown's lectures on the Philosophy of the Mind and revising my French a little; so that, all things considered, I hope our project will not eventually suffer by my detention here. I ought to mention also that I have been successful enough to procure the Abbé Sicard's works, which I have been reading. My present plan is to visit Paris in the spring. In some of my late letters I have mentioned that it would be well to add a little to my pecuniary resources. It is best to be in season with things of this kind. I have resolved to ask whether it would be thought quite consistent with the *strictest* adherence to propriety, to allow me while abroad something more than my *mere expenses.* I have one reason for making this request, the wish that I have to improve the opportunity I enjoy of purchasing a few books. But do not mistake me. *I have no wish to push this matter.*

Whether it be pride or a better principle, I do hope
that my settled plan of life is to devote myself to
the service of God and to trust to His providence to
make provision for me, without being at all particular on this point in any dealings which I may have
with my fellow-men.

I close this letter in haste, as I have just received
a letter from my brother who expects to sail from
Liverpool in a few days. Give my best remembrance to all inquiring friends. My health has suffered a little from the extreme variableness and
humidity of the Edinburgh winter; but I hope to
revive in the spring. May the Giver of all good
continue to yourself and family this invaluable
blessing and shower down upon you the more
delightful blessings of His grace. My best regards
to Mrs. W. and your family.

Yours truly,

T. H. GALLAUDET.

Among Mr. Gallaudet's papers numerous
evidences appear of the efforts he speaks of
making "to procure acquaintance among
persons of influence" who might aid him in
his efforts to break down the Braidwood monopoly.

His diary mentions a "breakfast Thursday
morning, August 31st, with Rev. D. Dickson,
D. D. ;" of a "dinner with Dr. Duncan, senior,
Friday, September 1st ;" of a "dinner with Mr.

James Carmichael, Saturday, September 2nd ;"
of a "dinner with Dr. Anderson, Sunday,
September 3d ;" of a "breakfast with Rev. Dr.
Hall, Monday, September 4th, at Pulan's farm-
house, half a mile from the Lunatic Asylum
Morning-side village, Lenton Road ;" and a
dinner at a "festival of Pomona, Oman's
Tavern, St. Andrew's Square, Tuesday, September 5th." Among the friends he made was
Lady Anna Maria Elliott, a daughter of the
Earl of Minto, to whom Mrs. Dugald Stewart
had introduced him. Lady Anna was a friend
of Mrs. Braidwood, and expressed the hope to
Mr. Gallaudet that "Mrs. Braidwood might
perhaps listen to the representations of an
impartial person, sooner than to those who
may be supposed to have a nearer interest in
the matter." But the Braidwood monopoly
was equally proof against the blandishments
of personal friendship and titled rank, as
against appeals in the name of Christian
charity.

To Mr. Gallaudet, and as he says, to *some* of
his advisers, the contract with Mr. Braidwood
seemed as one without legal force, and this
view he did not hesitate to express openly.
But when the incidents of his experience in
Edinburgh were made, somewhat later, the

subject of comment in the public journals, he was virulently assailed, accused of the " sin of violating the obligations of gratitude and truth," charged with " obtuseness of understanding " and a " defective moral system," all because he had ventured to characterize the Braidwood bond as an *illicitum pactum.*

While remaining in Edinburgh Mr. Gallaudet received an interesting letter from his far off pupil, Alice Cogswell, which will be read with interest as showing the progress she was making under the instructions of Miss Huntley [Mrs. L. H. Sigourney].

HARTFORD, Wednesday, October 11, 1815.

MY DEAR SIR :—I remember story Miss Huntley was tell me.   Old many years Mr. Colt little boy Name man Peter Colt very much curls little boy hair Oh ! very beautiful mama lap little boy comb curl love to see O beautiful.   Morning long man preacher coat black come bow ask mama give little boy hair make wigs very beautiful preacher give, mama no preacher. yes oh· yes talk long man say come back little boy scissors cut hair white hair curls all in heap make wig preacher am very much glad proud little—little boy head very cold mama tie handkerchief warm, tears no more mama very sorry.   I hope my hair never cut make wigs—This morning study all in school away Geography all beautiful a school all very beautiful very still very good noise no—the Play no, Miss Huntley work and two go Norwich all school come not—me very sorry come back little while—O all very glad,—O beautiful—I love you very much—

Your affectionate,
ALICE COGSWELL.

In a letter from Dr. Cogswell, of the same date, Alice's letter is explained as follows :—

As soon as I knew of Mr. Upson's sailing I proposed to Alice to write you by him. She readily consented, but said she was at a loss what to write. I told her to write the story Miss Huntley related to her from Mr. Colt—the circumstances I will relate, that you may the better understand it : Mr. Peter Colt, from Patterson, was lately here on a visit ; he told her [Miss Huntley] what happened to him, when he was a little boy. It seems he had a very thick head of white curled hair; a clergyman who was visiting his mamma, took a fancy to it, for the purpose of making himself a *wig;* his mamma, at first, refused, but after a little urging, *talk long,* as Alice calls it, she consented, and the hair was cut off and the wig made. You will observe that the conversation between his mamma and the preacher is somewhat in the form of a dialogue. You know so much of her manner, that I believe you will understand it. Miss Huntley communicated the story to her by signs. Miss Huntley, as you will perceive by Alice's letter, is at Norwich, on a visit. The letter

is all her own, without any assistance or correction.
With every wish for your success and happiness,

I am affectionately yours,

MASON F. COGSWELL.

MR. T. H. GALLAUDET.

Mr. Gallaudet remained in Edinburgh until
toward the close of the winter, making good
use of his time, as may be understood from
his letters, although he failed to accomplish
the special object of his visit. The memo-
randa found in his notebooks show him to
have been indefatigable in his endeavors to
improve himself in every possible way. He
made many acquaintances among the cultivated
people of Scotland—visiting Dugald Stewart
at his home near Edinburgh, and Thomas
Chalmers at Glasgow—both of whom, as well
as Mrs. Stewart, became his warm friends, Dr.
Chalmers sustaining a voluminous correspondence with him after his return to America.

Mr. Gallaudet during his stay in Edinburgh
wrote a letter to Dugald Stewart, describing
the case of Julia Brace, a blind deaf-mute
whom he had visited before leaving America.
Some extracts from this letter will be of
interest, particularly in view of the fact that the
teaching of this child antedated by several
years the education of Dr. Howe's more dis-

tinguished deaf and blind pupil, Laura Bridgman.

Mr. Gallaudet says, under date of September 26, 1815 :

When about four years and a half old, this little girl was afflicted with a violent fever of long continuance, on her recovery from which it was found that she was entirely blind and deaf. She had before this enjoyed the use of all her senses in perfection. . . . . For a short time after her loss of sight and hearing she retained the use of speech, which she employed to make her wants known to those around her. But in this she soon became imperfect and incoherent. Still she would delight to repeat in their order the little lessons of words she had before learned in her spelling book, and what was most distressing to hear, to pour forth, occasionally, an incessant volley of oaths and imprecations, which were, no doubt, first taught her by the force of a pernicious example, and now furnished by memory on every occasion of perturbation or anger ; for at this time she was the victim of a temper so furious and ungovernable, that nothing short of absolute confinement could restrain it ; and this, as the mother acknowledged, was unfortunately too seldom employed. Her circle of words daily contracted within narrower and narrower limits, so that when I saw her she uttered nothing more during the space of a few hours than two or three inarticulate sounds which seemed to be the result of some emotions, though they were entirely unintelligible. And these imperfect remains of speech must soon be lost, so that she will in a little while be as absolutely dumb as she is now deaf and blind. Her senses of touch and smell have been gradually growing more acute and discriminating. She could go to any part of the house without assistance, and even into the yard, which she sometimes did with a basket for the purpose of gathering chips. . .

When any new object was given to her she first felt every part of it, moving the ends of her fingers over it with peculiar minuteness and delicacy. She then applied it to her upper lip, on which she rubbed it for some time, as if there was the seat of a more nice sensibility of feeling, and after smelling it, all of which she did with much apparent eagerness and delight, she immediately placed it in her sister's hands, still retaining hold of it herself, and with her fingers directing her sister to the same process of touching and smelling through which she had just passed, and the pleasure of which she seemed to wish to enhance by making it a social one.

Speaking of a fear of strangers, and especially men, which Julia had, and which could be traced to a dread of her physician, who had applied painful blisters to various parts of her body during her illness, Mr. Gallaudet says :

When I saw her this fear had very considerably abated ; . . she freely felt us, rubbing our hands

with her own, which she afterwards applied to her
nose, as if still retaining on them the peculiarity of
our smell, which by this curious mode of transmis-
sion she seemed to acquire with wonderful accuracy.
An experiment that we several times repeated furnished satisfactory evidence of this.

We put our watches into her hands. While doing
it, she rubbed our hands with one of her own, which
she immediately applied to her nose, in order to
determine to whom the object belonged. Then she
passed through her usual process of feeling and
smelling the watches, with their appendages, and of
soliciting her sister to do the same. After she
appeared to be satisfied with doing this, each of us
attempted to take from her the watch which did not
belong to him. She invariably perceived the deception, would not suffer the wrong commutation, as
she might deem it, to take place, but returned to
each his own watch. . . . New clothes are
highly gratifying to her. . . . She has sometimes a disposition for sport, particularly in the way
of playing off tricks of youthful merriment on her
brothers and sisters. . .

After detailing some incidents, Mr. Gallaudet expresses the opinion that a certain amount
of instruction might be imparted to this unfortunate child—claiming, however, much less
important results than were actually attained
when Julia came, a few years later, under his
care in the school he established at Hartford.

After having gained much useful knowledge in school, Julia Brace lived happily for many years in the institution at Hartford, performing certain duties in an exemplary manner, and enjoying the society of a circle of friends to whom she was warmly attached, and with whom she communicated with considerable facility through the medium of the language of signs. She never attained to any great proficiency in verbal language.

On the 12th of February, 1816, Mr. Gallau-det left Edinburgh for London, where he spent a couple of weeks before proceeding to Paris. It was during this stay in London that he made the acquaintance of Major-General Macaulay and his brother Zachary, the father of the great historian.

With Zachary Macaulay, who was then the editor of the *Christian Observer*, Mr. Gallau-det formed an intimate and valued friendship which was broken only by the death of Mr. Macaulay. Many long letters, on subjects of public, as well as private, interest passed between the two friends, one of which will be found at the end of this chapter.

Mr. Gallaudet arrived in Paris on the 9th of March. Within three days he was cordially received by the Abbe Sicard, then at the

head of the Royal School for Deaf-Mutes,
and offered every possible facility for the
achievement of the object he had been vainly
pursuing in Great Britain.

The benevolent Abbe permitted Mr. Gallaudet to have access to the several classes of
the school, beginning with the lowest and proceeding in regular order through those of
higher grade.

He also arranged that Mr. Gallaudet should
have private lessons from his distinguished
pupil and assistant Massieu.

For two months this work of training went
diligently forward. On the 20th of May an
important incident occurred, which is recorded
as follows in Mr. Gallaudet's diary:

In a conversation had with Clerc this day he
proposed going to America with me as an assistant,
if the Abbé Sicard would give his consent. I think
of addressing the Abbé on the subject.

Clerc was a young deaf-mute about his own
age, who had been a favorite pupil of Sicard's,
and was then teaching a class in the Paris
institution. He was a man of more than
ordinary ability, well versed in all Sicard's
methods of instruction.

His proposal to accompany Mr. Gallaudet to America was most opportune, for the latter was beginning to feel somewhat impatient to return to his native land, and begin the work for which he had been so long endeavoring to prepare himself.

Mr. Gallaudet lost no time in seeking the Abbe's consent to part with Clerc, sending him the following letter within twenty-four hours after Clerc had offered to accompany him to America.

To the Reverend Mr. the Abbe Sicard:

Director of the Institution for the Deaf and Dumb, member of the National Institute of France, etc., etc.

Reverend and Esteemed Sir:—On Sunday last I unexpectedly met an American friend, the commander of a vessel which is soon to sail for the United States, who very strongly solicits me to return with him to my native land. His request is seconded by another of my friends, who has been engaged in this city for twelve years past, in commercial transactions, and who expects to return to America in the same ship. The conveyance would be peculiarly convenient and agreeable to me. I suggested this circumstance to Mr. Clerc, at the same time expressing my fears that it would be quite out of my power to enjoy it, as I doubted whether I could be sufficiently qualified for my intended employment, the instruction of the deaf and dumb. I also observed, that could I procure some deaf-mute as an assistant, I should not hesitate to do it. Mr. Clerc, of his own accord, offered to go with me in this capacity. I told him I could not think of proposing any arrangement of this kind without first securing your approbation, and it is for this reason I now take the liberty of addressing you.

I am fully sensible, Reverend Sir, that in asking you to part with so faithful and valuable a pupil, I solicit, on your part, a great sacrifice; and I should have but little hope of succeeding in my request, were I not satisfied that the *interests of humanity* in the western world will plead strongly with you in my behalf. To *these interests*, in Europe, your life and genius have been devoted, and I can assure you the pleasure which I should feel in transmitting, from your hands, so great a blessing to my countrymen would only be equaled by their gratitude in receiving it. They are by no means ignorant of your justly acquired reputation, and could I thus commence the establishment in New England for the instruction of the deaf and dumb, under your auspices, the name of *Sicard* would be as dear to *America* as it now is to *France*.

My country is already under great obligations to you, Reverend Sir, for the very great kindness with which you have given me free access to the advantages of your important establishment, but how would those obligations be increased, could you consent to send Mr. Clerc with me, as an illustration of the wonders you have performed in redeeming the human mind from the darkness of ignorance, and in illuminating it with the rays of knowledge and virtue. In such a gift the world would see an illustrious proof that *philosophy* and *humanity* equally prevail in the breast of the *Father* of the Deaf and Dumb in France, and that his *benevolence* can surrender for the good of mankind what his *genius* has adorned with the most useful and endearing accomplishments.

Very unexpectedly, and in a manner quite unsolicited on my part, Mr. Clerc expressed his willingness to go with me should it meet with your approbation. Should you consent, Reverend Sir, to grant this approbation, I have no doubt that Mr. Clerc and myself could enter into arrangements which would be deemed advantageous for him, both by himself and friends. For the establishment which I hope to commence, having already excited considerable interest in New England, being under public and respectable patronage, and having a town for its intended situation which is less than two days journey from the large cities of Boston, New York, and Albany, will, I trust, if properly conducted, soon be in a flourishing condition.

I have taken the liberty, Reverend Sir, of expressing my thoughts in writing, for I thought I could do this with the most clearness and precision, and could you furnish me with your reply in the course of a day or two, I shall esteem it a great favor. I am, Reverend Sir, with sentiments of unfeigned respect,

Your very obedient servant,

THOMAS H. GALLAUDET.

PARIS, May 21, 1816.

The venerable Abbe, now nearly eighty years of age, hesitated at first from parting with his favored pupil and valued teacher, but not many days passed before the eloquent appeal of Mr. Gallaudet produced its effect and the consent of the Abbe was communicated in the following note :

J'ai repondu, ce matin, à neuf heures à mon cher eléve Clerc, et je lui donne mon approbation, avec des conditions qu'il vous communiquera. J'espere, monsieur, que vous serez content de moi. Je fais, avec plaisir, le sacrifice que vous m'avez demandé. ce 27 mai, 1816.

L'ABBE SICARD.

Mr. Gallaudet felt himself justified, though not authorized in any way to bind the gentlemen under whose patronage he was in Europe, in entering into a contract with Mr. Clerc for three years. The provisions of this agreement were very advantageous to the young Frenchman, and he turned his face toward the New World under favoring conditions rarely accorded to men. He was called to bear an important and prominent part in a philanthropic work in a new country, being at the same time free from any considerable responsibility or anxiety for the undertaking ; a

handsome income was assured to him, with the
privilege of returning to his native land after
three years ; and he went as the friend of the
chief actor in this new enterprise.

Having secured the services of Clerc, Mr.
Gallaudet lost no time in returning to America.

Within three weeks, or as soon as Mr. Clerc
could complete his arrangements for leaving
home and friends, they sailed from Havre
on the 18th of June.

The records of Mr. Gallaudet's stay in Paris
show that he lived a life of intense activity
during the fourteen weeks that he remained
there.

The best hours of every available working
day were devoted to the school-rooms of the
institution for deaf-mutes. Private lessons
from competent teachers supplemented these
zealous labors. Time was found for numerous
social engagements and some sight-seeing,
and besides all this Mr. Gallaudet acted as
pastor to an English speaking congregation,
preaching no less than fifteen sermons, which
were afterwards published in a volume.

A number of these sermons were prepared
in Paris ; and the entire collection, coming as
it did from one with little previous experience
as a preacher, received such high praise from

the critics of the day as to call for more than
a passing notice in this connection.

Mr. Gallaudet, in his dedicatory note to
Mrs. Hannah More, with whom he had formed
an intimate acquaintance while in England,
speaks as follows of the sermons and the
occasion of their delivery :*

Most of them were delivered while I was prosecuting in Paris, under the auspices of the venerable
Abbé Sicard and his interesting pupil, Clerc, my
present fellow-laborer, the object of qualifying myself to instruct an unfortunate and too long neglected
portion of my countrymen, the deaf and dumb.
Several of your Nation and my own, taught in their
own lands to hallow the Sabbath of the Lord, felt a
desire to do this in the splendid and voluptuous
city where they had assembled, as their surest safe-
guard against its fascinating seductions, and, at the
request of this little flock of strangers I became
their temporary preacher in the Chapel of the Ora-
toire, to which we were kindly allowed access.

The volume, which was published in 1818,
received warm commendation in America, but
nowhere was it more highly approved than in

---

* Discourses on Various Points of Christian Faith and Practice ; most of which were delivered in the Chapel of the Ora-
toire, in Paris, in the spring of 1816, by Thomas H. Gallaudet.
New York : 1818.

England, in the columns of the *Christian Observer*, London, in July, 1818, two years before Sidney Smith flippantly inquired, " In the four quarters of the globe, who reads an American book?"

The *Observer*, after a long extract from the closing sermon, which was one delivered at the opening of the school for deaf-mutes in Hartford in 1817, says:

From the length of this quotation it may possibly be inferred that we consider the last discourse as the best in the collection; and perhaps, at the moment in which we are writing these lines, there may be some justice in the remark, so far, at least, as regards the touching eloquence of the composition. But in truth a similar kind of impression has accompanied us in the perusal of almost every sermon in the volume. It is impossible to read one of them, without perceiving the deep seriousness of the writer, and the elevated character of his mind. His subjects are of high importance; and he appears to be capable of adorning any subject which falls within the range of his Christian ministrations. His views are scriptural and correct; his imagination lively, but under due control; his language, at all times, or with very rare and trifling exceptions, perspicuous, elegant and chaste, and often remarkable for its vivid and glowing eloquence; and the arrangement of his materials is so easy and natural, that every thing seems to have fallen without effort into its proper place. Many of his subjects are common, but he has the art of throwing over them an air of novelty; and while we consent implicitly to every statement as he proceeds, we do it with the sort of pleasure experienced by a traveler in passing on a road with which he was formerly acquainted, but the beauties of which he does not recollect to have sufficiently observed. He remembers the great features of the country around him, but there is a certain freshness in the air, or a luxuriance of vege- tation, or a general liveliness in the landscape, which had hitherto in some way escaped him; and he is glad to dwell upon ancient recollections, with so many circumstances of additional interest and unex- pected gratification.

It is, further, the uniform tendency of these dis- courses to invest Christianity with an amiable and dignified character. We feel that there is some- thing ennobling in religion, and are almost *com- pelled* to love and to admire it. Some of the topics of inquiry would lead many preachers into the thorny paths of controversial disputation; but the mind of Mr. Gallaudet is of too high an order to be thus beguiled. He appears to have drunk of the pure streams of Christianity—pure as they flow from the fountain of holy truth—and the words which he speaks are words of truth and soberness. If his views be elevated, his religion is also practical; and few intelligent persons can peruse these discourses without perceiving both the reasonableness and the excellence of the principles which they inculcate. We venture in conclusion, to recommend them as admirable specimens of compositions for the pulpit —equally remote from coldness and enthusiasm; animated, interesting, and judicious. And many as are the valuable sermons produced by the divines of our own country, we shall rejoice to be frequently favored by such importations from America.

The following letters, selected from among a great number, must serve as illustrations of the correspondence which grew out of Mr. Gallaudet's stay in Great Britain.

Letter from Rev. Thomas Chalmers, D. D.

GLASGOW, March 2, 1817.

MY DEAR SIR:—I beg leave to transmit for your acceptance a volume of sermons published by me within these few days. I received all the pamphlets about the Peace Society, and also your volume of sermons. I am compelled to say that I have, as yet, been able to look very little into either of them. I am glad to understand that your volume has been very favorably noticed in the *Observer.* But really for myself, I am so excessively engrossed, and I am so miserably in arrears, both with unread books, and unanswered letters, that I must for some time store it unread. I have been sadly pressed to take an active part in the business of a Peace Society established here. This I can not do, and all that I can possibly afford in behalf of this object, is my testimony in its favor.

I had, not many weeks ago, an application from Mr. Farquhar Gordon, of Edinburgh, for your sermon and report on the subject of the deaf and dumb. He had not seen them at that time. And I have, since I sent them, had another letter in which he fully exculpates you. I have learned that he was the author of the article against you in the *Instructor*, though I do not think that it is at all in harmony with the temper and principles of the man.

I cordially acquiesce in all you say about the dangers of conformity. I at one time thought that much would be done to conciliate the support of worldly men to the good cause, could its accommodation to the interests of civil society be cunningly held out to them. I am now far less sanguine of any good from their co-operation, and am veering toward the opinion, that the more broadly the aspect of peculiarity and separation is flashed upon the public eye, so much the better. Let us not partition this matter, or give countenance to the doctrine that there is any compatibility between the spirit of the Gospel and the spirit of natural and unconverted men. At the same time I rejoice in the belief, that Christianity is making progress; that evangelical statements are more tolerated by the public at large, and are entering with demonstration and power into a great number of individual hearts; that the national impulse at present is on the side of religious education; and that amid the conflict and operation of all the elements of darkness, there is an element of grace, working and growing and making such progress, as will at length subordinate and, like the rod of Aaron, swallow up all the others.

It is my earnest prayer, in your behalf, that as you have experienced the fulfillment of the one saying, ' In the world ye shall have tribulation,' so you may experience the fulfilment of the other, 'that in Christ ye shall have peace.' May this peace rest in your heart, and the world will not take it away. Do, my dear sir, pray for the entire *simplification* of your aim. ' Let your eye be single, and your whole body shall be full of light.' Oh, at what a distance do I feel from the principle of doing all things for the glory of God, and in the name of Jesus.

Your observations respecting the philosophy of mind, as illustrable by the phenomena of education in your seminary, are highly striking and just. And this suggests to me the mention of a work just now published by Thomas Brown, professor of moral philosophy, Edinburgh, on "Cause and Effect." I used to admire his former pamphlet on this subject, and I am prepared to expect a very profound and accurate exposition of this subtle and interesting argument. I have just begun to read it, and I think you will like it, not merely as a characteristic of, but highly creditable to the Scottish metaphysical school. I am, very dear sir, yours most truly,

THOMAS CHALMERS.

Letter From Mistress Hannah More.

BARLEY WOOD, NEAR BRISTOL,
28th April, 1818.

REV. AND DEAR SIR:—I would not return you

my thanks for your kind letter and very valuable volume, till I had nearly finished your admirable sermons. You are not one of that numerous class of authors whom it is prudent and safe to thank for their books before one has looked into them, as the only way of preserving both one's veracity and good breeding. I declare my judgment is not bribed by your too flattering and most undeserved dedication, when I assure you I think " The Discourses " are of a very superior cast. Though deeply serious they are perfectly uninfected with any tincture of the errors of a certain new school in theology. Your style and manner are in thorough good taste, a garb in which I delight to see sound divinity arrayed. By the blessing of God, I trust they will do much good. The circumstances, too, under whîch they were delivered, as well as the *place*, make them still more interesting to the reader. I was going to point out to you the sermons with which I was particularly pleased; but I found the recapitulation would be almost universal. I would not except any. I was charmed and deeply affected with the sweet letter of my dear little dumb correspondent. [Alice Cogswell.] What heart-felt joy, dear sir, must it afford you to have been the honored instrument of rescuing this, and so many other forlorn little creatures, from a state of almost nonentity! " Inasmuch as ye have done it to one of the least of these, ye have done it unto me," says our divine Master.

I have taken the liberty to convey to your hands, through Mr. Macaulay, a ten-pound bank note, as a small token of my admiration of your admirable institution, to be disposed of in such a way as your judgment shall direct for its benefit.

Adieu, my dear sir. May it please Him without whom nothing is strong, nothing is holy, nothing is successful, to shower down His blessings on you, and on the great work you have, by so much labor, such perilous voyages, and such great difficulties, accomplished; and may many of your pupils thank you in Heaven for having been the favored instrument of bringing them thither.

I remain with sincere esteem,

Your very faithful and obliged,

H. MORE.

Letter from Zachary Macaulay, Esq.

LONDON, 7th November, 1818.

MY DEAR SIR :—I immediately forwarded your letter to Miss More. I have not heard from her since—indeed, there has scarcely been time : but I can not doubt that she will readily accede to your wish of having her likeness to adorn the library commenced by her donation. She has, of late, been suffering from severe attacks of illness, which have produced a considerable prostration of her strength ; but her mind, amidst the infirmities of sickness and age, retains all its pristine vigor, and she labors to employ her remaining hours in elevating the views and aims of all around her, from earth to heaven.

The luminous account you gave me of the superiority of the French mode of instructing the deaf and dumb over the English, you will already have seen in the pages of the *Christian Observer*.

I should have been glad to have seen the specimen of American typography which you have sent me; but it was conveyed to me through the post-office, with a charge of £4 5s. on the cover. I have hesitated to pay this and the packet is still unopened. Whatever is put up in the form of a letter, if it comes by the packet, pays the full packet postage of 8s. 8d. per oz., and if by a merchant ship, half the packet postage, besides the inland postage. I have, of late, had many such parcels addressed me from America, which I have been obliged to decline receiving, on account of the enormous expense attending them. Some of my American friends also choose to address their letters to me by name, as editor of the C. O. This alone forms a reason against my receiving them. It would be a formal acknowledgment of a fact, which I have never acknowledged except to some private friends, and which, indeed, is not known at all to vast multitudes in this country, and only surmised even by the religious world generally.

I· thank you for your kind inquiries respecting my son Thomas Babington. He is now in good health, and prosecuting his studies with ardor at the University of Cambridge. God has been pleased to endow him with very considerable powers of mind, and with a very strong desire for knowledge. My prayer—and indeed I am thankful to say, my hope is that they may be sanctified and made subservient to His glory.

. . . . I have, of late, been much occupied with the congress at Aix-la-Chapelle. You will wonder at this. But the slave trade was my object. I have strong hopes that something effectual may be done, before the sovereigns separate, for that cause. I framed an address on the subject, which was put into their hands, and has been well received. The Emperor of Russia read it, he said, with the most entire satisfaction. He perfectly approved of the proposal to make slave trading piracy, and would do all in his power to effect this object. He gave copies of the address, with his own hand, to the kings and ministers assembled. " It was not to be endured," he said, " that Portugal should continue to resist the united wishes of Europe, by retaining the trade for a single day after other nations had abandoned it. As for the miscreants who should continue it, after it had been universally reprobated, their only proper designation and punishment were those of pirates. I take shame to myself," he added, " before God, that we should have left this great work unfinished at Vienna. I now see that we were guilty of a great and criminal omission, which must not be repeated. When I consider what I owe to the kindness of Providence in rescuing me and my people from the hand of the oppressor, I should be the most ungrateful of men if I did not labor, with all my might, to liberate those who groan under a worse oppression, and especially our wretched fellow-creatures in Africa." This was said to a friend. Lord Castlereagh and the Duke of Wellington are cordially co-operating with him.

The emperor spoke to the same friend, on the subject of the Peace Societies. He said " he could disapprove of no society which had for its object to hasten the happy time, which he firmly believed would come, when nations should have war no more. The great thing to be done, however, was rather to cure the passions which lead to war, than to declaim against war itself. He hoped to be able to induce the governments of Europe to concur in some plan of arbitrating their differences, which might supersede an appeal to arms ; it was impossible, however, to effect this suddenly."

In thinking over the utility of Peace Societies, both here and in America, it occurred to me that there was a way in which they might be infinitely more beneficially employed, than in publishing general declamations against war and its evils. If *our* Peace Societies would take pains to correct all the misrepresentations and exaggerations respecting the state of feeling towards us in America, and to produce kindly feelings towards her, by exhibiting the various circumstances of a favorable kind, which might be noticed ; and if *your* Peace Societies were to pursue a similar conduct, with respect to this country, I can have no question it would do more to preserve peace, and prevent war between the two countries, than all the general reasoning on the subject of war they either have employed or can employ. This would be a practical and practicable object. The pursuit of it would prove the sincerity of their professions and the strength of their principles; and I think would make them popular in both countries.

Mrs. Macaulay and my brother, the general, who is now with us, unite in every kind wish, and in all assurance of esteem and regard, with, my dear sir,

Yours, very sincerely,

ZACHARY MACAULAY.

CHAPTER IV.

1816–23.

Return to America—Efforts to Interest the Public in the Education of the Deaf—Public Addresses in Many Cities—Organization and Opening of the School at Hartford—Favorable Action of State and National Legislatures—Munificent Grant of Land from Congress—Erection and Dedication of Permanent Buildings for the Institution—Rapid Increase of Number of Pupils—Difficulties in Management—Attempt in the Board of Directors to Remove Mr. Gallaudet from Office.

EAGER as Mr. Gallaudet was to commence in America the work to which he had devoted himself with such enthusiasm, he was destined to experience a trial of his patience on the homeward voyage. Calms and head-winds hindered the progress of his vessel, and fifty-one days passed after leaving Havre before he landed in New York. These days, however, were not wasted, for they afforded an excellent opportunity for him to perfect himself in the art of deaf-mute instruction with the aid of his assistant Clerc, and gave the latter time to improve his knowledge of the English language, which was slight when he left France.

Mr. Gallaudet landed in New York on the 9th

of August, 1816, and spent some days in that
city, reaching Hartford on the 22d of the same
month, having been absent on his mission a
little more than fifteen months. The interest
manifested, everywhere, in Mr. Gallaudet's
undertaking was, naturally, very great ; for it
must be remembered that in 1816 no public
charitable institutions of any sort, except a
small hospital for the insane in Virginia,
existed in our country ; unless, indeed, alms-
houses could be spoken of as such.

The following letter from Nathaniel F.
Moore, a professor in Columbia College and
later its president, to Rev. John McVickar,
for more than half a century a professor in
the same institution, written within a fortnight after Mr. Gallaudet's arrival in New
York, gives a graphic picture of the attention
shown to him and his companion.

NEW YORK, August 21, 1816.

MY DEAR SIR :—Knowing the interest you take
in the subject, I have procured for you from Mr.
Gallaudet a report published by the Edinburgh
Institution for the Education of the Deaf and the
Dumb, containing some specimens of their composition ; and I also send you a minute of the conversation we had day before yesterday with Mr. Clerc,
the deaf and dumb companion of Mr. Gallaudet.

This gentleman, you know, was sent abroad by the Connecticut institution that he might qualify himself to take charge of a school to be established at Hartford. He had not intended to return so soon, but this Mr. Clerc, who was seven years a pupil of the Abbé Sicard and eight years more a teacher in his institution, and who when Mr. Gallaudet became acquainted with him had charge of the highest class, having offered to accompany him, he thought it quite unnecessary to wait any longer, considering Mr. Clerc as capable of forming either the teachers or the pupils of the institution here as the Abbé Sicard himself would be.

Mr. Clerc does not speak except by signs, by means of which we saw him and Mr. Gallaudet communicate with each other as expeditiously, almost, as we could do by words. With strangers he converses by writing. Mr. Gallaudet says that Mr. Clerc knew very little of English before they embarked together. You may judge yourself of his progress in it. My father saw him several days ago at the house of Mr. Gallaudet's father, and wrote upon a slate, "I hope you are pleased with New York." He wrote in reply, "Yes—so well that soon I shall not regret France." When he called the day before yesterday with Mr. Gallaudet to return my father's visit my father wrote, "I hope you continue to be pleased with this country." He wrote, "Yes—better and better," and before my father could read his answer he reached out his hand for the slate and added:—"I meet with a good reception everywhere, and the kindest attentions are shown me." I wrote—"We are surprised at your progress in English, your method of learning must have something peculiar in it, or your industry must be very great." He wrote:—"By dint of studying I have got some progress, but my friend, Mr. Gallaudet, has been my best methodic." Before I had time to read his answer, he asked Mr. Gallaudet by signs whether he had not committed an error in the last word, and being told he had, he stepped up to me and rubbed out the two last letters. I wrote:—"It is no wonder that you make mistakes, but that you make so few of them." He wrote in reply:—"Ah, I make many mistakes, and very often, I assure you." When I read this he reached his hand for the slate and wrote:—"Before having seen me, and being informed that I was deaf and dumb, did you know there were deaf and dumb? What idea had you of them? Did you think them unhappy or did you think their situation could be alleviated by learning to read and write?" I replied that "We had heard a great deal in this country respecting the Abbé Sicard and his predecessor, and we took great interest in the deaf and dumb, and consequently knew that their situation might be alleviated." He wrote:—"I thank you for it, and the interest you express for us poor *unfortunates.*"

Sarah, at Mr. Gallaudet's request, entered into a French correspondence with him by writing:—"*C'est etonnaut que vous écrivez si bien l'anglois, je serois bien contente de pouvoir ecrire le françois aussi bien.*" The sight of his own language seemed, as Mr. Gallaudet said it would, to please him very much, and he wrote :—

"*J'etois agréablement surpris, vous écrivez trés bien le françois, et je crois qu'un peu plus agée, vous l' ecrivez encore mieux.*" We had more conversation, both French and English, which was transcribed by Sarah, or written down from recollection by me immediately after, but as my epistle has already run out to a great length, I must suppress a part of it. I am not afraid of having tired you, because I am sure you will be, as we all are, very much interested in this poor unfortunate, as he calls himself; though he has, as I told him, almost lost all claim to that name. I have not been able to learn how abstract ideas are communicated to the deaf and dumb, but as an example of the justness of their notions I give you the following definition of virtue which Mr. Clerc wrote down *verbatim* and *literatim*, as you have it below, on my father's asking him what idea he had of virtue :—"It is the disposition or habit of the soul to do good, to avoid evil, and to observe what divine and human laws order and what reason dictates."

I think the Connecticut institution will open under the most favorable auspices—the talents and experience of Mr. Clerc, and the great progress Mr. Gallaudet had made even before his late visit to Europe authorize very sanguine expectations of the success of their joint exertions.

Believe me, with sincere respect and esteem,

Yours,

NATHANIEL F. MOORE.

The REV. JOHN MCVICKAR, Hyde Park, N. Y.

While Mr. Gallaudet was still in Europe, his supporters and the friends of the deaf in Hartford were not idle. They secured an act of incorporation from the Legislature of Connecticut for the new institution in May, 1816, and raised a considerable sum of money by private subscription, not, however, enough to warrant the opening of the school. The solicitation of funds, therefore, became Mr. Gallaudet's first work. In October, 1816, the Legislature of Connecticut granted five thousand dollars in aid of the enterprise, which is believed to have been the first appropriation of public money made in America in behalf of a benevolent institution. In New York, Philadelphia, Boston, Albany, and a number of smaller towns, the cause of the deaf was successfully urged by its young and zealous apostle. He enlisted the generous support of such men as Elias Boudinot, of New Jersey; Stephen Van Rennselaer, of Albany; Daniel Wadsworth, of Hartford; William Phillips, William Gray and Israel Thorndike, of Boston; and Robert Oliver, of Baltimore. Many donations of less amount followed the liberal subscriptions of these men, and before the opening of the new institution upwards of seventeen thousand dollars was secured.

Mr. Gallaudet's sagacity in bringing an educated deaf-mute from France was proved by the effect produced by young Clerc in their solicitations. His intelligence, and the fact of his being well educated, made it impossible for any one to question the feasibility of the work proposed to be done. And yet, strange as it may now seem, there were those who had declared, even from the sacred desk, that the proposal to educate the deaf was absurd, quixotic, involving a useless waste of money.

The records of the Board of Directors of the institution show that it was no easy task to effect its organization. These public spirited men were setting out on an untrodden path, at least in their own country, and it was difficult to obtain information from any source that might give them the experience of others.

It was thought desirable, since it was necessary to make the new institution a boarding-school, that a suitable person should be employed to take charge of the domestic department. In their search for such an officer the directors were for a number of months singularly unsuccessful, and so serious did this difficulty become, as the time for opening the school drew near, that a day was appointed by vote of the board on which the Divine assistance should be formally invoked. A special meeting of the directors was held toward the end of February, 1817, at which the several pastors of Hartford were invited to be present and conduct religious services. This occasion was in effect a solemn dedication of the new institution to the service and honor of the Almighty, and His especial blessing was asked on all its operations.

Soon after this meeting the organization of the institution was completed and public announcement was made that pupils would be received.

It was on the 15th of April, 1817, a date deserving to be commemorated as the birthday of organized philanthropic effort in America, that Mr. Gallaudet's heart was made glad by the actual opening of the school, for the establishment of which he had labored in the face of obstacles which would have seemed insurmountable to many men.

It is not difficult, when his singleness of heart is remembered, and the devotedness of his self-sacrificing spirit, to imagine with what joy he must have contemplated the triumph of that day.

And yet, great as had been the burdens

already borne, the difficulties overcome, labors far more severe were before him, happily unforeseen, the strain and stress of which his sensitive spirit and delicate frame were to endure ere his work for the deaf of America could be accomplished.

The devotion and self-sacrifice which he brought to the arduous duties he was now called upon to assume is well shown in the following extract from a letter addressed a fortnight earlier to the gentleman in whose hands the domestic management of the institution was to be placed :

And I do hold it to be our sacred duty, to do all in our power in our respective provinces to make the school flourish, although we should just get through the first year and save nothing, and have to complain of the want of generosity in the public or even in our directors.

It will be time and money and labor lent to the Lord and He will take care of us. Start then in your department upon a liberal, not an extravagant plan.

Go a little beyond what would be considered even a fair fulfillment of your engagements. To speak like a man of the world, I know if we make the institution respectable and flourishing during the first year, we shall have a power over the public and over the directors which is always the result of a man's proving himself to be worth something : and,

my Christian brother, I want to prove, what you so
forcibly suggested in one of your letters, and what
men of business are not wont to believe, that a sense
of responsibility to God and of devotion to the cause
of Jesus Christ can lead men to nobler plans of conduct than all that is falsely called honor by this
world.

Former biographers of Mr. Gallaudet have
had little or nothing to say of the difficulties
and annoyances that beset him from the out-
set of his career as the recognized head of the
first public benevolent educational institution
in America. They have pointed to the rapid
development, ample endowment and firm
establishment of the school, giving him due
praise for his masterful management, and have
stated the bare fact that after fourteen years
of faithful service he was compelled on account
of failing health to resign his office as principal.

In undertaking to give, more fully, the story
of his labors while at the head of the school
of which he was the founder, the writer begs to
disclaim all desire to criticise or condemn the
actions, and far less the motives of others who
had to do with the management of the institution. He is willing to believe they acted
always from convictions of duty—that they

had the interests of the institution at heart,
that they meant no injustice to any one. They
were novices in their work—they were men of
varying degrees of ability—and for their
errors of judgment the writer bespeaks the
charity of the reader as he begins a narrative
which in the light of to-day will seem astounding and even, perhaps, incredible.

In Mr. Gallaudet's diary the following
entry appears under date of Sunday, January
25, 1818 ·

During the time which has elapsed since the
opening of the school [ten months] I have had to
encounter great trials. Now I am quite exhausted
in health and strength. Oh! that God would appear
for me, and make haste to help me. If I know my
own heart I long for but one kind of happiness, that
of zealous and cheerful activity in doing good. I
have of late begun to ponder a good deal on the
difficulty of my continuing to be the principal of
such an establishment as this with which I am now
connected will probably be. Most gladly would I
hail as my superior here and as the head of the
institution some one of acknowledged piety and
talents and of more force of character than myself.
Alas, how is my energy gone! How I shrink from
·difficulties! Oh! Almighty God, in thy wise providence thou hast placed me in my present situation.
—Thou seest my heart—Thou knowest my desire is

to be devoted to thy service and to be made the
instrument of training up the deaf and dumb for
heaven. Oh! turn not a deaf ear to my request.
Oh! raise me from this bodily and intellectual and
religious lethargy which has now so long prostrated
all the energies and deadened the affections of my
soul! Oh! show me clearly the path of duty, and
teach me submission to thy holy will—more self-
denial and humility—more patience and perseverance.

Thus did an over-burdened, fainting man, cry
out in self-condemnation and self-distrust, laying on himself blame that belonged, if there
was blame, elsewhere. With more of daily
labor, hourly care, ever present sense of
responsibility, oft recurring worry, frequent
annoyance and opposition where cordial co-
operation was to have been expected, all of
which combined to form a burden too heavy
for the strongest man to carry, this invalid
with a heart of gold and a soul of steel, patient
and persevering in the extreme, self-denying
and humble to a fault, wrote himself down
incapable, proud, impatient and negligent of
duty, allowing his conscience to castigate his
upright spirit when he was merely suffering
from an entirely natural and inevitable attack
of nervous prostration.

From the time he assumed charge of the institution Mr. Gallaudet's duty was to give six hours daily to the teaching of a class that had no other instructor: he was expected to receive those, and they were many, who desired to visit the school : he maintained a large correspondence with the relatives and friends of pupils : he arranged and conducted exhibitions of pupils for the purpose of enlisting the interest of legislatures and the public in the institution : though not understood to have charge of the domestic concerns of the school he had more trouble with them than would have been the case had he been clothed with proper authority to manage them : it was necessary that he should take time needed for rest to train new teachers for their work : he gave up days of his vacation for the preparation of Annual Reports to which the name of the Clerk of the Board of Directors, and not his own, was appended : he was appointed by vote of the directors to membership on some of their committees and asked to attend and give advice at the meetings of the board, and then was called intrusive and impertinent by members of the board because he had complied with such requests.

Ample evidence of these facts is in the hands

of the writer, to give all of which would unnecessarily burden these pages.

Two quotations from letters to the directors will suffice.

On the 4th of September, 1817, less than five months after the opening of the school, Mr. Gallaudet addressed a long communication to the board in reference to the management of the domestic affairs of the institution. These had been placed under the control of a gentleman and his wife who were supposed to be competent and trustworthy. This not proving to be the case, abuses were reported to Mr. Gallaudet, who felt compelled to interfere in behalf of those who had suffered.

Mr. ——, says Mr. Gallaudet to the directors, is bound by his contract to take care of the pupils on the Sabbath. Commodious seats in church were provided for them by the committee; but Mr. and Mrs. —— absolutely declined sitting with them. The care of them has, of course, devolved on some of the directors and the principal, who will continue cheerfully to accompany them to church on one condition, that Mr. —— be made explicitly to understand that in this particular, he is to exercise no control over them, and especially, that he is not in the face of the whole congregation to make signs of rebuke at them, thus situated under the care of the principal, very much, as has often been the case, to the mortification of the elder pupils, especially the young ladies.

I am told by my friend and fellow laborer [Mr. Clerc] that he is sometimes neglected in the gratification of so simple a want as that of a piece of white bread, and that when the mistress of the family, who is well acquainted with his wishes in this respect, makes not provision to have them always gratified, and when he has asked the servant for so small a favor and been told that "the house can not furnish it," with his accustomed good nature he has contented himself with a draught of milk alone.

After speaking of many other complaints, which he feels are well grounded, Mr. Gallaudet concludes as follows :

I would beg leave, respectfully, to inquire whether the principal of the institution is not entitled to some kind of authority within its walls; whether the pupils are to regard him as quite on a level, out of the school room, with themselves ; or whether he is to have the right of interposition or control, should he see the pupils ill-treated, their conduct and language, as it has often been, very much misapprehended, and themselves incapable of understanding the signs which are awkwardly and vehemently made to them? Are they to feel themselves destitute of redress in case of grievances ; of an interpreter in case of a mistake ; of a friend in case of abuse? These things are suggested not, I hope, from feelings of wounded pride, as has been most ungenerously attributed to me, nor from a wish to exercise authority, which is by no means, to me at least, a pleasant task, but from the conviction, and surely it is a sober one, that the usefulness of that man is soon at an end, who, filling a public station of responsibility, and called to form the minds and conduct the education of those who look up to him as their teacher and guide, suffers the loss of that respect without the enjoyment of which both himself and his office must soon become contemptible.

The other communication to the board is so short that it may be given entire :

March 18, 1818.
To the Directors etc., Gentlemen :
When your board first began to hold its meetings, I felt reluctant to attend them, and I did not until I was told by many gentlemen that my attendance would be very acceptable. I was even urged to go on the ground of my having been sent abroad on purpose to collect that information and experience, the knowledge of which might prove highly useful to the directors in their deliberations. '.You will be wanted as our chaplain,' was said to me, ' and you must be on committees for the transaction of business, which committees will have to report to the directors, and your presence therefore, so far from indicating any thing like intrusion, is really made necessary by the fact of your being

placed on these committees. I, of course, began habitually to attend the meetings of the board, and to express my opinions on subjects relating to the welfare of the institution. Instances have occurred when I have hesitated about giving my opinion and have been told that no apology was necessary, but to express my mind freely. It was with feelings of surprise, therefore, that I have heard it suggested that my attendance at the meetings of this board has, in some instances, I know not by how many of the members, been deemed incorrect. Whatever rights may be supposed to belong to the principal of an establishment like this with regard to his attendance on the meetings of the directors, whatever value may be attached to his opinions on subjects touching the interests of the school, how great ought to be the confidence placed in one, or how much the indulgence, if indeed it deserve this name, shown him, who has been a laborious servant of the deaf and dumb—how far an invitation to this effect has virtually been given by placing him on several committees—these are considerations, gentlemen, which I would not wish to urge for one moment. After being invited and solicited to attend the meetings of this board, I retire from them, only requesting at the same time that the directors would please to express an opinion on this subject and to inform me what their views are with regard to the propriety of attending their meetings, a thing which I did not at first solicit and which I have not the least wish to repeat should it be unacceptable to this respectable board. I am, etc.

The embarrassment as to Mr. Gallaudet's attending meetings of the directors was happily relieved some months later by the contribution of one hundred dollars from a friend in Baltimore, whose name was not disclosed, for the purpose of making him a member of the board for life. And his unfailing modesty appears in his unwillingness to accept even this solution of the difficulty, until the directors had by a formal vote declared that they saw no impropriety in his becoming a director while holding the office of principal.

It must be said in this connection that Mr. Gallaudet's distrust of his own ability, and indisposition to assume and exercise authority which was not definitely conferred upon him, proceeding no doubt from his sincere modesty and his strict sense of justice, had the effect on certain occasions to impair his efficiency, and oftener to add greatly to his cares and worries.

The directors apparently failed to understand Mr. Gallaudet in this matter. When he hesitated as to his ability and showed a disinclination to accept power, they would take him at his own estimate, providing for the government of the institution in ways that were ineffective and cumbersome, and which were sure to end unfortunately, as they did.

A clearer discernment on the part of the directors of Mr. Gallaudet's ability to manage the institution, in all its departments, would have led them to give him full powers—an arrangement which would certainly have saved a vast amount of exhausting friction on all sides.

But this clearer vision did not come to the directors, nor did Mr. Gallaudet ask for those broad powers which naturally belonged to his office. As a consequence the fourteen years in which he continued to act as principal of the institution were full of exasperating difficulties growing out of the mistaken policy of the board as to the method of government.

In July, 1818, the directors adopted a series of regulations recognizing the existence, defining the powers, and prescribing the duties of a *Faculty*, consisting of the *Principal*, the assistant *Teachers* and the *Superintendent*."

In certain matters the faculty were to act by vote, the members having equal power. Certain duties were assigned to the principal, and he was to perform them without interference from the faculty or the superintendent. Certain other duties were given to this last named officer, who was, so far as they were concerned, made equally independent.

Under such a divided organization the wonder is, not that there were serious difficulties and an utter lack of harmonious management, but that the institution was not overwhelmed with disaster and left to break down by its discouraged and handicapped nominal head.

The writer believes he is not awarding undue praise when he claims that few men could be found who would have shown the tact, forbearance, boundless patience and supreme charity in all judgments of associates that was ever exhibited by Mr. Gallaudet while he continued to hold the office of principal.

Evidences of the unwisdom of the "Faculty" organization abound in Mr. Gallaudet's papers.

A few months after the adoption of the regulations described above, which made the assistant teachers of equal authority in the faculty with the principal, Mr. Gallaudet received a note from one of these teachers, Mr. Clerc, in which he expressed his purpose to return to France, at least for a time. Mr. Clerc concludes as follows :—

Tell me frankly if you desire me to return to the United States, and if so, how many years do you wish me to stay? Do not say *forever*, for I am not willing to do it. Tell me likewise if you would have any objection to my having a salary larger than your own?

Mr. Gallaudet responds:

In reply to your note of this morning I tell you frankly that it is the first and most ardent desire of my heart that you would not go to France at all, and that if you must go you would return as soon as possible. It is indeed my earnest prayer that we may continue to labor together in doing good to the dear immortal souls by whom we are surrounded. If you can not conclude to spend your days with us, can not you engage after your return to stay five or six years? I do not urge this point. I would rather have you return to stay only two or three years than not to return at all. With regard to my salary, while I remain single, I shall be perfectly satisfied with my present income, unless some very unexpected change in the affairs of the institution by the liberal increase of its funds should make it convenient for the directors to increase it without injury to the institution. Nor shall I feel at all disappointed if your salary is made to exceed mine.

Strange as it may now seem, the suggestion of Mr. Clerc as to salary was, at a later period, acted upon favorably by the directors, and more astonishing yet, other instructors, whose services were considered of less value to the school than those of Mr. Clerc, received for years salaries larger than Mr. Gallaudet's.

In spite of these annoying experiences, the affairs of the new institution moved on in a full current of prosperity.

In the winter of 1818 it was thought best to solicit the aid of Congress and it was proposed that the principal should visit Washington for the purpose of pleading the cause of deaf-mute education at the capital. Mr. Gallaudet felt that the appearance of an educated person of the class for which aid was to be sought would have great effect, and advised, quite unselfishly, that Mr. Clerc go in his place : since they could not both be absent at the same time.

This advice was followed and the influence exerted by Mr. Clerc at Washington was such as to secure the hearty co-operation of many prominent men. A year later an earnest and formal appeal for aid was presented to Congress through the representatives from Connecticut, Hon. Nathaniel Terry, Hon. Thomas S. Williams and Hon. Timothy Pitkin. This movement was warmly supported by many philanthropic members in both branches of Congress, prominent among whom was Hon. Henry Clay, then Speaker of the House. An

HARTFORD SCHOOL FOR THE DEAF.

act was speedily passed appropriating a township of wild land, more than twenty-three thousand acres, from the sale of which an endowment for the institution was ultimately realized amounting to more than three hundred thousand dollars.

Following closely upon this favorable action of Congress came the permanent establishment of the school in buildings and grounds of its own, which were ready for occupancy early in 1821. On the 22d of May in that year dedicatory services were held in the new building, Mr. Gallaudet preaching a sermon from 2 Corinthians v : 1 : " For we know that if our earthly house of this tabernacle were dissolved, we have a building of God, an house not made with hands, eternal in the heavens."

This sermon, and the dedicatory prayer which .followed it, are remarkable for the intense spirit of dependence and devotion to God which pervade them, and they illustrate in what rare proportions the highly spiritual and thoroughly practical were blended in the mind of their author.

We see before us, he says, a little group of our fellow-beings, who are called in the mysterious providence of God to endure affliction. This affliction may become comparatively light to them, and as it were, enduring but a moment, could it be made instrumental of working out for them a far more exceeding and eternal weight of glory.

They are just introduced into an earthly house well calculated for their accommodation, but it becomes both them and all of us, who feel interested in their welfare, to keep constantly in mind, that this goodly edifice, with its various sources of instruction and improvement, is one of the things which, though seen perhaps with grateful satisfaction, is still temporal, the worldly advantages may prove uncertain and must be transitory, and at which, therefore, we ought not to look with any sense of strong and undue attachment, but rather, raise the eye of our faith, and persuade these sufferers to do likewise, to a better home, to that building of God, the house not made with hands, eternal in the heavens. When I say the worldly advantages of this institution may prove uncertain, do not understand me as wishing to disparage their true importance and value. To do this would be alike unwise and ungrateful. It would be unwise; for godliness hath the promise of this life as well as of that which is to come, and it is only a misguided enthusiasm which can aim to prepare youth for a better world, without, at the same time, training them up to a faithful discharge of all their duties in this. It would be ungrateful; for every creature of God is good, and nothing to be refused if it be received with thanksgiving; and we might as well close our eyes to the budding beauties of this season, which the kind Author of nature is now unfolding to our view, as to shut our hearts against that general aspect of convenience, and that prospect of future comfort to the deaf and dumb, which the same Giver of every good and perfect gift deigns to shed over the establishment which we wish this day to dedicate to Him. But the brightest hopes of spring sometimes fall before an untimely frost, and human establishments of the fairest promise have often been so perverted from their original design as to become the nurseries of error, or so conducted in their progress as to promote the views of personal interest, or so decked out with the pomp and circumstance of greatness, as to serve rather for the ornaments with which ambition would love to decorate itself, than as the plain and useful instruments which the hand of unostentatious charity would employ to dispense our simple and substantial benefits to the suffering objects of her care. Believe me, these are the rocks on which this institution may be ship-wrecked. Its very prosperity should serve as the beacon of its danger.

The following is the key-note of the dedicatory prayer :

Almighty and most merciful God, in behalf of those whom thou hast called in thy Providence to direct and govern its concerns, we do now dedicate this whole institution to thee; to thee in all its departments of intellectual, moral and religious instruction ; to thee in all its privileges of worship, prayer and praise; to thee in all its domestic regulations, and various means of comfort and usefulness; to thee with all its benefits both spiritual and temporal, beseeching thee to accept the offering and to make it subservient to the promotion of thy glory, to the honor of thy son Jesus Christ, and to the building up of His kingdom in the hearts of all who have been, who now are, or who may be the objects of its care.

No sooner was the school for the deaf in Hartford suitably housed, than Mr. Gallaudet began to labor for the extension of its benefits. Pupils from several of the New England States, besides Connecticut, had been admitted on the payment of their expenses by their friends, but up to this time public provision for the poor was lacking. Mr. Gallaudet visited the capitals of the several New England States, exhibiting to the legislatures the happy results attained with many of his pupils. He delivered on numerous occasions a sermon from the text, "But as it is written, to whom he was not spoken of, they shall see ; and they that have not heard, shall understand." Romans xv : 21.

So eloquent and effective were these appeals that within a short time grants of money were made by all the New England legislatures for the education of the deaf, and the number of pupils rose soon after the completion of permanent buildings to one hundred and twenty-eight.

In the midst of all this prosperity and while Mr. Gallaudet was working far beyond the limit of his physical ability, a tempest rose about him that few men would have had the courage or the discretion to outride.

It was the natural outcome of the system, unwisely adopted by the Board of Directors, of placing the institution under the charge of two men, neither one controlled by the other.

The superintendent, to whom was committed the domestic management of the establishment, was jealous of the prominence and importance attaching to the office of principal —he being the nominal head of the institution, though not controlling the superintendent, as he ought to have been allowed to do.

Under such an arrangement friction was inevitable ; and so serious did this become that a movement was made in the board to secure the removal of the superintendent.

No evidence appears that Mr. Gallaudet took any part in this effort, but the "other

head of the institution," as he sometimes
styled himself, believed it to have been inspired
by him, and took such active measures in
retaliation, that when on the 15th of September, 1823, the directors voted to discharge
the superintendent, a resolution was introduced " That the Rev. T. H. Gallaudet, the
principal, be requested to resign his place."
Action was deferred until the next meeting of
the board and Mr. Gallaudet was informed
that such a measure was pending.

The excitement among those interested in
the institution was most intense during the next
forty-eight hours.   So far as can now be ascertained Mr. Gallaudet made no effort to prevent
the adoption of the resolution requesting his
resignation.   Indeed, there is good reason for
believing that he was disposed to resign and
step out from under the heavy and unreasonable burdens which had been heaped upon
him, without waiting for the possible passage
of the hostile resolution.   But those who
knew best how valuable his services were to
the cause of which he had been thus far the
leader, would not listen to a suggestion of his
retirement.

On the 17th of September a meeting of the
directors was held at Morgan's Hotel, on

State Street, to take final action on the pending resolution.

Twenty directors were present and the
meeting continued for several hours.

The assistant instructors, five in number,
had signed a paper resigning their positions
and had placed this in the hands of the clerk
of the board, with the understanding that it
was to be presented at once in the event of the
adoption of the resolution asking for the
resignation of the principal. These teachers
were at the hotel in a room adjoining the one
occupied by the board. Communication
between them and the directors was frequent
during the progress of the meeting.

The attitude of the teachers was regarded
by many of the directors as an unwarrantable
attempt at coercion and resented accordingly.
Passion rather than reason controlled the
minds of many, and the resolution failed only
by a tie vote, most of those who voted for it
being regarded as warm personal friends of
Mr. Gallaudet up to that time.

No stronger evidence of a willingness to
sacrifice personal feelings to a sense of duty
could be found than in Mr. Gallaudet's action
under the circumstances. His desire was to
resign at once. He felt himself wounded in

the house of his friends.   His pride could ill
brook the idea of retaining a position that ten
out of twenty of his associates on the board
had asked him to vacate.   He had made a
brilliant record.   His name was sure to stand
in history as the founder of a great philanthropic enterprise.   He had been underpaid
and overworked.   He could have risen easily
and quickly to eminence in the profession of
his early choice, which he had relinquished
for the cause of the deaf.   But he was made
to feel that his work for the children of silence
was not yet completed.   Those who reasoned
calmly urged with justice that his retirement
would inflict an almost fatal blow on the
young institution ; that no one could be found
who was competent to *fill* his place ; that having outlived the storm he must keep his hand
on the helm until all the angry elements were
at rest.   These counsels prevailed and Mr.
Gallaudet kept on the even and laborious
tenor of his way, holding back nothing of time
nor strength from the work he loved until,
indeed, as the sequel will speedily show, the
drain upon his vitality became too great for
even his self-sacrificing endurance.

THOMAS HOPKINS GALLAUDET.
(Taken in 1822.)

CHAPTER V.

Marriage to Sophia Fowler, One of the Earliest Pupils of the School—Characteristic Letter written Two Days after the Wedding—Description of Mrs. Gallaudet—Happiness in the Married Life.

BEFORE concluding the story of Mr. Gallaudet's active labors as principal of the school for the deaf at Hartford, an interesting event must be spoken of which exercised a most important influence over his life.

The laws of romance would have made Alice Cogswell his wife in due time. But she was not twelve years of age when she became regularly his pupil, while he was thirty.

And besides, there was among his earliest scholars " a rare and radiant maiden " just on the threshold of womanhood, whose unusual attractiveness turned other heads and touched other hearts than her teacher's.

One who knew her only in the last years of her long life, but who gave her that loving homage which none could withhold who ever came within the circle of her influence, and to whom she had confided much of the story of her life, writes thus of her early days and development :*

Her parents belonged to the hardy, independent, pious, and active minded race of farmers from whom have descended a great majority of the many distinguished sons and daughters of New England. Lying a short distance back from Long Island Sound, in a region of fertile hills and vales, abounding with towering elms and luxuriant wild roses, her home was equally well placed for health, for beauty, and for the business of its inmates.

It will require no small effort, even from those who are well acquainted with the affliction of deaf-mutism, to realize the depth of anguish into which the parents of this house were plunged when the knowledge was forced upon them painfully and slowly, yet inflexibly, that their girl-baby would be forever incapable of responding to their voices. For it was a far more terrible misfortune then than now. Only in one way could it be alleviated. The parents might be comforted, and the babe grow up useful and happy, if they knew any means by which the

---

*Sophia Gallaudet—American Annals of the Deaf—Vol XXII, No. 3., July, 1877, by Amos G. Draper.

intelligence of the little one could be evoked, and drawn into sympathy and communion with those whose faces bent anxiously above it. But there was then no such knowledge, either among the friends of the child or in the community at large. There was not a single school for the deaf in America, and only three in the world. Even the existence of these three was scarcely known on this side the Atlantic; while of the systems on which they were based, and of the methods they employed, there seems to have been no knowledge whatever in America in the year 1800.

It will not seem strange, therefore, that as the child grew the deficiencies of her intellectual acquirements, as compared with those of her young associates, became painfully evident. In all else, in mirthfulness of spirit, in vigor of physique, she was perfectly fitted to delight in their companionship. This she could do in certain games and amusements. But if they partook of an intellectual character her pleasure vanished. Did the group, tired of play, subside to conversation upon the grass-plot; was a book introduced; did the merry jest or sparkling story pass round the happy circle—she could but sit silent, troubled, gazing in mute wonderment upon the swiftly-moving lips, the responsive glances, eager to share, but unable even to comprehend what was to her an undefined, subtle enjoyment, no less mysterious than precious.

So she passed through childhood to young womanhood, with scarcely a glimpse at the ample page of knowledge. She received no mental instruction, save through the disconnected natural signs of her friends, which could hardly treat of more than the objects of vision.

But if her mind remained largely undeveloped, not so her spirit. That could be reached in a measure, and, moreover, it was at work by itself. She early gave evidence of possessing those lovely and attractive traits which afterwards distinguished her. Unconsciously following the guidance of her own sense and the best models about her, she learned to discriminate between the false and the true, and grew up modest, kindly, conscientious, and cheerful even to gayety. Of definite religious knowledge at this time she had little or none. It may almost be said to have been confined to a dim impression that there was a power *above* who looked down benignantly upon good actions, and frowningly upon bad.

During these calm years, also, was laid the foundation of that superb physical condition which attended her through life. In the regular and quiet performance of household duties, in all of which she became an adept, her frame acquired the vigor, grace, and elasticity which afterwards, under the softening influences of metropolitan life, gave her a rare personal comeliness, without ever losing their sustaining qualities. Her hair was black; her eyes large, dark, and inquiring. Her features betokened a sanguine temperament, and her manner was vivacious and pleasing to a remarkable degree.

Such was Sophia Fowler in character and appearance as she stood at nineteen on the threshold of womanhood; happy in the performance of her daily

SOPHIA FOWLER GALLAUDET.
(*Taken in* 1822.)

home duties, scarcely ever having passed beyond the borders of her native town, unconscious of the widening paths that stretched before her, apparently destined to pursue without interruption the noiseless tenor of her sequestered way.

In the spring of 1817, her father learned that some gentlemen at Hartford were about to establish a school for the deaf. Soon after, hearing that these gentlemen were at New Haven, he went there in order to meet them, taking her with him. He told her by signs of his hope that they would be able to teach her to read, to write, to cipher,—to acquire, she afterward said, it seemed to her, knowledge without end. She grew radiant with the prospect of satisfying the only craving of which her nature felt a need.

Not long after the meeting at New Haven, Mr. Gallaudet visited the home of the Fowlers, in Guilford, and the same spring Sophia became a pupil in the Hartford school. Her name appears as the fifteenth in the order of those received at the opening, Alice Cogswell's being the first.

Of her progress as a pupil it is possible to judge only by her later development. Those who are familiar with the difficulties to be encountered will understand the fact that for a number of years her acquirements were confined to the common English branches. Owing to her zeal and vigor of mind, her advancement in these was rapid. In the spring of 1821, however, just at the period when a bright deaf-mute pupil may be expected to attain a fair degree of proficiency in the subjects indicated, her studies were interrupted in a manner quite unanticipated by all the parties concerned except one.

This interruption was occasioned by nothing less than a proposal of marriage from Mr. Gallaudet. It appears that for more than a year previous he had carefully concealed his feelings out of regard for the young woman's position as a pupil; his bearing toward her, up to this time, was in no way distinguished from that which he observed toward the other female pupils under his charge.

The first sensations excited in the bosom of the young lady when she perceived his wishes give assurance of this. There is nothing to show that her previous feelings for him were other than those which would naturally flow forth toward an able, kind, and sympathetic instructor. In after life she said that her first feeling, when she comprehended his meaning, was one of almost unmixed surprise.

When, to this, other and warmer feelings succeeded, they did not blind her to what she considered her lack of qualifications for such a great change of station. She pleaded her want of knowledge of the world; he averred that this would soon be remedied by travel and society. She lamented that her education was but just begun; he promised that it should be pursued, with himself for a guide and helper. Considering the character and relations of the suitor and the sought, it is not surprising that this period of hesitation did not long endure. They were married on the 29th of August, 1821, and went on a wedding journey to Saratoga.

The marriage was announced by the bridegroom in the following letter :

SAYBROOK, August 31, 1821.

MY DEAR FATHER :—I wrote you a few days since from Guilford. I am here on a little excursion with one to whom my fortunes are at length united —Miss Sophia Fowler that was—Mrs. Gallaudet that now is. We were married on Wednesday evening. It is an event to which I have been looking forward for some time, and, all things considered, I deemed it best to have it take place now. I can not but hope that it will increase my means of usefulness among the deaf and dumb to whom I feel myself devoted. Yet I feel more than I ever did the shortness and uncertainty of all things human. Oh! that we could be always ready for a better and happier state. I am now obliged to write in great haste. You shall hear from me again soon. Sophia joins me in best love to yourself and our dear sisters and brothers.

Your dutiful son,

T. H. GALLAUDET.

Fifty-six years later, shortly after the death of Mrs. Gallaudet, a packet carefully enveloped was found in her writing desk containing ten letters received from her husband before her marriage.

The first bears date New York, April 20, 1818, and was written during a vacation following Miss Fowler's first year at Hartford. In order to appreciate what may seem a rather commonplace letter, it must be considered that the person to whom it was addressed, although an adult in years, was no more than an infant in the use of verbal language. On entering school eleven months earlier Miss Fowler was absolutely ignorant of the meaning of words, she had no power of communicating her own thoughts and feelings except through rude gestures and facial expressions. That she could now understand and enjoy such a letter as her teacher addressed her gives evidence no less of zeal and skill on his part than of industry and intelligence on hers. It may interest the curious to know that the letter given below contains two hundred and nine-teen different words, of which seventy are nouns, sixty-five verbs, thirty-two adjectives, twenty pronouns, fourteen adverbs, twelve prepositions, three conjunctions, two articles, with one interjection.

Mr. Gallaudet's First Letter to his Future Wife.

My Dear Friend :—To-day I received your kind letter. I read it with great pleasure. It was com-posed very well. I understood it all. I am very

glad your father and you and Parnel * arrived home
in good health. I am glad all your friends are well.
You remember Mr. Woodbridge † and my sister and
Mary R—— and myself rode away in the stage on
Thursday morning. We rode till sunset. It was a
very unpleasant day. It rained and snowed, and it
was very cold. My sister was very sick; she was
faint and ate nothing. Mary R—— was very well.
God took care of us. We passed Friday in New
Haven. I saw Mr. Orr; he will come to teach the
deaf and dumb in May.

On Friday evening, when it was dark, Mr. W. and
A. and M. and myself went aboard of the steam-
boat. We soon went to bed. We sailed all night.
In the morning I rose early. I soon met my sister
and M. I shook their hands. I asked them if they
were well. They were very well. We arrived in
New York on Saturday at noon. I got a coach.
Four of my brothers met me on the wharf. I was
glad to see them. Ann and Mary and my brother
James and myself, with all our trunks, rode in the
coach. I stopped the coach and I spoke to my
father at his book store. He was well. We again
rode very far. We arrived at my father's house. I
saw my dear mother and brothers and sisters and
aunt, who were all well. Mary R. slept at our house
two nights. On Tuesday she went to Albany with
her father. I did not stay long at home. I went
to Newark. I passed Sunday with Mr. Woodbridge.
I saw his father and mother. On Sunday evening

---

* A mute sister.   † An instructor.

thirty ladies and gentlemen met at Mr. W.'s. I told them about the deaf and dumb. Three men prayed ardently for all the deaf and dumb, that God would bless Mr. Clerc and Mr. Woodbridge and me, and give all the deaf and dumb clean hearts and enable them to trust in Christ and repent of all their sins. The thirty persons sang hymns and some of the ladies cried very much. I heard them weeping. How kind they were to pray for the deaf and dumb! Oh! do not forget God and Christ. Pray for a very clean heart. Trust in Christ. Avoid all sin. And may God bless you, my dear pupil, both you and your sister and your dear father and mother and brothers and grandmother and all your friends.

I returned to New York on Monday one week ago. I have been very busy in buying books and pictures for the deaf and dumb. Alice [Cogswell] will be here probably to-morrow. I will show her your letter; how glad she will be to see it! I had a letter to-day from Loring;* he writes thus: "I love very Miss Sophia Fowler." Loring was very well. I received a letter from Comstock;† he was well and all the deaf and dumb were well. When Mr. Clerc comes to your home give him my best love. Tell him I have already written him two long letters. I hope he will stay and see you some days. I wish I could be at your house also. Give my kind regards to Parnel. I hope she is quite well.

---

*A class-mate from Boston.

† A class-mate from Newport.

Give my kind regards to your grandmother and your father and mother and brothers and all my friends. I shall soon see you again. Next year we will learn more, and I hope love God and Christ more and become more and more wise and holy.

My father's family, especially my sister Ann, send their best regards to you and your sister.

I am your sincere friend,

T. H. GALLAUDET.

In other letters written during 1818, '19 and '20, Mr. Gallaudet addresses Miss Fowler as " My esteemed pupil," or " My dear pupil," signing himself " Your affectionate teacher," or " Your sincere friend ; " but late in the latter year he begins a letter " My dear Sophia," and signs himself " Your affectionate friend," in which he shows a much deeper interest than that of a teacher.

Two letters written in the spring of 1821 show plainly that an engagement had taken place, for arrangements are alluded to for Miss Fowler to board on her return to school with friends of Mr. Gallaudet's, to whom he has "spoken frankly about our expected prospects."

These letters of Mr. Gallaudet to his future wife are unusual in two particulars— they show a great desire to add to the knowledge of his pupil, and the greatest possible solicitude for her development in spiritual and religious matters.

One little yellow folded bit of paper, addressed in a beautiful hand, such a note as might naturally carry a sentimental message between lovers, and being no doubt such a love missive to the mind of him who though consciously a lover was still the faithful teacher and guardian, on being opened reveals only these words :

The ornament of a meek and quiet spirit is in the sight of God of great price.

Another note, written with equal care and preserved to a later day by her to whom it was addressed, is as follows :

Pray in secret every morning and evening.
Ask God to teach you how to pray.   .
Ask God to give you His Holy Spirit.
Ask God to warn your conscience.
Think of God often.
Think of Christ often.
Every evening think if you have been wicked during the day ;—ask God to forgive your sins.
Trust in Christ alone to save you.
Trust in Christ alone to enable you to avoid all sin.

Often examine your heart to see if you truly love God, and obey Him and trust in Christ·

Be humble. Be meek. Be kind. Avoid pride, vanity, ambition.

Serve Christ every day.

Teach the young pupils, and talk with them about God and Christ.

Be cheerful. Be contented.

Oh ! do not forget God and Christ.

May God bless you and keep you from all sin.

A little well worn pocket notebook, with a calendar of Saints' days in French, for the year 1818, perhaps a gift from Mr. Clerc to Miss Fowler, contains the following meditation written very carefully and legibly in pencil by Mr. Gallaudet :

Oh! Jesus, my Saviour, I love thee. I wish to imitate thee, to be kind as thou wert kind, to be humble us thou wert humble.—Oh! give me thy Spirit to keep me from sin. Oh! enable me to serve thee and to be kind to all and to do good every day. And oh! prepare me to eat the Lord's Supper.

That these lessons, given when the mind of Sophia Fowler was at its most impressionable period of development, took a lasting hold on her spiritual organism was proven a thousand times through her long and not uneventful life.

When heartrending sorrow came to her,
she did not need to cry,

> "Oh ! for a faith that will not shrink
> Though pressed by every foe,
> That will not tremble on the brink
> Of any earthly woe."

For at such times hers was indeed,

> "A faith that shines more bright and clear,
> When tempests rage without ;
> That when in danger knows no fear
> In darkness feels no doubt."

Of this faith and its influence over Mrs.
Gallaudet's life her friend quoted above writes
as follows :

A prominent characteristic was her joyous and
undoubting faith in the religion of Jesus Christ.
When they came to her, she accepted the truths of
revelation so readily and implicitly that it seemed
as if they did but bear out and confirm the dim
intuitions of her uninstructed childhood. Not only
did she love and practice all the Christian virtues ;
not only, as one who knew her long and well has
said, was she "most exactly just and perfectly truth-
ful and sincere, exemplifying in an eminent degree

all the virtues described by the apostle when he exhorted us to think on whatsoever things are true, honest, just, pure, lovely, and of good report" —but Christ, the embodiment of all excellences, was to her a real and present person. When threatened with blindness, in the last year of her life, and feeling its dread approach, more than once she was seen to pray to Him, with fervor, as if He stood in her chamber, that He would spare her such a grievous affliction; she was aged and deaf, she said, and if now her sight must be taken she would lose the little joy that remained to her; then, in a moment, and in a different spirit, she would tell Him that, though she felt it hard to bear, she wished what *He* thought best should be done, and she would strive to be resigned.

It will not surprise the reader to be told that the marriage of Mr. and Mrs. Gallaudet was pre-eminently a happy one. His physical weaknesses and natural tendencies to depression of spirits were often overcome by the vigor and cheerfulness she was able always to impart to their united life: while her mind, eager for knowledge, could easily supply the deficiencies of her early education by an appeal to her ever-present teacher.

Mr. Gallaudet has been heard to say that many trials and difficulties had come upon him in the course of his life which he could hardly have endured or overcome, but for the sympathy and encouragement his brave and loving wife was always quick to give him.

CHAPTER VI.

1823—1830.

THE years following Mr. Gallaudet's marriage in 1821 were happy years though full of toil.

The occupancy of enlarged and permanent buildings by the institution was followed by an increase in the number of pupils, necessitating the employment and training of new teachers. This growth brought added cares and labors to the principal of the school. But he shrank from nothing, rejoicing in work that was thoroughly congenial. He was a born teacher, and a teacher of teachers, as well as of children.

His skill in adapting methods borrowed from France to the needs of American children was great. He possessed peculiar and natural endowments for the special work of instructing the deaf : prominent among which was a really marvelous grace and clearness in all kinds of pantomimic expression.

He was the first to suggest and use in schools for the deaf the language of signs in religious exercises and lectures. His eloquence in this language has never been surpassed and rarely equaled.

He had an unusual facility in communicating thought by means of facial expression and movements of the body without any resort whatever to motions of the hands or arms.

This process is described in an article published three years before his death, long after he gave up teaching.

One day our distinguished and lamented historical painter, Col. John Trumbull, was in my school, room during the hours of instruction, and, on alluding to the tact which a certain pupil had of reading my face, he expressed a wish to see it tried. I requested him to select any event in Greek, Roman, English or American history of a scenic character, which would make a striking picture on canvas, and said

I would endeavor to communicate it to the lad. "Tell him," said he, "that Brutus (Lucius Junius) condemned his two sons to death, for resisting his authority and violating his orders."

I folded my arms in front of me and kept them in that position, to preclude the possibility of making any signs or gestures, or of spelling any words on my fingers, and proceeded, as best I could, by the expressions of my countenance, and a few motions of the head and attitudes of the body, to convey the picture in my own mind to the mind of my pupil.

It ought to be stated, that he was already acquainted with the fact, being familiar with the leading events in Roman history. But when I began, he knew not from what portion of history, sacred or profane, ancient or modern, the fact was selected. From this wide range, my delineation on the one hand, and his ingenuity on the other, had to bring it within the division of Roman history, and, still more minutely, to the particular individual and transaction designated by Col. Trumbull. In carrying on the process, I made no use whatever of any arbitrary conventional look, motion, or attitude, before settled between us, by which to let him understand what I wished to communicate, with the exception of a single one, if, indeed, it ought to be considered such.

The usual sign, at that time, among the teachers and pupils, for a Roman was portraying an aquiline nose by placing the fore finger crooked, in front of the nose. As I was prevented from using my finger in this way, and having considerable command over the muscles of my face, I endeavored to give my nose as much of the aquiline form as possible, and succeeded well enough for my purpose.

Every thing else that I looked and did was the pure, natural language by which my mind spontaneously endeavored to convey its thoughts and feelings to his mind by the varied expressions of the countenance, some motions of the head, and attitudes of the body.

It would be difficult to give any thing like a complete analysis of the process which I pursued in making the communication. To be understood it ought to be witnessed and accompanied with the requisite explanations. The outlines of the process, however, I can give. They were the following :—

A stretching and searching gaze eastward, with an undulating motion of the head, as if looking across and beyond the Atlantic Ocean, to denote that the event happened, not on the western, but on the eastern continent. This was making a little progress, as it took the subject out of the range of American history.

A turning of the eyes upward and backward, with frequently repeated motions of the head backward, as if looking a great way back in past time, to denote that the event was one of quite ancient date. The aquiline shape of the nose already referred to, indicating that a Roman was the person concerned. It was, of course, an old Roman.

Portraying, as well as I could, by my countenance, attitude, and manner, an individual high in authority, and commanding others, as if he expected to be obeyed.

Looking and acting as if I were giving out a specific order to many persons, and threatening punishment on those who should resist my authority —even the punishment of death.

Here was a pause in the progress of events, which I denoted by sleeping as it were during the night and awaking in the morning, and doing this several times, to signify that several days had elapsed.

Looking with deep interest and surprise, as if at a single person brought and standing before me, with an expression of countenance indicating that he had violated the order which I had given, and that I knew it. Then looking in the same way at another person near him as also guilty. Two offending persons were thus denoted.

Exhibiting serious deliberation—then hesitation, accompanied with strong conflicting emotions, producing perturbation, as if I knew not how to feel or what to do.

Looking first at one of the persons before me and then at the other, and then at both together, *as a father would look,* indicating his distressful parental feelings under such affecting circumstances.

Composing my feelings, showing that a change was coming over me, and exhibiting towards the imaginary persons before me, the decided look of the inflexible commander who was determined and ready to order them away to execution. Looking and acting as if the tender feelings of *the father* had again got the ascendency, and as if I were about to relent and pardon them.

These alternating states of mind I portrayed several times, to make my representation the more · graphic and impressive.

´ At length the father yields, and the stern principle of justice, as expressed in my countenance and manner, prevails. My look and action denote the passing of the sentence of death on the offenders, and the ordering them away to execution.

Before I had quite completed the process, I perceived, from the expression of his countenance, and a little of impatience in his manner, that the pupil felt satisfied that he was fully in possession of the fact which I was endeavoring to communicate. But for the sake of greater certainty, I detained his attention till I had nothing more to portray. He quickly turned round to his slate and wrote a complete and correct account of the story of Brutus and his two sons.

Mr. Gallaudet follows with other instances of such communication and adds :

There was another use which I found it practicable to make of the mere expressions of the countenance, in conveying not only ideas but *words* to the mind of this pupil.

On a journey to Maine, we sat, one day, directly facing each other in the stage-coach. I proposed to him that we should invent an alphabet of expressions of the countenance, and see if we could not, in a short time, become so familiar with it, as to make it subservient to the spelling of words quite as surely and quickly as could be done by the finger alphabet. We began and settled it as follows :

The simple expression of awe was to denote the letter *a ;* of boldness, *b ;* of curiosity, *c ;* of despair, *d ;* of eagerness, *e ;* of fear, *f ;* of gladness, *g ;* and so on. We made various trials of this new alphabet of the looks, and found it to succeed. It is easy to see, that if I expressed by my countenance distinctly, and with slight intervals between the expressions, the emotions of despair, eagerness, awe and fear, the letters *d, e, a,* and *f,* would be denoted, and, of course, the word *deaf,* communicated.

Simple as this process is, it would still appear very surprising to a person ignorant of it, after being requested to furnish any word, no matter how difficult or abstruse its meaning, to see it immediately *looked* by the teacher into the mind of the pupil, and the latter writing it down correctly on his slate.

These, and other experiments of a similar kind, made by a teacher of the deaf and his pupils, may, perhaps, seem to be matters of mere amusement, and not of any practical use. But amusements have their uses in all schools, and especially if the teacher can, at suitable times, take part in them with his pupils.

Mr. Gallaudet had strong convictions as to the value of the sign language as a means of instruction, of which it may not be amiss to speak in these days, when not a few men of intelligence are found who would banish them . from all schools for the deaf.

In an article on "The Natural Language of Signs ; and its Value and Uses in the Instruction of the Deaf and Dumb," published long after he had given up teaching, Mr. Gallaudet says :—

"My object is to show the intrinsic value and, indeed, indispensable necessity of the use of natural signs in the education of the deaf and dumb. . . . In attempting this I wish I had time to go somewhat at length into the genius of this natural language of signs ; to compare it with merely oral language, and to show, as I think I could, its decided superiority over the latter, so far as respects its peculiar adaptation to the mind of childhood and early youth.

"In what relates to the expression of pas- sion and emotion, and of all the finer and stronger sentiments of the heart, this language is eminently appropriate and copious.

"So far as objects, motions, or actions addressed to the senses are concerned, this language, in its improved state, is superior in its accuracy and force of delineation to that in which words spelled on the fingers, spoken, written, or printed are employed."

Mr. Gallaudet, after treating at length of the capabilities and value of gesture language as a means of instruction, says in closing:

Instructors of the deaf and dumb should appreciate the great importance of being masters of the natural language of signs,—of excelling in this language; of being able to make delineating and descriptive signs with graphical and picture-like accuracy; of acquiring the power to have the inmost workings of their souls,— their various thoughts and feelings, with their fainter and stronger shades of distinctive character,—*beam out* through the eye, countenance, attitude, movement, and gesture ; and of doing all this with spirit, grace, and fluency, and for the love of doing it.

The labor is not small, indeed, that must be undergone, in order to possess these indispensable qualifications of an accomplished instructor of the deaf and dumb. To acquire them, the new and inexperienced teacher must consent, carefully and perseveringly, to take lesson after lesson of the older teacher who is a proficient in this language, while the older teacher must have the patience to give these lessons. For the language of signs is not to be learned from books. It can not be delineated in pictures, or printed on paper. It must be learned, in a great degree, from the living, looking, acting model. Some of the finest models for such a pur-

pose are found among the originators of this language, the deaf and dumb. The peculiarities of
their mind and character, and the genius of that
singularly beautiful and impressive language which
nature has taught them, should be the constant
study of those whose beneficent calling it is to
elevate them in the scale of intellectual, social, and
moral existence; to fit them for usefulness and
respectability in this life, and for happiness in that
which is to come.

Mr. Gallaudet's practice as a teacher was
consistent with this earnest preaching. He
loved the language of signs and made a life-
long study of it. That he was such a master
of it is due in part to his patience and pains-
taking as a student of it. But his eminence
in pantomime was, no doubt, in large measure owing to inherited natural ability derived
from those Italian ancestors of whom mention
was made in the early pages of this book.

Though continuing, while he remained principal, to have the entire daily charge of a
class in the school, as required by the board,
he exerted himself in many other directions,
than in the rather narrow one of elementary
teaching.

Demands for public addresses in aid of the
cause of deaf-mute education were frequent,

and were cheerfully responded to. Exhibitions of pupils before legislatures and to the general public had often to be given, and in them Mr. Gallaudet showed his great skill in enlisting the sympathy and co-operation of others.

These occasions brought him in contact with the leading men of his time, and though a drain upon his strength were congenial to his tastes.

Representatives of several states outside of New England appealed for counsel and aid in establishing schools for the deaf within their borders, and in meeting their applications much time and effort was expended by Mr. Gallaudet.

His services as a preacher were often sought to supply vacant pulpits, and in most of the organized public movements of the day his support and active co-operation were considered essential.

No man, however vigorous, could have led a life of such constant activity and involving so much of ever-present care and responsibility for many years without showing signs of breaking; and the wonder is that with so fragile a physique these signs did not sooner appear in Mr. Gallaudet.

He became painfully conscious during the latter part of 1829 that he was overtaxing his strength and felt that he must be relieved of some of his duties, or relinquish them altogether.

Up to this time he had taken little thought as to his pecuniary interests, accepting such compensation for his services in the institution as the directors saw fit to vote him. But the presence in his household by this time of three sons and two daughters led him to wonder how all the little mouths were to be fed, the bodies clothed and the minds instructed as time went on.

So almost for the first time since he had been in relations with his board of directors, now more than fourteen years, he asked their serious consideration of his personal affairs in a communication that needs to be read entire to be fully understood.

Mr. Gallaudet, to the President and Directors, etc.

HARTFORD, January 11, 1830.

GENTLEMEN :—I have been led, for several years past, seriously to consider, how much longer my health and strength would enable me to sustain the confinement and labor necessary for the daily instruction of a class, together with the performance of other duties, as principal, in the institution over the interests of which you preside.

While making known these sentiments from time to time to those more immediately connected with the management of the school, and especially to the instructors, I have perceived that the actual amount of time and of labor which I have been obliged to bestow from the commencement upon its internal and external concerns, in addition to that employed, in common with the other instructors, in the daily care of a class, has been but imperfectly understood ;—and, on this account, it has been thought by some rather unreasonable that I should propose, in any way, to have my labors diminished.

As I still feel it to be a duty which I owe to myself and family, to state explicitly that I can not any longer undertake the daily instruction of a class, and thinking it not improbable that this may lead to the dissolution of my connection with the institution, I beg leave, gentlemen, to lay before you a brief statement of what labors I have sustained in the discharge of my various duties, since I have been in your employment. In this way I hope to satisfy you that, in my past wishes, and present determination not to be confined to the daily instruction of a class, I have been actuated only by those views and motives which should influence the conduct of every prudent man. I make this statement, as I know your candor will do me the justice to believe, not from the desire of vain-boasting, nor from a wish to induce you to think it would be for the interests of the school that my connection with it should be continued (for I am ever doubtful in my own mind whether this would be the case), but from that feeling which is common to us all, to show to our friends that we have not been wholly unreasonable in our plans and conduct. Such a statement, also, will, I think, not be without use, in presenting to the consideration of the directors some views with regard to both the internal and external concerns of the institution, and, especially, the duties which the principal, whoever he may be, ought to have abundant time allowed him to perform, that may, heretofore, have escaped their notice. Should the issue be, that you deem it best to have some other person occupy the station which I now hold, a decision in which I shall cheerfully acquiesce, I can not but urge the importance of your affording him every needful facility for sustaining the responsibilities which he will assume, and every suitable encouragement for making this institution what it already aspires to be, one of the most useful and respectable in the world.

During the twelve years and a half that I have labored here, I may safely say that I have devoted full as much time to the discharge of my official duties, as is devoted by any of the presidents, professors, or tutors, in our colleges, to the business of their respective institutions,—and, even much. more than this during the early stages of the work. In most of the colleges, there are three months of vacation in each year; and, in addition to this, many of the labors of the president and professors are suspended from the time of the examination of the senior class in July, to the commencement in September. Our vacations are but two months in the year; during some of these, it has fallen to my lot, in common with the other instructors, to remain and take a general oversight of the establishment, and of such of the pupils as did not ·return home, and during others, and nearly all of the vacations in the spring, I have been detained by the business of the annual meeting happening at that time, and by the preparation of the annual reports, twelve of which I have written, and arranged and prepared the original compositions of the pupils for the press: a labor demanding no small amount of time and care.

The Elementary Book which has been used in the various classes was prepared by me, while teaching a class, and consumed no small portion of my time out of school hours; for this labor I did not receive, nor, indeed, did I expect, any compensation. In the same manner, with the assistance of Mr. W., I also prepared the Catechism of Religious Instruction which has been used.

I have given, out of school hours, much private instruction to the younger teachers, and especially a long and elaborate course of lectures to Mr. P. For such services, from the very commencement of the institution, Mr. Clerc has received a liberal compensation, to which, indeed, he was justly entitled, at first from you, and, afterwards, from the instructors. For similar services, I have never received, nor asked, any compensation.

The correspondence of the institution, more especially that which relates to its external relations, to the many inquiries made from different parts of

the country with regard to the terms of admission
and to the peculiar circumstances of the pupils as
connected with their accounts with the treasurer,
has occupied no inconsiderable portion of my time.
With regard to the last particular, I may venture to
refer to the recollection of the treasurer for the
correctness of my statement. The principal degree
of responsibility with regard to the admission of
new pupils, and the recording of their names, and of
other interesting particulars respecting them, in a
book kept for this purpose, has devolved upon me,
and, also, their organization into a class, and their
getting started in the course of instruction, especially
when they have been under the care of a new and
inexperienced instructor. One part of my labors,
as principal of the institution, which has not, indeed,
attracted much observation from those employed
more immediately in its concerns, but which has
consumed, in the aggregate, a vast amount of time,
and been attended, out of school hours, with great
additional fatigue, is the attention which I have
been obliged to show to visitors. Among these
have been the patrons and friends of the school,
respectable strangers coming with letters of introduction, and others introduced by some of the
directors, or by their friends in the city, and who
always expect and are entitled to receive respectful
attentions from the principal of a public institution.
Such attentions I have always cheerfully rendered,
but, it ought to be recollected, that it has more
particularly fallen upon me to render them ; that
they have often made it necessary for me out of

school hours, to gratify such visitors by an exhibition of the pupils in the school-room, that I have been liable, from my residing near at hand, to such demand upon my time very frequently, and that such time, after the exhaustion occasioned by the labors of the school-room, I have often needed for relaxation and exercise, and also, to devote to the domestic concerns of my family. It is very important, however, for the interests of an institution depending on public patronage for its character and usefulness, and increasing, too, like ours, in public estimation, that the principal should be at liberty, at almost all times, to exhibit its internal management, and the progress of the pupils, in such a way as to excite a deep and permanent interest in the minds of intelligent visitors.

For a somewhat similar reason, too, I have had peculiar labors to perform and embarrassments to contend with, even during school hours, in advancing the class of which I have most usually had the charge. This class has consisted of those pupils who had made the most progress, and on whose attainments, and especially on their original compositions published in the annual reports, the character of the institution has chiefly depended.

This class I have had to advance in their studies, while subject, during school hours, to peculiar interruptions from various sources,—from some of the younger instructors resorting to me for signs, from persons coming to my room for the transaction of business; from visitors, some bringing letters of introduction, and most of all such wishing to visit the class taught by the principal, and he, of course, having afterwards to provide for their being admitted into some of the other classes. Of late, a person has been employed to receive visitors at the door, and to conduct them to some one of the school-rooms. Previous to this arrangement, and for a long course of time, the interruptions which I experienced from this source were so frequent as to create no small embarrassment in the attention which it was important I should bestow upon the class immediately under my care.

I have devoted also considerable time to the religious instruction of the younger classes, where the teacher has himself as yet been a novice in the art of making signs.

I have long regretted that my confinement to the daily instruction of a class has prevented me from spending more time in what I apprehend would have greatly contributed to the prosperity of the institution in maturing improvements in the general course of instruction—in communicating signs, and the results of my experience to the other instructors, and especially to the younger ones, both by private lectures out of school, and by explanations and suggestions in school in the presence of their classes, and in the preparation of a series of books for the use of the deaf and dumb. To this latter object I have been for years endeavoring to give its true importance, while at the same time I have as constantly stated that, while engaged in the instruction of a class, it was impossible for me to prosecute it to any effect. Surely, while confined daily to the exhausting employment of making signs, having the common responsibilities of an instructor of a class, and the more peculiar ones of principal of the institution, it was not to be expected that I could find time for the arduous task of preparing such books as would be useful to the pupils and creditable to the institution. I experience no small degree of satisfaction in finding that my general views with regard to the importance of having such books prepared correspond precisely with those expressed in a late circular of the institution for the deaf and dumb at Paris. The employment of making signs daily for twelve years is one demanding vigorous health. I have found it, together with the pressure of my other duties, making deep inroads upon my bodily constitution. During the last term, in consequence of a statement which I made to you, gentlemen, I was released from the instruction of a class, with reference more especially to the preparation of some books for the deaf and dumb.

The result of my labors I beg leave to lay before you, and to state also the other duties which I discharged during that period of time. In that period I prepared the annual report for publication; I carried on that part of the general correspondence of the institution which has usually devolved upon me (some general view of the time employed in which the treasurer may be able to state from recollection); I officiated in turn in the various religious exercises of the school; I devoted every Saturday forenoon to the instruction of three of the lower classes, with their teachers, in their religious lessons; I spent

some time in aiding the younger instructors in their
school-rooms ; I delivered for one month a course
of daily lectures on signs, one hour each, to the
younger instructors, including Mr. H., who, expecting soon to go to Ohio, was very anxious to have
the benefit of my experience; for this I declined
receiving any compensation, but the instructors presented me with a few books as an expression of their
thanks.   I attended also to many visitors, who were
of such a character that it was indispensable that
they should be treated with respectful attention by
the principal.

Besides these more general duties, I prepared a
book of about fifty pages, which was much needed
in four of the classes.   This book was ready for
publication in September last.   Delay on the part
of the engraver in New York has prevented its publication.   I have made an arrangement with the
publisher that I shall be able soon to furnish, free
of all charge, seven or eight hundred copies, sufficient
to supply the new classes for years to come.   I have
also made considerable progress in the preparation
of a vocabulary for the deaf and dumb.   The preliminary steps which I deemed necessary for the
completion of such a work in order to render it both
creditable to the institution, and permanently useful.
to this and other similar schools, required an amount
of patient labor which no one but those familiar
with pursuits of the same kind can duly appreciate.
Some estimate can be formed of the amount of this
labor when I state that it was necessary for me to
go twice through the English dictionary from A to

Z, examining carefully each time thirty or forty thousand words in order to make the proper selections, and to arrange them in classes. In addition to this, I have transferred to a series of charts one principal class of these words, relating wholly to sensible objects, and also to other charts classes of words of a different kind. By no other process which I could devise could I see any mode of obtaining the materials necessary for the formation of a vocabulary for the deaf and dumb. I am aware that it has been thought that such a vocabulary might be formed in the space of a few weeks. If this were practicable, it is rather singular that it should not ere this have been done in some of the European institutions, for the late circular of the Paris institution, published in September last, to which I have already referred, states that the preparation of such a vocabulary is a work of great importance, and that the instructors in some of the European institutions are now actually engaged in it. The preliminary steps which I have taken are precisely those recommended in this circular, showing a remarkable coincidence of views in this respect, and what is more, stated to be absolutely indispensable. In the completion of this work there is still needed no small amount of time and labor, and I would most cheerfully put all my manuscripts into the hands of any person who would undertake to bring it to a conclusion; and if originally such a vocabulary could have been prepared in three or four weeks, the task will now be a much lighter one, as many of the more difficult preliminary steps are already accomplished.

In the review of my past connection with the institution, I have much to lament of deficiencies and error in the discharge of my duties; yet justice to myself leads me to state that I have performed services out of school for which a compensation might reasonably have been asked, and that the actual amount of time and labor, which for twelve years I have expended in order to promote the prosperity of the school, is fully equal to what any president or professor or tutor in any of our colleges has devoted in the same length of time to a similar object, while the kind of labor, that of teaching the deaf and dumb, is more exhausting, and makes deeper encroachments upon the constitution and bodily health than that endured in almost any other pursuit or profession. I ought to state also that from the first moment when I concluded to go to Europe on my responsible and difficult undertaking to this hour, I have never urged any pecuniary claims, nor received any thing for any extra services. I have taken just what the directors have seen fit to allow me, and with this have always been contented.

When I allude, therefore, to the fact that some of the instructors have been receiving for years past a much larger compensation than myself, and that others have found it perfectly consistent with their duties to add by other labors to their income; while it was impossible for me, when confined to the daily instruction of a class, and to the duties both of an instructor and the other peculiar ones connected with the office of principal, to engage in any pursuit by which to add to my income: when I allude to these facts, and also to one other of a striking nature known to every body, that the presidents and professors in colleges, and also many settled clergymen, find time, after discharging the appropriate duties of their stations, to publish books and to do other things as means of increasing their resources,—I hope, gentlemen, I shall be considered as presenting for your consideration only what I owe to myself and family, when I state that after having spent the very prime of my life in your service, I have deemed it but reasonable to be released from the instruction of a class, and also to have sufficient leisure to command enough of my time to devote to some objects by which to add to my means of providing for my family and educating my children, and of laying up a little something for the exigencies of those future days rapidly approaching, when the life and animation of an actor of pantomime, calling into artificial exercise the most intense effort of thought and of feeling through the mysterious medium of the eye and the countenance and the gestures and attitudes of the body, must settle down into the tranquillity and even feebleness of declining years.

It ought not to be concealed, that I entertain views, with regard to what the principal of such an institution might accomplish, if released from the instruction of a class, so as very much to promote its welfare, with which those of most, perhaps all, of the other instructors, do not coincide. They think,

as I am informed by the chairman of the committee,
and this without any reference to myself personally,
that the true interests of the school require, that the
principal should, in addition to his other peculiar
duties, be engaged in the instruction of a class.
They also think that the peculiar duties of the
principal, out of school, need not occupy more than
one hour daily. Consider this estimate as correct,
though in my opinion it is far from being so, taking
into account the performance of all that I have
stated to have been performed by me, in addition to
the instruction of a class—and what time will be
left for the principal to devote to the general progress
of the classes, to the training up of instructors, to the
delivering of lectures on signs, to the maturing improvements in the course of instruction, to the religious instruction of the lower classes, to the preparation of suitable books, to the general good order and
prosperity of the institution, both in the school-room
and the workshops, and to the publication of the
annual reports. Are such objects worthy of the
active and zealous efforts of such a person as is fit
to be held up to the public as competent to discharge the duties of principal; and if so, how can
he justly be held responsible for the faithful discharge of the duties growing out of this important
trust, while he is obliged to exhaust a great portion
of his strength, and consume the most considerable
part of his time, in the daily instruction of a class?
It is to be recollected, also, that he needs time to
attend to his family concerns,—to take a sufficient
degree of relaxation and exercise for the preservation

of his health, and surely to enjoy the opportunity of keeping pace with his cotemporaries in the improvement of his intellectual powers, which is, through him, to affect the reputation of the institution.

My confinement, for years past, to the daily instruction of a class—an employment, in itself, quite as exhausting as the whole amount of the daily duties performed by the presidents or professors in our colleges—while numerous responsibilities, connected with the state of other classes and the general concerns of the institution, have, for want of any other appropriate person, been constantly referred to myself, and yet no adequate time allowed me to discharge them; this, together with the wide field of enterprise for promoting the prosperity and elevating the character of the school opening before me, could I but have been released from the care of a particular class, has tended very much, I am free to confess, to damp the former ardor which I had during the early progress of my work; has had no trifling effect upon my general health and spirits, and has furnished reasons, at times, for my friends to fear that the spirit of resolution and of effort had quite forsaken me. And yet I have held on my course, and may I not be permitted to ask, referring to all the past history of the institution, when has your principal once failed in the accomplishment of any great object connected with its prosperity? It was an ardent and enthusiastic spirit which first led him to embark in an undertaking considered by many as wholly visionary, and the same spirit has always been ready to kindle whenever any important object

has been proposed by which to add to the usefulness or the reputation of the institution. But for
any one to plod on in the same round of èlementary
instruction to twelve or fifteen infantile minds for
twelve years, with no hope of being released from it,
while, at the same time, he sees various ways in
which his time and talents could be brought to bear
with a hundred-fold more effect upon the prosperity
of an institution, which under Providence he has
been one of the principal instruments of raising up
to usefulness and reputation,—all this is calculated,
especially where a feeble constitution has to contend
with the pressure of nervous disease, while engaged
in one of the most exhausting of all employments—
to weaken, to dishearten, nay to paralyze hope,—
although once the brightest, and resolution the
strongest, and enterprise the most undaunted.

To one point, gentlemen, permit me to invite
your particular and candid attention. Ought the
services which I have rendered to be estimated by
the exact number of hours and minutes consumed in
their performance, and ought they to be placed on a
level with those of the other instructors?

Before I went to Europe in your employment,
I had received a very expensive education. I
had graduated at Yale College; I had been a
tutor in that institution two years; I was licensed
to preach, and, in addition to all this, I had
received a pretty thorough mercantile education.
All this cost money, and enabled me to enter upon
the discharge of the trust that you assigned me in
the origin of the school, and has since enabled me to

discharge additional ones, with so much the greater promptness, dispatch and success. In support of this position, may I allude to the peculiar difficulties which I had to encounter, and which, by the blessing of God, I overcame while in Europe; to the amount of funds which I was instrumental in raising; to the successive annual reports which I have prepared; to the impressions made by means of addresses, and sermons, and public exhibitions, on legislatures and the inhabitants of some of our largest cities, and on the Congress of the United States, favorable to the prosperity of the institution; to the securing, by previous correspondence and by my own personal attendance on their respective legislatures, the appointment of commissioners from the New England States, and the abandonment of projects almost ripe for execution, for the establishment of other schools, and the concentration of public patronage on one for all New England; to the conducting for years a very delicate and difficult controversy, if it may be so called, with the New York institution, and affording complete satisfaction to the commissioners chosen on the part of that state to visit the institution of the superiority of our mode of instruction; to the enlisting the feelings and good will of hundreds of respectable visitors from all parts of the Union; to the carrying on a correspondence with distinguished individuals and officers of government, with regard to the interests of the deaf and dumb generally and the welfare of this institution more particularly; to the making improvements in the course, and manner of instruction, and

in the religious exercises of the pupils; to the educating some pupils who are now assistant teachers,
and to the furnishing in the early progress of
the school specimens of the attainments of the
pupils which excited surprise even in the older
establishments in Europe; and in these, and
other ways, to the securing to this institution,
while yet in its infancy, the approbation and
patronage of our own country, and an elevated rank
among those of long standing in foreign countries.

So far as I have been instrumental, under the support of a kind superintending Providence, in the accomplishment of these objects; and, so far as I have
performed the more ordinary business of the institution with promptness, dispatch and success, ought
not a proper regard to be had to the qualifications
in the possession of which I originally entered into
your employment?

Are not the services of all public agents and professional men estimated in this way, and ought my
services, then, to be estimated by the precise number of hours and minutes that it has taken me to
render them; or ought I, in this respect, to be
placed on a level with younger men, who have not
had the same advantages of experience and of education as myself?

If we examine the arrangements of any extensive
establishment of a commercial or manufacturing
kind, or those of the naval, the military, or the civil
department of our government, do we ever find
that those occupying important stations of trust are
obliged, in addition to the responsibilities growing

out of these stations, to labor, also, in the details of business in the more inferior departments?

Is the estimate placed upon their services, and the compensation which they receive for them, ascertained by the precise amount of time employed in rendering them, or are they placed, in this respect, on a level with those having less experience and occupying subordinate stations? On the contrary, are not their services estimated according to their experience and skill—and do they not often receive double the amount of pay for spending much less time than is employed by one in an inferior station? These principles are acted upon in institutions of a similar kind in Europe, and none of the prominent ones for the instruction of the deaf and dumb require of the principal to be devoted to the daily instruction of a class.

Nothing but the very peculiar circumstances under which I am placed, would lead me thus to allude to topics, to mention which, on almost any other occasion, would look too much like vain-boasting. But it seemed to me indispensable to make such a statement—in order to place in its true light the reasonableness of my views with regard to releasing the principal, whoever he may be, from the daily instruction of a class, since no one but myself, however kindly disposed, is sufficiently acquainted with all the facts of the case, to be able to state them fully and accurately. Such a statement, for various reasons, I wished to leave on your records—and having thus considered the past, the great question recurs, what is to be done with regard to the future.

After much deliberation, with the advice of several judicious friends, I have formed my judgment on two important points—that I ought not to be confined any longer to the daily instruction of a class, and that, in justice to an increasing family, I ought, in some way or other, to add to my present income.

Whether, under these circumstances, the continuance of my connection with your institution will be consistent both with its true interests, and with the duties which I owe to myself, and to my family, is a question which I am free to confess I feel myself much at a loss to decide, until I am made more fully acquainted with the views of the directors, and also with those of my colleagues, on the various points involved in this communication.

Other spheres of usefulness, of great importance, have been presented to my consideration and offers made to me, within a year or two past, more compatible with my health, and more productive, in a pecuniary point of view, than that which I now occupy ;—and as these have all related to the great department of education toward which both the efforts of my mind and the feelings of my heart have long been intensely directed, and in which the dearest interests of our common country are most deeply involved, I confess, that I have been often led to hesitate whether to such objects it might not become my duty to devote my future labors. In addition to this, so long as the other instructors retain the views that they have expressed to the committee, it is manifest that they can not consider the other services which the principal of the

institution might render if released from the instruction of a class, of sufficient value to justify his being
retained in his present station.

Under these circumstances, is it not obvious to
every mind possessed of any feelings of delicacy and
of self-respect, that the continuance of my connection
with the institution must be attended with much to
depress any generous feelings of enterprise and usefulness?

The general question at issue, is, I am aware, but
matter of opinion. My colleagues may be in the
right, and myself in the wrong. It may be establishing an injurious precedent to release the principal
from the daily instruction of a class; and should
you, gentlemen, be of this opinion, I will submit
most cheerfully to your decision; not disappointed,
should it thus prove to be the will of Providence, in
being permitted to resign a station of great responsibility, full of anxieties and cares, and to discharge
the duties of which, as they ought to be discharged,
demands no small portion of both bodily and mental
labor. I will retire, in perfect good-will toward all
parties; retaining a grateful recollection of the kindness and indulgence which I have experienced at your
hands, and pledging myself, so far as any means or
influence may be left to me, to do all that I can to
promote the peace, the prosperity, and the happiness of the school.

On the other hand, should you conclude that it is
desirable still to continue me in your employment, as
principal of the institution, in accordance with the
views which I have stated, I must say, with the same

frankness which I have endeavored to preserve throughout all this communication, that my decision with regard to the course of duty will depend, not merely on the nature and extent of the duties which may be assigned to me, but quite as much on the views and feelings which this may produce on the part of my colleagues.

For it must be obvious to every one, that without harmony and confidence between the principal and his associates, his own comfort, and of course his usefulness, must be greatly diminished ;—his health impaired by a constant series of anxieties, and thus, his efforts to promote the prosperity of the institution rendered, in a great degree, ineffectual.

I am, gentlemen, with sentiments of esteem and respect,

Your obedient servant,
T. H. GALLAUDET.

This letter was not without its effect on the directors, and within a week after its presentation they voted to release Mr. Gallaudet from the duty of teaching a class for a year, with the evident intention of making the arrangement a permanent one. Not so ready, however, were the assistant instructors to do what might have retained their principal in his place. They had already expressed their view that he ought not to be excused from teaching. Not sustained in this by the board they entered into an earnest controversy as to the proper mode of governing the institution, insisting that this should be done by a faculty in which the principal should have little if any more authority than one of them. It will be remembered that in 1818 the experiment of governing the school by a faculty was made. This method proving unsatisfactory at that time was not continued. Two sets of pro-posed regulations were submitted to the directors, one by Mr. Gallaudet and one by his assistants.

When it became evident after almost inter-minable correspondence that their suggestions did not command the approval of the direct-ors, and when they found their course of con-duct was actually driving Mr. Gallaudet to resign, the instructors undertook to withdraw much they had said, and expressed a disposi-tion to acquiesce in the decision of the board and to give Mr. Gallaudet their support if he would remain.

Too much argument, however, had been car-ried on, and the differences of opinion were too radical to allow a hope of harmonious action to be had.

Mr. Gallaudet, therefore, on the 7th of April, 1830, forwarded his resignation to the directors.

To one who has studied with care the many documents that go to make up the record of this seemingly unfortunate history, the charity shown by Mr. Gallaudet towards those who had been opposing him appears little short of sublime.

While giving suitable prominence to the differences of view existing between the instructors and himself and showing how unlikely it was that harmony could be expected even though the directors should fully sustain and the assistants acquiesce in his policy, as both seemed disposed now to do, he still declared his willingness to make the attempt of continuing to direct the affairs of the institution, were he not convinced that his health would no longer bear the strain. He closes his letter of resignation as follows :

Trusting, gentlemen, that whatever opinion you may form of the expediency of the course which, after long and deliberate reflection, I have adopted, you will let my motives share the exercise of your candor, I resign into your hands the office of principal, cherishing towards all connected with the establishment the most friendly sentiments; grateful for the kindnesses which I have received; sensible of my many deficiencies in duty and errors in judgment; and beseeching Almighty God so to

guide and bless all concerned in its management
that the institution, over whose interests you, gentlemen, have so long and so successfully presided,
may go on to increase in favor with the public, and
in usefulness to that interesting and yet very
numerous class of our fellow-men, for whose benefit
it was, under the guidance of a merciful Providence,
originally established.

In their annual report following Mr. Gallaudet's resignation the directors thus record
their appreciation of the value of his services :

It is well known that to this gentleman, as the
agent of the board of directors, the cause of
humanity is primarily indebted for the introduction
of the art of deaf-mute instruction into the United
States, and for the general spread of that information necessary for prosecuting it successfully in public institutions, of which all in operation in the
country are now experiencing the benefits. It is,
however, in our own establishment that the importance of his services can be best appreciated. These
are and have ever been most highly valued by the
board. To them they attribute primarily and chiefly
the success of their institution hitherto, as it apper-
tains either to the patronage of public bodies, the
favor of influential individuals, the benevolent wishes
and the contributions of the charitable, and the
actual instruction of several hundred deaf and dumb
persons. Retaining his connection with the institu-

tion as one of its life-directors, Mr. Gallaudet will
still be enabled to exercise an important influence in
its management; and while his associates in the
board rely upon the aid of his experience and counsels in their future operations, they can not but
express their cordial desire for his own continued
prosperity and happiness, in whatever sphere of usefulness he may be called to engage.

It would burden these pages to relate how
often and in what manner Mr. Gallaudet's
"experience and counsels" were of special
value to the institution in whose board of
management he retained a seat, after ceasing
to be its executive head.

These services covered a period of more
than twenty years: they were given without
thought of pecuniary reward; and that the
directors recognized later the obligations of
the institution to Mr. Gallaudet growing out
of these labors, by voting him a sum of
money, detracts nothing from the unselfish
spirit in which they were offered.

Not the least important of them was rendered almost immediately after his resignation, and before his successor had been
appointed. It was to urge upon the directors
with an earnestness which good taste, and his
natural modesty, forbade him to show so long

as they concerned himself, all those measures
he had proposed concerning organization and
division of duty and authority in the institution.

These measures were promptly adopted by
the board, and Mr. Gallaudet's successor
found himself clothed with all needful power,
required only to perform such duties as were
natural to his office as principal—and these
not of an exhausting character—and in the
receipt of a salary much larger than had ever
been paid to Mr. Gallaudet.

That the directors of the institution, or the
teachers, intended to do injustice to Mr. Gallaudet need not be charged at this late day,
and it would probably be wrong to impute
such motives to them. That he was unjustly,
even cruelly, treated is evident from the
record. It is known that he felt himself to
have been so dealt with. But through all this
bitter experience he broke no friendship, he
accused no man of unworthy motives. He
had, with wonderful energy, discretion and
devotion, carried a great public work to a
brilliant and substantial success, in consideration of which the least the directors could, in
justice, have offered him would have been a
year of absolute rest, that he might, if possi-

ble, regain the health which had broken down in their service.

But it does not appear that this, or any such measure, was even suggested in the board, and it was left to Mr. Gallaudet to see that the consideration he had long deserved was bestowed on his successor.

CHAPTER VII.

BEFORE relating events which followed
Mr. Gallaudet's resignation as principal
of the School for the Deaf it will be necessary to speak of the services he rendered to
many objects of public interest while still filling that arduous office.

His mind was too active, his sympathy too
broad, and his interest in his fellow-men too
alert to allow him to become narrow even
while carrying the heavy official burdens that
were upon him.

Whatever movement was set on foot for
the benefit of humanity, for the uplifting of
the oppressed, and especially for the advancement of the cause of general education, was

sure to find him among its earliest and most
zealous supporters. Nor did he always wait
for others to start such undertakings.

In the periodicals of the day many articles
and addresses may be found from his pen on
subjects other than those connected with his
specialty, such as the Mission to the Sandwich Islands in 1819, the Tract Society, and
a series of elaborate articles on General Education in Poulson's *Daily Advertiser*, Philadelphia, in 1820, Teachers' Seminaries in 1826,
Female Education in 1827, the case of the
Moorish Prince Abdul Rahhamann in the
same year, and the Philosophy of Language
in 1830.

The following suggestions in a letter to his
intimate friend, S. V. S. Wilder of New York,
well known to some now living as a prominent and influential merchant of his time, were
written thirteen years before the first Normal
School was established, and of which, as the
sequel will show, Mr. Gallaudet was invited
to take charge.

Letter to Mr. Wilder.

HARTFORD, Dec. 10, 1824.
MY DEAR FRIEND :—I am going to jog your elbow,
as you sit by your fire with your dear wife and chil-

dren, about my project. I shall be as brief as possible; for hints to the wise are sufficient. How can we expect any great moral change to take place in the world, until the education of children is conducted on the best plan, and, I would add, on evangelical principles? The talents, and character, and fidelity, and skill of their instructors is of immense importance. Make the business of an instructor of youth as much a profession as that of divinity, law, or medicine. We have theological, law, and medical institutions. Why not have an institution for the business of education? Give it what name you please. Fix it somewhere in New England. Let it be under the control of judicious, pious men. Let it have its professors;—men of talents adapted to the object. Let them deliver a course of lectures on the theory and practice of education, so far as it relates to the instruction of children and youth in the branches of what is called a good, *common English education,*— and on the best modes of teaching them practical, moral, and religious truths. Let the institution have a library, to contain all the books, theoretical and practical, in different languages, on education; and also the various apparatus employed for this purpose. Let there be placed at the institution a sufficient number of youth to form a school for practice, so as to reduce the theories of the professors to actual experiment. Let young men go to this institution to qualify themselves to become instructors. Let them stay till they are well qualified, and receive a diploma or certificate.

The advantages of such an institution are so many

and great, that I have not time to enumerate them.
Many of them will doubtless occur to you. They
would result, however, in producing throughout the
country, *an uniform system of education* on *the best
plan*, and *in elevating the character of instructors*, and
in producing public confidence in them, and *in saving
a great deal of time, labor, and money*.

This plan may need modeling and maturing (let
wiser heads than mine do it); but of the utility of
its general features can there be a doubt?

The object of having a certain number of youth
at the institution would be to have them daily
taught by the young men who are qualifying themselves to become instructors, under the direction of
the professors. Thus, in a few years, a mass of experience would be accumulated that would lead to
the most profitable result. Such an institution, too,
would soon become the place where the *best school
books* would be prepared; and, indeed, all sorts of
books intended for the improvement of the youthful
mind. What an engine of doing good, if well conducted!

Let me add, that such an institution would be the
means of developing and establishing those correct
principles of education, which would be of immense
use to the missionaries who go to teach heathen
people, and who, of late years, are beginning to find
out and to tell us, that the great hope of Christian-
izing those among whom they labor, lies in *instructing the rising generation*. Oh! for a reformer to
arise on this subject of the education of youth!
Our apparently weightier projects of doing good

have caused this to be too much neglected. We spend our labor upon the old trees ; we too much disregard the young shoots.

Yours in the bonds of Christian love,

T. H. GALLAUDET.

In 1828, Mr. Gallaudet visited Washington at the request of the managers of the Pennsylvania Institution for the Deaf and Dumb, to aid them in an effort to secure Congressional aid for their young institution. This school was, at that time, under the charge of Mr. Lewis Weld, who had been trained for his work by Mr. Gallaudet, and who, two years later, was called back to Hartford at the latter's suggestion to become his successor.

Mr. Weld accompanied Mr. Gallaudet to Washington with a number of pupils of the Philadelphia school, and an exhibition of their attainments was given to Congress, of which John Quincy Adams gives a full and discriminating account in his diary.

While in Washington Mr. Gallaudet was invited to preach in the Hall of the House of Representatives. Of his sermon Mr. Adams speaks as follows :—

Feb. 17, 1828.   Rev. Thomas H. Gallaudet preached in the Hall of Representatives from Ro-

mans xv., 21 : "But as it is written, to whom he was
not spoken of they shall see ; and they that have not
heard shall understand."

Mr. Gallaudet considered the deaf and dumb as
Gentiles of our own age and country.

This sermon, written in an unambitious style,
was fervent in manner and cogent in reasoning.
It was listened to with deep attention. Mr. Gallaudet is the first founder of the schools for the
deaf and dumb in this country, and may, without
imputation of arrogance, compare his own condition
and services to his fellow mortals with those of the
apostle of the Gentiles.*

The incident of Mr. Gallaudet's interest in
Abdul Rahhamann occurred not long before
the visit to Washington.

This remarkable man, after having been
many years a slave in Mississippi, was met
and recognized by a surgeon in the United
States navy, Dr. Cox, as a Moorish prince he
had known in Tumbo, and by whom he had
been treated with great kindness when he was
sick in that place. Dr. Cox made an unsuccessful effort to secure the freedom of the
prince—but left such statements on record as
induced the United States government a few
years later to send an agent to Natchez to

---

* Diary of J. Q. Adams, vol. vii., pp. 434-438.

procure his liberation, and his master, Colonel Thomas Foster, manumitted him without compensation.

"The prince* was then sixty-six years old, having been a slave forty years. He had a wife, five sons and eight grandchildren, all in bondage. His wife was soon bought and set free by benevolent individuals in Natchez and the neighborhood. The object was to send them back to their own country; but they could not bear to go and leave their children and grandchildren behind. A large sum was required for their ransom, and how was it to be obtained? In the number of the *African Repository* for October, 1828, I find the following notice of the agency by which the purchase money was raised:"

We have before mentioned the prince's desire to obtain the redemption of his entire family, and that he had gone to the Northern cities to solicit aid. We rejoice to find, that the Rev. Mr. Gallaudet, principal of the Institution for the Deaf and Dumb at Hartford, and so well-known to the public for his truly Christian and charitable enterprise, has generously devoted himself for two or three weeks past to this unfortunate stranger; examined and made

---

* Rev. Dr. Humphrey's Life of Dr. Gallaudet, p. 229.

himself familiar with his history; brought the facts of it before the public in New England, and finally visited New York, where he made a powerful appeal in the Masonic Hall to the generous and wealthy of that city.

The address was published, and greatly aided in raising the sum required. I can not refrain from quoting a part of the closing paragraph from that eloquent appeal. It was thought worthy of the man and of the sacred cause of humanity and religion.

"The prince was born and spent his early youth in Timbuctoo, and recollects that no one was disturbed for religious opinions, and that the Alcoran had given the people a curiosity to see the Bible. During all his trials the prince has not forgotten his Arabic, but reads it fluently and writes it with neatness. The finger of God seems to point to great results arising from his return. His life appears like a romance, and would be incredible if the evidence were not undeniable. We see in these events, that God's ways are not as our ways, nor His thoughts as our thoughts. We see why the prisoner was not to return with his Moorish disposition and his Moorish sword; that Providence continued him here, till grace had softened his heart. He will now return a messenger of peace. Blessed be God, that we are permitted the honor of co-operating with him. Methinks I see him, like a patriarch, crossing the Atlantic, over which he was taken forty years since, with his flock around him, and happy in doing good. I think I see benighted Africa taking her stand among the nations of the earth. I think I see Egypt, as heretofore, pouring a flood of light into Greece, and Carthage arising in former glory.

" I think I see Africa, one hand pointing to the tablet of eternal justice, making even us Americans tremble, while the words are pronounced, 'Vengeance is mine, I will repay, saith the Lord ;' and with the other pointing to the golden rule of the Gospel."

Soon after their emancipation, the prince and his family emigrated to Liberia, where he died in a short time, and where Mr. R. R. Gurley, secretary of the American Colonization Society, visited his widow not long after his death. She handed him an old pocket-book, in which he found the following letter from Mr. Gallaudet :

Letter to the Moorish Prince.

HARTFORD, May 15, 1828.

MY VENERABLE FRIEND :—I have read with deep interest the late accounts respecting you, and how, with the blessing of God, and by the liberality of kind friends, yourself and wife have obtained freedom, and are soon to return to your native land.

I saw in this city, a few days since, the Rev. Jonas King, who has lately been a Christian missionary in Palestine. He told me, that when he should arrive in New York, from which place he expects soon to embark for Greece, he would send you an Arabic Bible. I hope it will reach you in safety.

I also send you (and of which I beg your acceptance as a small token of my esteem and friendship), a small book in Arabic, which was sent to me
a few years ago by a friend in England, the Rev.
Josiah Pratt, secretary at that time of the Church
Missionary Society, which has done so much to
enlighten the Africans in their native country.

Remember, my venerable friend, that it is the
religion of Jesus Christ alone which leads men to
do good to the souls of their fellow-men. What
other religion does this? I know there are those
who call themselves Christians (and it is easy for
men to call themselves by any name), and yet
act directly contrary to the commands of Jesus
Christ. Do not judge the religion of Jesus Christ
by such men.

Read attentively, I beseech you, my venerable
friend, the New Testament. You will see in the
character of Jesus Christ, and in all His precepts, a
religion which, if cherished in the heart and practiced in the life, would make men good and happy
both in this and in the futrure world.

Perhaps you have met a few persons who are
Christians in heart, and who imitate the example of
Jesus Christ. What do you think of them? What
do you think of that religion which has removed
darkness from their minds, and made their hearts
love God and love their fellow-men? Look at such
men. Are you not glad to have them for your
friends? They are the ones who wish not only to
do you good in this world, but to prepare you
after death (which, oh, my venerable friend, can

not be far distant from you and your dear wife), to
be happy forever in Heaven.

Was Jesus Christ, who set such an example and
taught such a religion, an impostor? You say, perhaps He was a good man. Well, if He was a good
man He could not have spoken falsehoods, He must
always have told the truth. But if He told the
truth, His religion must be the true one, and all other
religions which do not agree with it must be false.
He said He was the only Saviour, and that only by
repentance towards God for all our sins, and by faith
in Him as our only Saviour, we can be saved. If this
is not true, what a wicked person, what an
impostor Jesus Christ must have been! The Arabic
book which I send you, my venerable friend, shows
very clearly the truth of the Christian religion.

It was first written by Hugo Grotius, a very
wise and learned man, who lived in the United
Netherlands. It was translated into Arabic by Professor McBride, a very learned man who lives in
Oxford, England. I beg you to read it carefully.
I beg you to read the Arabic Bible carefully, which
I hope you will receive from my friend Mr. King.
I beg you at the same time, to pray Almighty God
that He would guide you by His wisdom into the
knowledge of the true religion; for, my venerable
friend, how important it is that we should find and
embrace the true religion! You, whose soul will so
soon be in eternity.

May the Holy Spirit lead you in the way of
truth, of safety, and of peace. Is not Jesus Christ
just such a Saviour, just such a teacher, just such a

guide, just such a protector, just such a friend as you and I need in a world like this, so full of disappointments, of sorrow and of sin? Shall we not need Him when we die, and when our souls appear at the judgment seat at the last day?

I heard yesterday that some family near this city had a long letter in Arabic, which you wrote when you first came to this country, in Charleston, South Carolina. I rode seven miles last evening to try to find this letter. I did not succeed, but I heard something about it, and I will try to procure it and send it to you. Please to write me as soon as you receive this letter, and tell me how soon you expect to embark, and to what place I shall direct another letter to you. Give kind regards to your wife and children, all of whom, as well as yourself, I commend to the protection and blessing of Almighty God, beseeching Him for the sake of Jesus Christ to guide you all, after the trials and changes of this short and uncertain life, to the mansions of eternal rest. I am, my venerable friend, your friend in truth, T. H. GALLAUDET.

A year before his acquaintance with the Moorish prince Mr. Gallaudet had become interested in the great question of the treatment of the blacks in our country, probably in consequence of the following letter received from the Rev. Edward Bickersteth, Secretary of the Church Missionary Society of England.

CHURCH MISSIONARY HOME, LONDON,
                    October 25, 1826.

MY DEAR SIR :—The committee of our society, having lost many valuable laborers in Africa, have turned their attention to a supply of teachers better fitted than Europeans to encounter the insalubrity of its climate. They have been strongly recommended to procure persons of color for this service, and have been led to suppose there may be many such in America, who have the requisite piety, talent and knowledge to fit them for such an office.

Their duty would be the religious instruction of the liberated Africans congregated in Sierra Leone from all parts of Africa.

We shall be much obliged if you will inform us whether there be, in your knowledge, any persons of this description who would be willing to devote themselves wholly to labor in Africa to diffuse the Gospel.

It might not, probably, be difficult for such persons to obtain ordination from the bishops of the sister church in America before they left there.

Such persons should pledge themselves to submit to the directions of the society, as to the stations in which they may labor, and their general conduct.

The remuneration for their services would be sufficient for their comfortable support; but on this point, and any other connected with the design, we shall be truly glad to have your free and full sentiments.   I am, dear sir, faithfully yours,

EDWARD BICKERSTETH,
                    Sec. C. M. S.

It being found impracticable to find in America many persons fitted to respond to this appeal, Mr. Gallaudet bestirred himself to secure, if possible, the establishment of a school or schools for the education of colored missionaries and teachers for Africa. The following letters will serve as specimens of a large correspondence on the subject :

Letter from Rev. James Milnor, D. D.

NEW YORK, February 21, 1827.

REV. AND DEAR SIR :—I should have returned an earlier answer to your favor of January, if I had been able to say any thing of importance in relation to the interesting subject. Similar communications have been received by some of the bishops of our church, and others ; and the society of our church for the promotion of domestic and foreign missions have taken the matter under consideration, and will no doubt make every inquiry in their power. I have, however, very little hope of many suitable missionaries being procured, except in the way you have suggested, and even that will be attended with great difficulty, both in the procurance of suitable characters, and providing them with the means of acquiring a competent education. There is an institution in an incipient state, whose location is designed to be in the vicinity of Newark, N. J.; but its funds at present consist only of the moneys bequeathed by Gen-

eral Kosiusco for such an object, and a great lassitude
seems to me to obtain in getting it into operation.
Much time must necessarily elapse, before efficient
aid in the supply of colored missionaries from this
country can possibly be rendered. To give a competent education to pious persons of this description, who have spent their earlier years in slavery
and ignorance, will very rarely be practicable. It
has seemed to me indispensable to begin with a
school of children and trust to the providence and
grace of God for their obtaining, along with the
benefits of secular learning, the spiritual qualifications requisite in the missionaries of the cross.

I sincerely hope that, in this age of Christian
enterprise, this very important means of extending
to injured Africa the benefits of Christianity, will
not be lost sight of. But in the present state of
things, it is neither practicable for me to suggest to
you any way in which you can further it, nor to do
any thing for its prosecution myself, except to present it, as opportunity offers, in all its interesting
bearings, to other minds, and thus assist in gradually exciting a spirit that may lead to determinate
measures in its favor.

I am, with great respect, Reverend and Dear
Sir, your obedient servant and brother in Christ,

JAMES MILNOR.

Letter from Hon. Gerrit Smith.

PETERBORO, N. Y., April 14, 1827.
DEAR SIR :--I received your letter with a great

deal of pleasure, and especially so, because it presents
to me, in yourself and Mr. Wright, a couple of valuable and earnest friends to the African cause—a
cause so neglected, that the few who come up to its
help are hailed with peculiar satisfaction. It was
with much regret that I saw in the *Freedman's
Journal* the article you, no doubt, refer to, respecting my purposes of good to this unhappy portion of
the human family. The reply which I immediately
sent to the editors of that paper will, I trust, go far
towards correcting the false impression on this subject. If that reply meets your eye, it will show you
that I am thinking a little about my duty in this
matter, and that I am hoping to begin to do it in a
year or two, should my life be spared so long.

I have, for a year, thought of establishing a
seminary in this place, in which to receive Africans
of from fifteen to thirty years of age, and to qualify
them for missionaries to Africa. Such being the
single object of the proposed school, none, of course,
would be admitted into it but such as were evidently
pious. I have not intended to carry them through
such a course of instruction as would render them
polite scholars and thorough theologians. Considering the character of the people with whom they
would have to do, such an education does not seem
to be necessary. A far less expensive one, such as I
propose, would qualify the individual, perhaps, nearly
as well for his duties, and at the same time, enable
me to double or treble the number of my school. A
common English education, and a careful instruction
in the fundamental truths of our holy religion (say

one year under a theological teacher), are the extent of the education I purpose to give.

This is something of my plan of beneficence to Africa. Of my little ability to do good to my fellow creatures, I have long thought Africa entitled to the largest share, and in no way can I serve her to any account, unless it be in some such way as I propose. The situation of my property forbids my helping her in any other way. I have no money, but a number of large and valuable farms around me. The grain of these farms will feed my school, and from the sheep that run upon them I can clothe it ; besides, I should get from each of my scholars two or three months' labor on my farms. Landed property here is scarcely convertible into money at any price.

There are many inviting features in your plan of taking African boys without reference to their character for piety. I think, however, of some objections to it. My correspondence on the subject has satisfied me that there are many more pious blacks in our country than it is generally supposed there are. I think I could get, without difficulty, fifty or one hundred of that description into such a school as I propose. I should be very loath to undertake the education of so many irreligious blacks. Aside from religion, the motives in our country for the black man to become a worthy person are not sufficiently powerful. Our institutions, political and social, the feelings and habits allied to them—a thousand causes, in short, conspire to make the black man worthless, by a power that is seldom successfully resisted where there is not grace in the

heart. True, the prospect of being speedily trans-
planted in Africa, there to be independent and
respected, would prove, no doubt, in the case you
mention, no inconsiderable stimulant to the young
African's ambition, and the improvement of his
character.

I am, very respectfully,

Your friend,

GERRIT SMITH.

Although the beneficent scheme of the
great abolitionist, as set forth in the foregoing
letter, was never realized, the proposal will be
regarded with interest when it is remembered
that Smith was at the date of the letter but
thirty years of age, and had, only a very short
time before, come into possession, from his
father, of that large property which was later
made the basis and source of so many munificent benefactions.

Their interest in the colored race exhibited
in their correspondence at this time led both
Mr. Gallaudet and Mr. Smith to give active
support to the Colonization Society, and the
former as secretary of the Connecticut
Auxiliary did very important work for that
cause in New England.

Mr. Gallaudet delivered an address at the
annual meeting of this society in Hartford in

1829 which was regarded of so great value and merit that it was published and widely circulated.

The limits of this volume will not allow even of mention of all the enterprises of a public character in which Mr. Gallaudet took an active and leading part. His interest in foreign missions can alone be alluded to before passing on to the next period of his life.

He was a warm personal friend of the Rev. Hiram Bingham, one of the earliest missionaries to the Sandwich Islands, and delivered an address in aid of the mission on the eve of Mr. Bingham's departure to enter upon his life-work.

The occasion on which this address was made was one of unusual and even romantic interest.

It was a meeting for prayer held in the Center Church, Hartford, in behalf of the proposed mission, and an incident of the meeting was the marriage of Mr. Bingham to Miss Sybil Moseley of Westfield, Massachusetts.

A personal friend of Miss Moseley, Mrs. Dr. George L. Weed, of Ohio, now living at a very advanced age, relates that an acquaintance of only thirteen days preceded this marriage, the betrothal having taken place on the morning after Mr. Bingham's ordination at Goshen, twelve days before.

Miss Moseley, given only twelve hours to consider the proposal not only of marriage, but of life as a missionary among a barbarous people, asked permission of her hostess to sit by the kitchen fire that she might "continue all night in prayer," and so reached a decision that was severely criticised in many quarters.

This condemnation, directed chiefly against the general policy, then almost without precedent, of allowing women to become missionaries, Mr. Gallaudet felt moved to combat, and did so in the following earnest language :

It is easy and pleasant for those of us who sit quietly by our own firesides, surrounded with comforts and luxury, to wonder at the rashness of those who embark in such hazardous enterprises; and while we shrink from self-denial, and do so little for the cause of Christ, we hope in some measure to palliate our neglect by finding fault with those who do more. And, strange as it may seem, woman—sent by heaven as an helpmeet for man; designed to share and soothe his sorrows; to participate in, and lighten his cares; to excite by her gentler influence, and invigorate by her kind remonstrances, his languishing efforts in the path of duty; woman—who may have less active courage, but more unbending fortitude, than man; whose instinctive good sense extricates from difficulties which his boasted sagacity can not surmount; woman—who, like the vestal virgin of old, keeps bright the lamp of domestic piety in the quiet of her retirement, while man suffers its flame to be almost extinguished in the tumultuous bustle of the world; woman—may be the admired heroine of a novel; or follow her husband through the fatigues of a military campaign and attend him amid all the horrors of war; or traverse with him the mighty deep, and spend years in some sultry clime while he is toiling to make his fortune—she may do all this, and receive the loudest plaudits of approbation for her intrepidity and constancy—but let her become the partner of some humble missionary, who goes to fight the battles of the cross, and to win an incorruptible crown, and to lay up treasure in heaven, and she no longer has any claim to magnanimity and fortitude of soul—she must consent to bear the reproach of weakness and rashness. Take up this reproach, ye daughters of Zion, and patiently endure it; followers of her, whose dust reposes in India, but whose spirit now rejoices in heaven over her past sufferings in the cause of Christ, and may the same arm which shielded Rebekah, who, at the call of Providence, left her kindred and home, even the Almighty arm of the God of Abraham, of Isaac, and of Jacob, ever sustain and protect you.

Mr. Gallaudet was for several years chairman of the executive committee of the Hartford County Auxiliary Foreign Mission Society, and presented at its sixth anniversary in September, 1829, a report which found as great favor and exerted as great influence as his address on colonization in the same year. With a few paragraphs from this report the record of the first natural important division of Mr. Gallaudet's life will be closed.

Why is it still necessary so often, and so earnestly, to urge upon Christians the spiritual necessities of the millions of the human family, who are yet " sitting in darkness and in the region of the shadow of death ? "

How quickly does every scheme of human enterprise, promising results favorable to the increase of individual wealth, or of personal aggrandizement, or of a town's prosperity, or of a nation's glory—command resources the most ample, efforts the most strenuous, agents the most competent, sacrifices the most heroic, perseverance the most indefatigable, zeal the most ardent, toil the most unremitting! Here, Avarice is put to the blush ; Apathy meets with reproach ; Self-denial is a virtue ; Patriotism is reverenced ; and even Enthusiasm, so much feared and ridiculed in all that relates to man's eternal well-being, is permitted to exercise, as worthy of such exalted objects, its free and unlimited control !

Here, you never have to encounter the objection, that your object is too distant in place, or its accomplishment too remote in time;—that it embraces too wide a field of operation;—that its results depend too much on broad and extensive relations, or on complex and uncertain contingencies;—or that it will serve to divert the stream of human effort and resources into channels stretching too far from the little spot or neighborhood, to which the eye and hand of prudent exertion should be primarily and principally directed!

In this respect, as in many others, "the children of this world are wiser in their generation, than the children of light." They study human nature. They act on the principles of common-sense. They take man as he is. They use motives that they can bring to bear upon his uniform rules of action; and they succeed.

They aim at great things and they accomplish great things. Look at this nation's struggle for independence. See how timidity vanished; how patriotism awoke to the contest; how courage encountered and overcame difficulties! Count the sacrifices of personal comfort, and of individual wealth that were cheerfully made. Estimate the sums of money expended; the amount of property lost; the number of lives offered up; the suffering, the toil, the hardships undergone. Consequences were calculated; enlarged views of national prosperity were taken; the vista of futurity opened in bright prospective, and the welfare of millions yet unborn was regarded with all the fondness of parental affection. And who now looks back, and regrets any thing that was lost, or expended, or sacrificed, for the attainment of the object, not only so productive of good to this individual nation, but to the cause of rational freedom throughout the world.

A whole people then rose, like one man, to their work; they "breathed united strength"; they achieved what they undertook, because they undertook it *on principle, with concentrated effort and with extensive aud harmonious co-operation.*

And what might not Christians accomplish, if they, too, would *thus feel, and plan, and act !*

What is the *struggle* in which they are engaged? Nothing less than the conflict between the powers of darkness and the Lord of Hosts.

For what are they *contending ?* For the deliverance of all mankind from the bondage of sin, and their introduction into the glorious liberty of the Sons of God !

What do they hope to *accomplish ?* The establishment of a universal empire of truth and righteousness and peace, throughout the earth; so that all men may dwell together as brethren in unity, acknowledging God as their common Father, and Jesus Christ as their only Saviour; and believing and practicing that religion, which is "pure, peaceable, gentle, easy to be entreated, full of mercy and of good fruits, without partiality and without hypocrisy."

What are their *motives* to action? The hope of rescuing millions of immortal souls from the domin-

ion and the curse of sin, and of preparing them for
an endless progress in knowledge, in holiness, and
in happiness;—the joy which they, in common with
the angels in heaven, will feel over every sinner that
repenteth;—that peace of conscience, that communion with God, that increase in every Christian
grace and virtue, that strengthening of faith, that
brightening of hope, that assured evidence of an
interest in Jesus Christ, that temperance in prosperity, that patience in adversity, that support
under affliction, that final victory over the pains of
death and the horror of the grave,—all of which
nothing so tends to promote, and cherish, and invigorate, as unremitting, self-denying, and benevolent
effort in *the active service of their Lord and Master.*

What are their *responsibilities?* Too many, too
weighty, too solemn almost to be enumerated.

*They have been bought with a price, even the pre-
cious price of the blood of the Son of God.* How can
they repay this love that passeth knowledge!
"Lovest thou me?" saith Christ to each of his
disciples; "then, feed my sheep."

All that they possess has been given to them.
They are but the stewards of God's bounty. Shall
riches be kept to foster pride; to gratify vanity; to
pamper luxury; to load the person with garments,
and the house with splendor, and the table with
delicacies? Shall wealth be hoarded up to enable a
succeeding generation to grow up in indolence; to
live in extravagance; to be exposed to temptations,
which fasten upon the sons and daughters of fortune as their legitimate prey; to mingle in gayeties

which stupefy conscience and ruin the soul ; to waste on worthless objects what might have soothed the couch of suffering, and supplied the cravings of want, and shed the light of the Gospel into the darkness and dreariness of sin ; and then die without hope, and leave behind no remembrance of any honored name, but sink forgotten and unregretted into an early grave ?

Do Christians yet feel their responsibility in this respect ? What self-denial do they practice ; what luxury, what useless comfort do they abandon, that they may do all in their power to relieve the numerous, the pressing, the affecting spiritual necessities of their fellow-men ?

CHAPTER VIII.

1830—1838.

IN writing of that period of Mr. Gallaudet's
life which immediately followed his retirement from the active service of the School for
the Deaf, his early biographer, Rev. Dr.
Humphrey, says :

"Whether he had distinctly marked out
for himself any particular course of life and
labor when he left the institution does not
appear. He had, indeed, cherished the hope
that he should, sooner or later, find time to

write school books in the elementary branches
of popular education and for the moral and
religious instruction of the young. What
else he should do, he seems not to have
decided. But, in the meantime, others who
highly appreciated his talents, and had heard
of his contemplated retirement from the field
which he had cultivated with such remarkable
success, were contriving how to allure him
into their favorite inclosures, as will appear
from the applications he received from almost
every quarter.

"It is believed that the services of no man
in this country were ever more earnestly
sought for in so many departments of philanthropic labor. The impression was almost
universal, as far as he was known (and where
was he not known?) not only that he was
eminently qualified to take charge of any
benevolent institution in the land, or for any
educational service to which he might be
called, but that he was the *first* man to be
thought of for places of the highest responsibility."

Within a few weeks after Mr. Gallaudet had
resigned his principalship, and before he had
been released from his duties, he received the
following letter :

Office of the Colonization Society,
WASHINGTON, June 6, 1830.
REV. AND DEAR SIR :—I am delighted with your report.* It is admirably drawn up, and must exert a powerful influence. May I beg you to favor me with three or four copies. Allow me to suggest that great good would probably result from giving it a wide circulation among the several state societies and other auxiliaries. I hope you have printed a large edition.

I am most happy to communicate the following resolution, which was adopted unanimously by our board at their last meeting:

"*Resolved*, that the Rev. Thomas H. Gallaudet be invited to accept of an agency for the society for a few months, in New England, and that he be particularly requested to visit Boston, and endeavor to establish in that city a state society, and to urge the objects of the memorial of the society, now before the Legislature of that state."

I hope you will consent to lend us, for a short time at least, the aid of your influence and talents in arousing the good feelings of New England to activity and energy in behalf of suffering and neglected Africa. You have done much by your pen; you can do much more by your intercourse with society, and the persuasive powers of your eloquence.

Several members of the legislature have promised their support. You will find Mr. Everett a

---

* Alluded to in the preceding chapter.

decided friend to our cause, and I have no doubt that Mr. Webster will give his countenance to the scheme. Mr. Charles Tappan, our local agent at Boston, has shown a very deep and friendly interest. The present is a very favorable time for bringing the subject before the citizens of Boston and of Massachusetts. I hope, therefore, you will not deny us your kind assistance.

Very respectfully and affectionately,
R. R. GURLEY, Secretary.

This letter was followed in a few days by another, giving notice of Mr. Gallaudet's appointment as permanent agent of the society for New England at a handsome salary.

The proposition, says the secretary, is for *yourself*. Our managers are unwilling to extend it to another. . . . I should rejoice to see you connected with our cause ; and can not doubt that, were you to accept the agency, such a connection would be permanent.

Strongly urging Mr. Gallaudet's acceptance of this offer came a preamble and resolutions from the managers of the New York Colonization Society most complimentary to him.

Declining these overtures, Mr. Gallaudet did not withhold his co-operation from the society, but served its cause so faithfully by labors not paid for in money, that after his death his friend Mr. Gurley writes as follows :

The society had, perhaps, never a more prudent, wise, sagacious, and determined friend. Profoundly acquainted with human nature; very conciliating but very firm ; ready always to concede in things immaterial, but resolute of purpose in things essential.

So prominent a friend was he of this cause that an appeal came to him, earnest but unsuccessful, from Gerard Ralston and others, managers of the Pennsylvania Colonization Society, to go into its active service in 1833.

Before Mr. Gallaudet was relieved of his office as principal of the Hartford School for the Deaf, in which he continued until October, 1830, the invitations alluded to by Dr. Humphrey poured in upon him.

Dartmouth College, the Oneida Institute, the Utica Female Seminary, the Norwich Female Seminary, the High School at Burlington, New Jersey, the New York High School, the Cincinnati Seminary, sought his services either as professor or as principal.

Two other propositions deserve more than passing mention.

A movement was set on foot early in 1830

to organize a school for the blind in Boston,
there being at that time no provision for the
education of such persons in America.

Naturally some of the promoters of this
enterprise visited Mr. Gallaudet in Hartford to
obtain his advice in the premises. Among
them were William H. Prescott and John D.
Fisher. So impressed were they with what
they saw and heard at Hartford, that they at
once urged Mr. Gallaudet to become the
founder of the education of the blind in
America, as he had been that of deaf-mute
instruction.

Although he gave them no assurance of a
favorable answer, Messrs. Prescott and Fisher
on their return to Boston called the trustees of
the institution together and they at once sent
a formal and urgent appeal to Mr. Gallaudet
to take up this new and important work; inviting him to visit Boston and confer with them
in person.

Mr. Gallaudet visited Boston as requested,
and the correspondence which followed showed
that he was strongly inclined to accept the
proposals of the Boston gentlemen, which were
of a most liberal and flattering character. The
salary offered was twice what Mr. Gallaudet
had received at Hartford—the duties required

were much less onerous—the prospect of doing good quite as great as that which attracted
him fifteen years before.

But he felt himself compelled to decline the
undertaking, for reasons which will directly
appear.

The other offer which he was strongly
tempted to accept was from the New York
University, which was then being organized.
And had the negotiations, which were begun
in December, 1830, been brought sooner to the
point of a definite proposition, it is probable
Mr. Gallaudet would have taken a professor-
ship in the university.

The chair offered him finally, some months
later, was that of the *Philosophy of Education*,
and the intention was to bring the influence of
the university to bear on the training of
teachers for common schools.

Dr. Matthews, Mr. J. Delafield, Comptroller
A. C. Flagg, and Mr. T. Dwight, Jr., were
greatly interested in securing Mr. Gallaudet's
services to the university, but when the pro-
fessorship was offered him, he was fairly
launched in an undertaking that was congenial
to his tastes and promised great usefulness.

In declining the offers of the trustees of the
institution for the blind Mr. Gallaudet makes

allusion to the state of his health and to his attachment to Hartford, which was very strong.

Hartford was then, as it has since been and is now, a place of residence of more than ordinary attractiveness, as well from the refined society and literary culture to be found there, as from its natural beauty of situation.

Bishop Chase, of Ohio, whose residence in Hartford was contemporary with that of Mr. Gallaudet—writes thus of the place in his " Reminiscences : "

In the bosom of an enlightened society, softened by the hand of urbanity and gentleness, my enjoyments, crowned with abundance of temporal blessings, were as numerous and refined as fall to the lot of man. Of the time I spent in this lovely city I can never speak in ordinary terms.

But warm as was Mr. Gallaudet's feeling for the city of his adoption, it was more his interest in the new work which engaged him that detained him there. And this was the preparation of books especially designed to interest and instruct children.

In 1830 no literature for the young existed.

Few story-books, even, had been published ; and in the United States Samuel G. Goodrich, known and loved by the boys and girls of that time and afterward as " Peter Parley," stood almost if not quite alone as a writer of children's books.

Mr. Gallaudet's peculiar labors as a teacher of the deaf had given him unusual opportunities to study the development of the mental faculties of children, and he was strongly impressed with the importance of the early training of youth, in many directions that had previously been much neglected. His particular scheme was to promote familiarity among children and youth with the teachings of the sacred Scriptures. He thought the Bible should be used as a text-book in the higher schools and colleges, and that books should be written, level to the understanding of children, which should convey in simple and forcible style the essential truths of the Christian faith. He corresponded with a number of prominent public men on the subject and received letters that sustained his own views. Two notable letters appear in this correspondence, one from Hon. Roger M. Sherman, the other from Hon. William Wirt, so warmly approving of Mr. Gallaudet's plans as to exert, perhaps, a deciding influence on his career at this juncture.

What now followed illustrates in a marked manner several interesting elements in Mr. Gallaudet's constitution and disposition.

Early in this year (1830) he had felt himself quite broken down in health, and resigned his principalship largely on that account. He was not released from the duties of that office until October—much of his time was taken up in considering the many propositions made to him to engage in other work. And yet so soon did elasticity and mental vigor return to him when he felt himself free, or likely soon to be, from the pressure of official duty; so entirely did change of work serve as the *rest* he needed and craved, that before the end of 1830 he had given to the world a remarkable book, The Child's Book on the Soul, followed in rapid succession by The Child's Book on Repentance, The Child's Book of Bible Stories, and The Youth's Book on Natural Theology.

Now altogether out of print, and scarcely known by the present generation, these volumes exerted, in their day, an influence it would be difficult to estimate. Thousands of copies were circulated—they were translated into many languages, besides being reprinted and largely sold in England. They were read as English reading books in the schools of the Foreign Missionary Societies, and through these channels made themselves felt in unexpected places : as will be seen in the following letter, which, though written some years after the time now under review, will find its most appropriate place here. The writer occupied the throne of Siam during the years of which Mrs. Leonowens has written so graphically in her " English Governess at the Siamese Court."

The King of Siam to Mr. Gallaudet:

CITY OF BANGKOK, SIAM, August 30, 1848.

SIR :—Having perceived your skill and contrivances effects, in some of the books of which you were author, prepared for child and youth, viz., Science of Human Soul, Natural Theology (conversations of Mrs. Stanhope and her son Robert), History of Joseph, and small English dictionary, that contains plain examples of every word, and received also your pious qualities from of the American missionaries who live in this country and speak of you, I was very glad to write you, and with much more satisfaction and gratitude to you, as I thought and imaged that I am alike your pupil on your absence, because I have known and remembered several English words from reading some the foresaid books, of which your authority was entitled on first pages, and which some of missionaries and English merchants have brought here for themselves, and were borrowed by myself from them, who had but one to read a few days, that they have limited with, I was therefore sorry that I could not learn much more lessons from your stilees, which were easily to be understood for me, and delightful and useful to me, as I am just studying this language about three years indeed.

I was therefore brave to write to you, asking you for some certain books, which you may image or presume that suitable to me, for easily reading; every book of which you were author, and which were printed, and still remained some at your hand, or every name and subjects of every idiom's book that you may denote to me in your answer.

I hope very surely that you will be graceful to me, reading this my manuscript, though I am your heathen, and was not acquainted with you at all.

I have now but one of books which you prepared. It is story of Joseph. It was bestowed to me by a lady of Captain Daniel Brown, who is my affectionate friend. I please much morely the small dictionary that contain example of every word, but I could not procure for myself in this country and neighboring states. Please reply me through care of some of the American missionaries who are living in our country, and with whom you are acquainted. I shall pay to them for the books which you mentioned their price, and sent me through here, American missionaries. Almost every one of them acquainted with me very exactly. Please pardon me if I mistake by unproper word and sentence, and overlook if my this letter were written ungrammatical, as I am just learning this language indeed.

I have the honor to be your friend, etc.,

THE PRINCE T. Y. CHAUFA MONG KUT,

One of high Buddhist priests.

P. S.—Please address me in your answer thus: To His Royal Highness the Prince T. Y. Chaufa Mong Kut, of Bangkok, Siam, as I am known by such manner of direction to most of foreigners who use English, that your letter would be handed to me soon.   T. Y. M.

Before this letter reached Mr. Gallaudet, he heard through a friend that Chaufa Mong Kut had been instructed in his books, and desired copies of them. Acting on this suggestion Mr. Gallaudet forwarded a number of volumes, which were already on their way to Siam when the Prince's formal request reached him. This will appear from the following letter ·

Mr. Gallaudet to the King of Siam.

CITY OF HARTFORD, STATE OF CONNECTICUT,

U. S. A., October 10, 1848.

TO HIS ROYAL HIGHNESS PRINCE CHAUFA MONG KUT.—SIR:—The Rev. D. B. Bradley, M. D., one of the Christian missionaries in Bangkok, tells me that you have, in a letter to him,

expressed your satisfaction in having read some
books of which I am the author, and that you
would be pleased to accept others should they be
sent to you.   In this I feel highly honored, by a
person so intelligent and distinguished as yourself. I
send by him, therefore, a few volumes, of most of
which I am the author, and of which I beg your
acceptance.

They are chiefly on religious subjects, and
exhibit the principles and precepts of the religion of
Jesus Christ, in which I most devoutly believe, for
I find evidence which perfectly satisfies me that the
Bible, which contains this religion, is a revelation
from God.   I find, too, that the Saviour whom it
offers for our acceptance, is just such a Saviour as
the erring and sinful beings of the whole human
family need.

How can we obtain the pardon of our sins, but
through the atoning sacrifices which this divine
Saviour made when He died on the cross? How else
can we be restored to the favor of God, whom we
have so much offended by our transgressions of His
most holy, just and good laws?   How else can we
secure an immortal existence of purity and blessed-
ness beyond the grave?   Is the Bible, which tells us
of this only way of salvation, truly a revelation from
God?   If it is, then *no other system of religion, as a
system, can be true,* for they all differ from the Bible,
and are opposed to it in many essential things.

May I venture to beg of you to examine and
carefully reflect on this great question? To read the
volumes, " The Bible not of Man " and " Bogue's

Essay," which I send you? To *read the Bible itself*, more particularly the New Testament, which contains an account of the life, the miracles, the teachings, the doings, the sufferings, and the death of Jesus Christ, and shows why He came into our world? In attending to this great subject, we need to pray to the Father of our spirits, to open our minds to the discovery of the Truth, and our hearts to the reception, love and obedience of the Truth. I pray that His Holy Spirit may be your teacher, guide, sanctifier and comforter.

Should you find leisure to let me know that the books have reached you in safety, and what you think of them, it would be a favor conferred on
Yours with sincere respect,
T. H. Gallaudet.

P. S.—I can not but hope that "The Practical Spelling Book" will aid you, by its peculiar system of classification, and its index, in overcoming (if you have not already overcome them), the difficulties attending the orthography of the English language, and that the little dictionary, even, will not be without some use.

Prince Chowfa Mong Kut, the actual, though not the recognized King of Siam when the foregoing letters were written, ascended the throne in April, 1851, and reigned until his death, which occurred in 1868.

Mrs. Leonowens speaks of his accession to power as follows :

In 1825 a royal prince of Siam (his birthright wrested from him, and his life imperiled) took refuge in a Buddhist monastery and assumed the yellow garb of a priest. His father, commonly known as P'tren-din-Klang, first or supreme King of Siam, had just died, leaving this prince Chowfa Mongkut, at the age of twenty, lawful heir to the crown ; for he was the eldest son of the acknowledged queen, and therefore by courtesy and honored custom, if not by absolute right, the legitimate successor to the throne of the Phra-batts. But he had an elder half-brother, who, through the intrigues of his mother, had already obtained control of the royal treasury, and now, with the connivance, if not by the authority of the Senabawdee, the grand council of the kingdom, proclaimed himself king. He had the grace, however, to promise his plundered brother—such promises being a cheap form of propitiation in Siam—to hold the reins of government only until Chowfa Mongkut should be of years and strength and skill to manage them. But, once firmly seated on the throne, the usurper saw in his patient but proud and astute kinsman only a hindrance and a peril in the path of his own crueler and fiercer aspirations. Hence the forewarning and the flight, the cloister and the yellow robes. And so the usurper continued to reign, unchallenged by any claim from the king that should be, until March, 1851, when, a mortal illness having overtaken him, he convoked the grand council of princes and nobles around his couch, and proposed his favorite son as his successor. Then the safe asses of the court kicked the dying lion with seven words of sententious scorn,— " The crown has already its rightful owner ; " whereupon the king literally cursed himself to death, for it was almost in the convulsion of his chagrin and rage that he came to his end on the 3rd of April. . . . Hardly had he breathed his last when, in spite of the busy intrigues of his eldest son, . . . the Prince Chowfa Mongkut doffed his sacerdotal robes, emerged from his cloister, and was crowned, with the title of Somdetch Phra Paramendr Maha Mongkut.

There seems to be no doubt that Mr. Gallaudet did wisely, *for the world*, in declining all the positions tendered him on his quitting the service of the school for the deaf, and devoting himself to the preparation of books designed to exert a wholesome influence on the rising generation. Of his success in the field he chose there can be no question, although his books are not now read and seldom seen. His first four volumes, already named, were followed by the Every Day Christian ; nine volumes of Scripture Biography, from Adam to Jonah ; the Child's Picture-Defining and Reading Book, and the Mother's Primer.

These works, says Dr. Humphrey, "enroll the name of Gallaudet among the most gifted and attractive writers in the department which he occupied."

The writer of these pages has been spoken to very many times concerning the Child's Book on the Soul, by persons he has casually met in Washington and elsewhere, merely because his name suggested the author of that little work. Such persons have invariably remarked upon the great effect produced by the book on them when children. Many have said that its clear and forcible style in treating of its important subject, had served to lay the foundation of a Christian faith which had stood for a lifetime.

Henry Barnard, LL. D., the distinguished promoter of public education, speaks of this book as "exhibiting Mr. Gallaudet's remarkable tact in bringing the most abstract subject within the grasp of the feeblest and youngest mind."

Most of the volumes which have been alluded to came, ultimately, to be published by the American Tract Society, and were issued for many years among their libraries for Sabbath Schools.*

---

* The American Tract Society have published eleven vol-

Two other books, not of a religious character, were prepared by Mr. Gallaudet with the assistance of Rev. Horace Hooker, which had a very large circulation. These were a Practical Spelling Book, and The School and Family Dictionary and Illustrative Definer. The publication of these works was continued for a number of years after his death.

Mr. Gallaudet worked mainly as a writer of books during a period of eight years. The nature of this employment left him much freer than before to engage as an unpaid promoter of public enterprises of a benevolent character.

He was prominent in the organization of the first "Teachers' Convention," held in Hartford in October, 1830, and which was presided over by Noah Webster.

Not long after, he prepared a tract entitled " Public Schools Public Blessings," which was

---

umes of Scripture Biography, the Bible Stories, the Child's Book on the Soul, the Child's Book on Repentance and the Youth's Book of Natural Theology. Of these sixteen books an average of about forty thousand copies each have been issued, making a total of more than six hundred thousand copies of Dr. Gallaudet's books put in circulation by the Tract Society alone. It is not possible to state with accuracy the number of copies printed of other works, or of these works in foreign countries, but it will be within the mark to say that the aggregate, including the issues of the Tract Society, will considerably exceed a million copies.

published by the New York Public School
Society for general circulation in the City of
New York, at a time when an effort was
made, which proved successful, to enlarge the
operations of that society.

His contributions to the periodicals and
newspapers of the day were numerous and
highly appreciated.

For the *American Annals of Education* he
wrote on The Philosophy of Language;
Methods of Teaching to Read ; Remarks on
Seminaries for Teachers ; Language of
Infancy ; Family and School Discipline, and
many other subjects of practical value. He
wrote frequently for the *Connecticut Common
School Journal* and for the *Mother's Magazine*,
and edited an American edition of "Principles of Teaching," by Henry Dunn, Secretary
of the British and Foreign School Society,
London, under the title of the " Schoolmas-
ter's Manual."

In 1833 Mr. Gallaudet became warmly
interested in the cause of industrial education,
and endeavored with a number of gentlemen
to secure the establishment of a " Connecticut Manual Labor School." In the interest
of this movement he was requested, with
Erastus Ellsworth, to visit the " Oneida Insti-

tute of Science and Industry," near Utica, N. Y. (of which it will be remembered he had been invited to take charge two years before), and the " Fellenberg Manual Labor School," in Greenfield, Mass.

Mr. Gallaudet's report on the condition and working of these two institutions expresses views which, read in the light of the present day, when the country is turning to the policy of industrial education as, perhaps, the only solution of some of the serious problems of the labor question, seem altogether prophetic. Had they been generally adopted, as they were not, hand labor would have been dignified, the acquisition of trades by boys would have been easy, and the element of monopoly in trades unions, which has since become so menacing, would have been practically neutralized.

In Sprague's "Annals of the American Pulpit," Rev. Horace Hooker, co-author with Mr. Gallaudet of several books, alludes to his readiness to suggest new plans for benevolent enterprises.

"The field of human wretchedness," says Mr. Hooker, " which some visit from a sense of duty, he delighted to explore, and never seemed so happy as when inventing schemes to relieve the suffering and raise the fallen. How many volumes have I heard him utter in our rambles in the outskirts of the city, respecting institutions for the relief of the intemperate, long before they were publicly advocated ; and how many ingenious plans have I heard him devise for institutions to shelter and give employment to the discharged prisoner until he can regain his character, and the confidence of the community. I can hardly realize that such institutions are not in being—so vividly were they sketched and so minutely were all the details presented to the mind."

At about this time Mr. Gallaudet took an active and prominent part in the establishment of lyceums and young men's institutes, and was instrumental in securing the delivery of the first course of popular lectures in Hartford, under the auspices of the Goodrich Association.

He acted for some months, to meet an emergency, as principal of the Hartford Female Seminary, with which Miss Catharine Beecher and Mr. John P. Brace were prominently connected, and lectured for a much longer period in that institution on English composition and moral philosophy.

In 1835 Mr. Gallaudet undertook a work which in the estimation of its promoters required the services of a man of very great discretion and ability. It was an enterprise which while, in a sense, of a public nature, it was felt to be of the highest consequence should be carried forward absolutely without attracting public attention.

A few earnest Christian gentlemen residing in Hartford and New York, whose names, even now, need not be mentioned, were impressed with the importance of making efforts in the interest of evangelical religion in the new states of the West, which might prevent the undue spread of the Roman Catholic faith in that section of our country —especially at points where large numbers of Germans were settling.

These eight or ten wealthy merchants provided all the means necessary. Mr. Gallaudet became their active agent, on a stated salary. The spirit in which he entered upon the work is indicated in the following brief note:

Thursday afternoon, January 15, 1835.

My Dear Sir :—In the strength of our Lord and Saviour the enterprise is to be begun to-morrow.

Yours truly,   T. H. Gallaudet.

Mr. —— ——.

Among a mass of papers and letters bearing on this enterprise the name of the association appears in no other way than the I.. U. P. O.—the meaning of which was a mystery to the writer of these pages until a very recent date, when the widow of one interested in the enterprise solved the riddle.

"*Look Upward, Press Onward,*" was the motto of the little band of earnest men whose aim was to help save the great North-west from becoming exclusively or largely Roman Catholic.

Mr. Gallaudet made arrangements to leave his family for a number of months.

His labors began, as he said they would, on January 16,—by the writing of a number of letters, the charge for posting which, noted in his L. U. P. O. expense book, was thirty-seven and a half cents. A week later he proceeded to New Haven and thence to New York, where he remained six days. Pausing for only two days at Philadelphia he made his way as rapidly as possible through Harrisburg, Pittsburg and Wheeling to Columbus, Ohio. He spent some time at various points in Ohio, and passed over into Kentucky about the middle of March. During the spring months he visited Missouri, Illinois and Indiana, returning east through Ohio and Pennsylvania, reaching Hartford on the 13th of June.

The only diary that appears of this interesting journey ·is Mr. Gallaudet's expense book, from which his route can be very distinctly traced, but which gives little insight into the object of his travels. Of their dangers and of extortions practiced even in those primitive days occasional glimpses are furnished, such as: "January 23, Life preserver (lost or stolen), $2.50:" "May 13, Supper, lodging and breakfast at Louisville, $1.50 ! ! ! !"

The actual work of the L. U. P. O. Association was done after Mr. Gallaudet's western journey, the purpose of which was to acquaint himself with the condition and needs of the then great North-west in religious matters.

He continued to act as the paid agent of the society for two years, and as its unpaid secretary for eight years more, or until 1845.

The work of the association may be briefly summarized as follows : a considerable number of young German theological graduates, mainly from Basle in Switzerland, were brought to the United States at the expense of the association, and were located at prominent western centers with the view of founding churches, and these young clergymen were maintained or aided by the society until they no longer needed assistance; loans and donations of money were made to many institutions of learning in the states visited by Mr. Gallaudet, with the view of aiding in the education of young men who were to labor in their own section as evangelical ministers of the Gospel ; tracts were printed and circulated in many quarters in furtherance of the great object of the society, and it is known that the influence of these led to the formation of other associations having the same end in view.

The history of the L. U. P. O. will probably never be written ; nor can any estimate be made of its achievements. Very many men were inspired by it and worked with enthusiasm for its objects without even knowing of its existence.

The writer of these pages has met and conversed with many persons who made Mr. Gallaudet's acquaintance on his Western tour, who felt his influence, but who never dreamed of his being at that time the agent of a society or the apostle of a special cause. Mr. Gallaudet preached constantly in prominent churches on this Western journey. He delivered many addresses on educational subjects. He was welcomed with enthusiasm everywhere as an eminent philanthropist, and was eagerly sought as an honored guest who was understood to be studying the general development of Western civilization, perhaps with the purpose of writing upon it.

Just as Mr. Gallaudet concluded his active labors for the L. U. P. O. he was called to perform another interesting duty, of which his friend and eulogist, Hon. Henry Barnard, LL.D., speaks as follows : *

In 1837 the County of Hartford, through the exertions mainly of Alfred Smith, Esq., erected a prison on a plan which admitted of a classification of prisoners, of their entire separation at night, of their employment in labor under constant supervision by day, and of their receiving appropriate moral and religious instruction. Mr. Gallaudet sympathized warmly with this movement, and in the absence of any means at the disposal of the county commissioners to employ the services of a chaplain and religious teacher, volunteered to discharge these duties without pay. He continued to perform religious service every Sabbath morning for eight

---

* Barnard's Tribute to Gallaudet, pp. 32, 33.

years, and to visit the prison from time to time during each week, whenever he had reason to suppose his presence and prayers were particularly desired. In such labors of love to the criminal and neglected, unseen of men, and not known, I presume to twenty individuals in Hartford, the genuine philanthropy and Christian spirit of this good man found its pleasantest field of exercise.

So long as Mr. Gallaudet continued to hold himself free from official engagements, offers of such were made to him at short intervals. A few of these are of sufficient importance to be noticed.

In 1836 he received a letter from Gorham D. Abbot, the purport of which will appear from the following extracts :

NEW YORK, June 7.

REV. AND DEAR SIR:—I have the pleasure to communicate to you a vote of the Executive Committee of the " American Society for the Diffusion of Useful Knowledge," at their meeting last night.

The Committee of Publication, through the Chairman, reported to the Executive Committee, that no time was to be lost in carrying into effect some of the plans, proposed by the Society, as the mischief which is daily done "by presses of an infidel and immoral tendency is incalculable." They also recommend as " an indispensable measure, the immediate employment of additional literary aid to carry forward the various departments of the society's contemplated labors."

Whereupon, it was " *Resolved*, That the Executive Committee proceed to the election of two individuals for this purpose.

" *Resolved*, That the salary of $2,000 per annum be offered to each of those individuals, with assurances of augmentation as the resources of the society shall justify."

The Committee went into election, by ballot, which resulted in the unanimous choice of the Rev. Jacob Abbot and the Rev. T. H. Gallaudet.

Flattering as was this proposal, Mr. Gallaudet declined it.

In 1838, he was the person, and the only person, had in view to fill the office of Secretary of the Board of Commissioners of Common Schools in Connecticut, when the bill was drafted for a public act "to provide for the better supervision of common schools " in Connecticut. The post was urged on his acceptance, with the offer and guaranty by individuals of an addition of one-third to the salary paid by the state. He declined, mainly from his unwillingness to absent himself as much from his family as the plan of operations contemplated, and also "because of the apathy as to the importance of the cause, which he had many reasons to know weighed not only on the public mind generally, but on the minds and hearts of good men, and even Christians,

who take an active and liberal part in other moral
and religious movements. To break up this apathy,
requires more of youthful strength and enthusiasm
than can be found in an invalid and a man of fifty
years of age." *

Mr. Gallaudet, however, did not fail to
co-operate actively and effectively in the work
he declined to superintend.

The measures of that board, and of their secretary, were determined upon after consultation with
him, and in all the preliminary operations their
resources had his personal co-operation. In company with the secretary he visited every county in
the state in 1838, and addressed conventions of
teachers, school officers and parents. He took part
in the course of instruction of the first normal class,
or teachers' institute, held in this country, in 1839,
and again in a similar institute in 1840. He appeared before the Joint Committee of Education in
the General Assembly on several occasions when
appropriations for a normal school were asked for.

Early in the year 1838, the events of which
are, chiefly, now being narrated, Mr. Gallaudet received an invitation which must stand
by the side of several others, already referred
to in this memoir, which show how often he

---

* Barnard's Tribute to Gallaudet, p. 30.

was thought of by those who knew him as a man most fit to head a new enterprise.

The following letter was from one whose venerable form, in his high-topped boots and knee-breeches, will be remembered by some still living in Hartford as the embodiment of the Historical Society.

Invitation to be Principal of the First Normal School in the Country.

Rochester, Mass., January 5, 1838.

Rev. and Dear Sir:—Before you receive this I think you will have a letter from Rev. Dr. Davis of Westfield. The Board of Education of this state, for the supervision and improvement of common schools, had their annual meeting in the Council Chamber in Boston, and resolved, as a leading measure of their proceedings, to establish a few schools for the instruction of teachers. I told them that you recommended such a measure, in a series of well-written numbers, in a newspaper, several years ago. The board hope to be able, eventually, to have enough to supply the wants of the state, yet as it is somewhat a matter of experiment, they will begin with three.

And now, Brother Gallaudet, we want you to take charge of the *first* Normal School. The object is to instruct the pupils in such a manner as will fit them for the best teaching and management of common schools. Probably something will be done in lecturing. It must, however, be left in a great degree to the principal. There will be no charge for tuition. The schools are to be furnished with the necessary apparatus and libraries. There are several important reasons why you should comply with our request.

First. I think this measure will be adopted in other states extensively, and the experiment ought to be made in the best manner.

Second. We want to manufacture the most of our school books. Once when you were in Dr. Hawes' study he desired you to turn your attention to that subject. I do not think a man could be found that would be so acceptable to all as yourself.

Third. Few men, if any, are so conversant with the human mind in its simple form as yourself. With great respect,

Your friend and brother,

THOMAS ROBBINS.

At the same time, or nearly so, that Massachusetts was urging Mr. Gallaudet to be the pioneer in her work for normal education, she was seeking his counsel concerning schools for the very youngest children.

The primary school board of Boston, represented by Lewis G. Pray, R. W. Bayley, J. F. Bumstead, George W. Otis, Jr., and Enoch Hobart, addressed a letter to Mr. Gallaudet in October, 1838, asking his counsel in meas-

ures they were taking "for the establishment
of a model school for children from four to
seven years of age."

The questions propounded called for and
elicited a lengthy reply — too much so for
insertion here — in which the whole subject was
covered with the writer's usual thoroughness.

Mr. Gallaudet thought it right to decline
the invitation to become principal of the first
Normal School. But there came soon a call
which carried conviction to his mind as well
as to his heart, in yielding to which he took
again the attitude of a pioneer in an important philanthropic work. At this period
no regular religious instruction had ever been
given to the insane, as a class. A few institutions for their humane and enlightened treatment had been established in the country,
and this branch of benevolent effort, like
every other, had Mr. Gallaudet's warm sympathy. He was actively interested in the
Retreat, which had been opened a few
years before in Hartford, and was the intimate
friend of many of its managers.

But his work for the insane was so important, and occupied so much of the remaining
years of his life, that it must be spoken of in
another chapter.

CHAPTER IX.

1838 — 1851.

Interest in the Insane — An Invitation to Preach at the Insane
Hospital in Worcester, Mass., and to become Permanent
Chaplain—A Similar Invitation from the Retreat at Hartford
Accepted — Extracts from the Chaplain's Diary — Sugges-
tions as to Treatment of the Insane.

"EIGHT years had now elapsed since Mr.
Gallaudet left the institution for deaf-
mutes, and it does not appear that he intended
ever to connect himself with any other public
institution. He had, as we have seen, declined many advantageous offers. He loved
retirement. Hartford was his home, where,
from his boyhood, he had spent nearly all of
his life, and to which he was strongly bound
by the cords of love. He had enough to do,
and just such work as he wanted. He could
write books for the young, and in many ways
aid the cause of popular education, which was,
in the largest and best sense, the dearest of all
causes to his ever active and philanthropic
mind.

THOMAS HOPKINS GALLAUDET.

(This portrait was drawn in 1844, on a leaf of Swift's Digest, in the court-room of the State House, by John W. Skinner, of New York, then a law student in Hartford.)

" But, though he was not to leave Hartford,
God was opening the way for his introduction
into a new sphere of public service, for which
he had been qualifying himself all the time of
his connection with the school for the deaf.
There, for thirteen years, he had been studying the human mind, in the earliest develop-
ments of its normal state. He had been
clearing the way and opening the door for the
emancipation of the imprisoned faculties of
deaf-mutes, and bringing them into joyful fel-
lowship with their sorrowing friends, and teaching them the relations which they sustained to
their Creator, of whom, before, they had no
knowledge.

" Now he was to be brought into daily contact with minds bewildered, deranged, cut off
from the possibility of enjoying the endear-
ments of home, and brought together where
they might have all the curative appliances
which the highest skill, the largest experience,
and the warmest Christian sympathies can
furnish.

" Mr. Gallaudet was to go from his retirement into an insane hospital to study the
human mind in this abnormal state ; to be the
religious teacher, friend and adviser of hundreds of persons suffering under almost every

variety and degree of mental derangement.
But whence? He did not court the service;
he did not expect to be called to it. But the
eyes of the managers of the insane hospital
at Worcester were turned upon him as the
fittest person they could think of to fill the
difficult and important place of chaplain.
Accordingly a correspondence was opened
with him through Dr. Woodward, for so many
years the beloved and distinguished superintendent of that institution." *

Dr. Woodward to Mr. Gallaudet.

WORCESTER, February 16, 1838.
MY DEAR SIR:—We have introduced religious
worship into our hospital, in a manner quite satisfactory, and with very complete success. I am very
desirous to have you come out and preach for us at
some time, and would name the first Sabbath in
March, or any one that you can name afterward,
excepting the second Sabbath in that month, on
which day we are supplied. I can offer you no great
encouragement, but will pay all your expenses of
the journey, and your board here at the American
Temperance House while you stay.

My object in writing to you now is, that I wish
to consult you on the subject of the chaplaincy.

---

* "Life and Labors of Rev. T. H. Gallaudet, L.L. D.," by Rev.
Heman Humphrey, D.D., p.p, 340 *et seq.*

We are hoping to have a regular chaplain next summer. We should be glad to procure a man, with a moderate salary, to preach for us on Sunday; if he can pursue some other employment a part of the time, it will be agreeable. We have thought of you, my dear sir, as a preacher of the character which we should like, and hoped that you could pursue book-making as profitably in our pleasant village as in the city of Hartford.

We have two hundred and ten patients, one hundred and fifty of whom attend our chapel, which, with our help and my family, make a snug congregation of two hundred. We have a beautiful room, of forty-five by thirty-two feet; have a very good choir of singers, all of our own household, and perform all the parts common in a New England congregation twice every Sabbath.

May I hear from you in the course of a few days?

I am truly and respectfully yours,

S. B. WOODWARD.

Mr. Gallaudet visited Worcester and preached to the patients of the hospital as invited to do.

At the time of this visit he met a young physician of the town, with whom he was destined to be associated, later, in very intimate relations.

This young man, now the venerable and

justly eminent Dr. John S. Butler of Hartford, spoke not long since to the writer of
these pages of the incident of Mr. Gallaudet's visit to Worcester in March, 1838.

He charmed us all. His ease of manner and
geniality won all hearts. The effect produced by
his preaching and personal intercourse with the
patients was remarkable. During one of the services
he showed in how high a degree he possessed that tact
and self-control that are necessary in the successful management of the insane. In his sermon he
was illustrating a point by an allusion to the circum-
ference of the earth, which he said was about
twenty-five thousand miles. A stalwart man sprang
to his feet and with one hand brandished high in
the air roared out, " That's a lie: it's only seven
thousand," and remained standing in a threatening
attitude. Mr. Gallaudet took the interruption as
though it were an everyday occurrence in his
preaching, and looking kindly at the excited patient
said with a smile: " Is that so ? Very well, we will
talk about it after service," going on at once with
his discourse. The patient sat down quietly and
made no further demonstration.

Dr. Woodward wrote to Mr. Gallaudet in
May, making a formal offer of the chaplaincy,
and urging its acceptance in the warmest
terms.

Negotiations continued for several weeks,

when the following letter conveyed Mr. Gallaudet's decision :

HARTFORD, July 6, 1838.

DEAR DR. WOODWARD :—Three weeks have not elapsed since last I saw you. I had hoped, however, even before this time, to give an answer to the invitation which the trustees of your institution had been so kind as to make, to have me occupy in it the situation of chaplain. Very peculiar circumstances have prevented me from doing so.

As I informed you before my last visit to Worcester, I had been appointed secretary of the newly organized Board of Education in this state; and although I could not, at that time, consider it my duty to accept of this appointment, I had agreed to postpone an absolute decision till my return and consultation with a committee of the board. The absence from Hartford of the acting member of the committee delayed the decision a week, when I declined the appointment.

In the midst of these deliberations, and wholly unexpected to me, the appointment of chaplain to the Retreat for the insane in this city was proposed for my consideration by the board of managers, about a week since. This placed me in a new and very trying position. To make it the more so, the committee of the Board of Education proposed, that should I become chaplain to the Retreat, and have any spare time, they would be glad to have my services in connection with their operations, and in

such a way as to call me very little from home, a
considerable absence from which, during the year,
was one of my principal objections to becoming secretary of the board. I found, on conferring with
Dr. Fuller [superintendent of the Retreat], that it
was his wish, at present, to have but one religious
exercise on the Sabbath, prayers once a day, and
such intercourse with the patients as might be
deemed judicious; so that I could devote considerable time to the Board of Education, and to one
or two other sources of support which promise well
if I remain here.

In addition to this, you can readily conceive and
appreciate other and powerful motives that would
influence me to continue in Hartford. I have lived
here forty years ; I have among our citizens many
old and long-tried friends; my wife finds here a
place of worship on the Sabbath, and a circle of
intimate acquaintances who know her language ; our
plans of living and of economizing are adjusted to
an experienced state of things ; a school taught in
my family, and which all of my children attend,
excepting one, has been for years in successful
operation, and can be enlarged to any extent ; and
here we are very near an aged mother and deaf and
dumb sister of my wife, and her near relations.
Some of these considerations, I know, are not to be
put in the scale as weighing much against the great
objects of benevolent effort in important spheres of
duty ; but they have a proper place where two, and
it may be, nearly equally important spheres of duty
present themselves. Still I was determined to say

or do nothing to forward the plan of my remaining here, unless the whole thing should move easily, and without any urgency on the part of my friends. I knew—for the managers of the Retreat had told me so—that what they could offer from the funds of the institution would be small; but they said a few individuals were ready to make up the deficiency. Under these circumstances, I consented to have the matter come before the Board of Directors, requesting my friends, *as a personal favor*, to let the thing take its own free course, and if any the least difficulties should present themselves, to drop it all, at once; in which case I would immediately let the trustees of the institution at Worcester know on what terms I would be willing to go there. The directors met a few days since, and proposed five hundred dollars from the funds of the institution, and two hundred and fifty from other sources, a year, payable to me by the treasurer, and made secure for five years, if I continue to discharge the duties of the office acceptably; seven hundred and fifty dollars being offered me as a salary for services which will occupy about one-half of my time. I concluded to accept the appointment. I have not made the least effort to bring about this result. Indeed, I was in a state of most perplexing, and I may say, distressing hesitancy, to know where my duty lay. Had there been no such unsought invitation to me to stay here, or after being made, had any thing occurred to arrest, temporarily, the course of action on the part of the institution or my friends toward its consummation, I should promptly and

heartily have taken the steps to lead me to Worcester, if our views as to the compensation had harmonized.

Providence has ordered it otherwise, and being
guided as I have been, and taking the course which
I have, I beg you particularly, and the gentlemen
comprising your Board of Trustees, and Mr. Foster,
and any other friends, to accept my sincere thanks
for the marks of confidence and kindness which have
been shown me in our late negotiations, and my
earnest wishes and prayers for the prosperity of the
noble institution which you have been instrumental
in raising to such a high degree of usefulness, and of
honorable character in our land.   In my humble
field of effort here, I shall aspire to be a fellow-
laborer of yours in your extensive sphere of benevolent exertions, and shall hope, in the particular department in which I shall be called to act, to receive
no small amount of aid from the suggestions which
I have already derived from the interesting inter-
views I have enjoyed with you, and from the future
results of your observation and experiences, which, I
am sure, you will be willing to impart.   I shall hope
to hear soon from you in reply; and in the meanwhile, present my very kind regards to Mrs. Woodward and your family, to Dr. Chandler, Deacon Ellis,
and other friends, both in and out of the institution.
You hardly know, my dear sir, the conflict of feelings through which I have passed.   Never have I
been called to a similar one in my life.   Every thing
inviting at Worcester, on the one hand (*co-operating
with yourself* in a noble department of benevolence,

the most important feature of the scene), and *Hartford*, with its sphere of duty, and some peculiar advantages, and a thousand *endearing* associations, on the other. The Lord bless and guide you and yours.

Yours truly,

T. H. GALLAUDET.

Of even date with this letter an entry in Mr. Gallaudet's diary reads as follows :

July 6th.—I called on Dr. Fuller to inform him that I was ready to enter upon the duties of my office. He said a committee of the directors, appointed for that purpose, would, in a few days, have the by-laws prepared respecting the duties of the chaplain, and then they would be ready to have me commence the discharge of those duties.

In all this affair, I humbly hope, I have acted from a sense of duty. I have continually prayed to God for His guidance.

Nine days later his work as chaplain began.

Sabbath, July 15, 1838.—This day at three P. M. I commenced my work as chaplain to the Retreat for the Insane in Hartford, Conn., by conducting religious service there, and preaching my introductory sermon. Out of ninety, the whole number of patients, eighty attended. The assembly, in all,

consisted of one hundred. The Rev. Mr. S——
and the Rev. Mr. R——, two of the patients, at
the request of Dr. Fuller, sat on my right and
left. One of the female patients, on account of
her incessant loud talking, just before the exercises
began, was led to her room. All the rest were
quiet, and conducted themselves with great propriety, except a very little chattering from a male
patient, which was stopped.

Dr. Humphrey in his biography says:
"Mr. Gallaudet kept a diary of his labors
in the Retreat up to his last sickness, from
which I have taken the following copious and
exceedingly interesting extracts. They show
the man, and his eminent fitness for the place;
his wisdom, his conscientiousness, his piety,
his quick and lively sympathies with the patients in their unhappy condition, and his remarkable skill as a spiritual physician in 'the
home of mercy.' It will be seen, too, that admirable as the curative arrangements and appliances were, he was all the time studying
how they might be increased and made perfect. As the result of his daily observations
and reflections, his diary abounds with suggestions, such as were at the same time occurring to the superintendent also, and which

have, one after another, been carried out by the directors."

Less than half of the extracts made by Dr. Humphrey from Mr. Gallaudet's diary can be here given ; but these may furnish suggestions of the kind of labors to which he devoted fully one-half of his time and more than half his strength during the last thirteen years of his life. Only suggestions, however, and insufficient at best : for none save the All-Seeing and All-Knowing One can ever justly estimate the value of those humble, devoted, Christ-like labors, given a hundredfold more for love than for money, in which the high privilege was to

> " Minister to minds diseased,
> Pluck from the memory a rooted sorrow,
> Raze out the written troubles of the brain,
> And with some sweet, oblivious antidote,
> Cleanse the stuffed bosom of that perilous stuff
> Which weighs upon the heart."

" July 23d, '38.—While conversing with three or four of the patients, one of them observed that there were a great many crazy folks and fools all around us. ' Yes,' says another, ' and it takes a very wise man to find out that he is a fool.'

" Aug. 8th.—Many visitors, who stayed to

prayers; the patients still. Mrs. H. L. Ellsworth reminded me of the fact, which I had forgotten, that at their house (the Dwight house in Prospect Street), her husband being one of the building committee, I first suggested giving the name of 'Retreat' to the institution. Mrs. Dr. Fuller told me how much she was struck with the peculiar and reverential appearance, as she sat at the window observing him unnoticed, of Capt. V——, one of the patients, in the yard, approaching the building and listening to the prayer.

"Aug. 11th.—Have nearly succeeded in teaching young L——, from Trinidad, the alphabet of the deaf and dumb, on the fingers. He also learns signs very quickly. He observed that if he had not neglected prayer, and forgotten his duty to God, he would not have been deranged. He lamented his past misconduct, and the grief he had brought on his aged father, and on his wife, and declared if he were ever permitted to return to his family, he would be a very different man.

"Aug. 19th, Sabbath.—Called on my way home to see Mrs. H., who has a husband in the Retreat, and had from her a particular account of his case. I am becoming more and more convinced that a judicious physical and religious education, on the simple principles of the Gospel, with early piety, constitutes the best security against mental alienation, and if it must come, affords the greatest facilities for the use of those means, which, under the blessing of God, will result in restoration. Mr. W———— rode home with me part of the way. He thought my confession of sin, in prayer, was too strong for the insane, that it might disturb and agitate them. This involves a point of deep interest—to what extent the simple truths of the Gospel may be brought out, in the religious exercises in the Retreat, with benefit to the patients. My impression now is, that the best course is, in a calm and kind manner, to bring out *these truths*, and to lead the insane to feel, so far as they have reason left, that *Christ, in His mediatorial character, is their great hope;* that He is ready to sympathize with them in their affliction, and *to save them as sinners.* But the *manner* of doing this must be looked to.

"Aug. 27th.—Commenced singing at prayers. One of the female patients very noisy and carried out. .

"Aug. 29th.—Rev. ———— ———— prayed at the evening service. He is a convalescent patient. His prayer was a very appropriate one.

"Sept. 30th, Sabbath.— Large number of visitors. Patients composed, excepting the deaf and dumb young men, who tittered considerably. Preached on the subject of prayer. After service Colonel W—— told me it was the best sermon he had ever heard me preach.

"Oct. 15th.—Interesting conversation with Mr. H——, who is a member of the Free Church, before prayers. He said he felt sorry for the manner in which he had expressed himself on the Sabbath, in the way of finding fault with his being detained in the Retreat, and charging Dr. Fuller and others with being unjust and cruel towards him. He observed that the cases of derangement, accompanied with religious excitement, seemed to be increasing; and he believed that, in many cases, if Christian friends would be faithful in doing their duty, they would not occur. He thought a little timely attention and sympathy on the part of his Christian brethren towards him, when his mind first began to be disturbed, would have saved him from coming to the Retreat.

"Nov. 20th.—Had some conversation with Mr. S. about the troubles in Canada. Observed to him that I hoped the time would come when all men would be at peace with

each other. 'Do you think,' said he, 'that the
Devil will ever become the friend of the
Almighty?' 'I do not,' I replied. 'Well,'
he added, 'when that happens, men will be at
peace with each other.'

"Dec. 20th.—After prayers, had a long interview with Mr. L. and Mr. B., who were together. Mr. L. considered himself as without
piety, and beyond the reach of the Gospel
salvation. He complained of having no feeling on religious subjects; of trying to pray
and not being able to do it. I tried to console
him but without effect. I told him of Cowper, of whose piety there is satisfactory evidence, and yet who suffered so much from
despondency and downright despair. But he
replied that it was by no means certain that
Cowper was a Christian. Mr. B. spoke, too,
of his own case as hopeless. He was possessed, he said, by the devil, and given over
to everlasting destruction. He said he had
committed the unpardonable sin. 'What is
the unpardonable sin?' said I. 'I do not
know,' was his reply. 'How, then, can you
know that you have committed it?' He made
no answer. He spoke of seeing shadows that
warned him of his doom. He said his voice
had been changed by a satanic influence, and

was unlike what it formerly was. I endeavored to give them both such counsel as I thought would do them good. Mr. B., his attendant tells me, sometimes kneels down by his bed, as if engaged in prayer.

"March 12th, '39.— Visited Mr. L. and found him very unwell, and exceedingly depressed in mind. More should be done to bring the insane under the influence, during the whole time, of a rational and cheerful piety. Those who have the care of them need such a piety themselves; and to act from religious, benevolent principle, feeling a pleasure in their employment, and regarding it as one of a truly elevating kind, inasmuch as they are, in an eminent degree, following the example of Christ, if they act from the motives which He presents to His followers. The insane should have vastly more means of interesting and useful occupation. Little parties of sewing and knitting should be formed for the females. Spinning wheels, large and small, should be introduced. There should be a spacious hall for exercise in bad weather, where battledore could be played, and India rubber balls used, and other innocent recreations. Instrumental music and singing should be encouraged, and drawing and painting. The

matron should devise various modes of entertaining the female patients; make parties for
them, with a little fruit and lemonade.

"There should be a reading-room for the
females, and one for the males, in which should
be suitable books, periodicals, newspapers and
pictures, and other entertaining objects; a
museum of natural curiosities, collections of
shells, minerals, etc. A course of lectures in
chemistry, natural philosophy, etc., might be
delivered; on history and biography, by the
chaplain. The females might cultivate flow-
ers in pots in their apartments, and the males
also. Singing birds in cages might be introduced. Workshops for the males should be
provided. Parties formed for the males, and
occasionally for both sexes to come together.
Checkers, backgammon and chess, but *not cards.*
1. They tempt the attendants. 2. They too
often fascinate too much the patients. 3. Patients who never played before acquire a fondness for this at the institution, and the habit
goes with them, to expose them to grievous
temptations. 4. It is revolting to the feelings
of many patients who have been educated to
regard it as an immorality. 5. It must be
very narrowly watched, not sometimes to lead
to gambling among the patients. 6. It often

leads to profanity and to boisterous and angry language, and in this way has annoyed other patients within hearing of it.

"Great pains should be taken to interest and improve the attendants. In their leisure time they should be provided with suitable books, newspapers, periodicals, etc. They should be regarded and treated as Christian fellow-laborers in the work of doing good. They should be encouraged to make suggestions in a proper way. In doing all these things, regard should, of course, be had to the peculiar state of the patient, to determine whether any, or how much, of these means of employment and amusement may be profitable. But who can be among the insane a little while, and not see how they need objects to occupy and interest their minds?

"April 20th.—Had some conversation with the male patients in the physician's room. One of them told me that he thought it would be much better to practice no deception with the patients. He complained of it, and said they would be vastly better satisfied to have it laid aside altogether, and if they were to be denied any thing, to be told so plainly and explicitly.

"May 2nd.—A dance this evening. I

did not stay. Dr. Fuller asked me if I had any scruples about it. I told him I thought it depended upon the manner in which it was conducted.

"May 10th.—A patient arrived, making a great noise, and using very profane language. Another patient, standing at the door and noticing this, said, 'If this is being crazy, it is bad enough; I'm sure I'll try and not be crazy any more.'

"Dec. 4th, '40.—Soon after dinner, called on Miss C., at Miss E.'s, who is in a deranged state of mind. Had a long conversation with her, and endeavored to persuade her to be willing to go to the Retreat. She said she would see me again to-morrow. At the request of Mrs. H., her sister, and of Mrs. E., I called on Mr. B., and requested him to call at Mrs. E.'s, and let Miss C. know that her friends had concluded that she *must* go to the Retreat, and to compel her to go if necessary. I advised this course in preference to any thing that involved deception or maneuvering. It was taken, and the object accomplished without any difficulty, she only protesting that she went against her will. She arrived at the Retreat immediately after prayers, at which time I officiated as usual. It has been my undeviating course, which I think is the only correct one, to practice nothing like deception or collusion with the patients, and to fulfill strictly all my engagements with them.

"Dec. 26th, '41, Sabbath.—Just after beginning the sermon, one of the female patients walked across the hall, rather suddenly, into the men's room, and was taken back with some difficulty. As she entered the men's room, young B. became greatly excited. For a minute or two the doors of the males' and of the females' rooms were closed and the exercises suspended. I soon began again, and there was entire quiet till the close. This is the first and only time, since I have been connected with the Retreat, that I have ever suspended at all the course of religious exercises.

"Oct. 9th, '47.—Visited E. early in the forenoon and asked him if I should pray with him. He said not now; I will let you know. I told him I was about going into the city, but would be back soon. In a few minutes he sent for me to the physician's office, where I was. I went to him. 'On the whole,' said he, 'I think you had better pray with me now; for we do not know what may happen within two or three hours.' I began to pray. He stopped me, saying, 'Excuse me; but I wish to have you make one special request.' 'What is it?' said I. He replied, 'I am a very great sinner; pray that God would soften my heart.'

"March 14th, 1848.—S—— B——, a maiden lady, who had worked in a factory at home, was talking to me about going home, and said it did not seem just like home to her at the Retreat. She said: 'I don't hear the tea-kettle siss.'

"The next day I handed her the following lines, which delighted her so much that she claimed them as her own, and read them often to her friends. She soon after went home cured."

LINES SUPPOSED TO BE WRITTEN BY A FEMALE PATIENT IN THE RETREAT.

O! how I do, I do desire
To see my own dear home — what bliss!
To sit around our blazing fire,
And hear the old tea-kettle siss.

O! how I'd stir about, I would,
And wash, and iron, cook and bake;
I'd strive to help them all I could,
And be the day long wide awake.

And while I worked I'd sing the song
I used to sing so blithe and clear,
Which helped me in my task along —
I try, but can not sing it here.

But I am crazy still they say,
   And do not act like other folk,
Choosing to have my own strange way —
   Perhaps they only mean to joke.

Perhaps they tell the truth, and so
   I'll be contented with my lot,
For sure the doctor ought to know
   Whether I'm crazy still or not.

I'll soon be well, quite well, and then
   I'll hie me home — what joy, what bliss !
To feel our blazing fire again,
   And hear the old tea kettle siss.

"April 12th, '48. — This day my wife and I received a bed-quilt with the accompanying note, in the handwriting of Miss R. C., a patient :

"'Presented to Mr. and Mrs. Gallaudet, by the ladies of the Retreat, April 12th, 1848.' On various parts of the quilt texts of Scripture are written by female patients, with their signatures. The following verses accompanied the present, by Miss M. G., a patient:"

This offering to thee we send,
And with it our affections tend ;
Perhaps you'll smile, perhaps you'll laugh,
We planned it for your better half.

The patchwork, though so intricate,
Is from a model drawn of late.
'Twas your good friend, Mrs. C.,
That first designed this plan for thee.

We all agreed with one consent,
And with the work right onward went.
The names subscribed in pen and ink
Are well ensconced in white and pink.

These passages of Scripture truth,
You've made familiar from your youth ;
But each of us has placed them here,
An emblem of our love sincere.*

The few quotations now given from Mr.
Gallaudet's diary while acting as chaplain at
the Retreat, furnish but imperfect suggestions
as to what his labors and influence in that
capacity really were.

He was a power behind the throne. Dr.
John S. Butler, who was the superintendent
during the last eight years of Mr. Gallaudet's
chaplaincy, has frequently spoken to the
writer in terms of grateful acknowledgment of
the valuable aid he constantly received from
him, and this often in ways quite uncalled for
in the line of his official duty as chaplain.

---

* The writer of these pages slept often under the " crazy
quilt," and remembered quieting his conscience for the morning indolence common to boyhood by studying, or pretending
to study, its tracery of Bible verses.

Important questions of management were discussed from day to day, the physician in charge looking on the chaplain as his ablest and most intelligent adviser. Dr. Butler regarded the influence of the chaplain on the patients as a most important curative force.

On one occasion Mr. Gallaudet brought him word that a certain Mrs. A——— was very anxious to be allowed to attend prayers. In health she had been a person of refinement and religious habits, her special manifestation of insanity being a disposition to break out into language of the foulest character. In asking to be admitted into the chapel she made the most solemn promises to keep absolutely quiet. Dr. Butler gave directions that she be allowed to take a seat near the door with an attendant, and said to her, " Mrs. A———, if you feel an impulse to speak out, twist your handkerchief hard in your hand." She sat through the service without making a sound, but was seen to twist her handkerchief with great energy once or twice. In speaking of her experience to the doctor the next day she remarked : " I could say *any thing* among the patients, but *nothing* in God's holy temple."

Dr. Butler regarded her self-restraint in chapel as the *punctum saliens* in the process of her recovery, which was rapid after the occurrence of this incident.

It was Mr. Gallaudet's custom to seek the physician in his office on his daily arrival for the purpose of making personal visits to the patients with the question: "What can I do to help you to-day, doctor?" Dr. Butler says that on occasions without number he has answered this question by a reference to cases in which he thought Mr. Gallaudet's quieting and cheering influence would do good on that particular day: and acting on these suggestions the chaplain would often accomplish results which could not otherwise have been attained.

Mr. Gallaudet was often appealed to, even in very extreme cases, his moral power being relied on when mere physical force would not avail. On a certain occasion a case of protracted violent mania was giving the physicians much anxiety, none of the attendants being willing to venture into the furious patient's room. The chaplain entered fearlessly, and when the maniac advanced with an uplifted chair to attack him, he said with an amused smile, "You would not assault a little man like me!" Instantly the patient was on his knees asking Mr. Gallaudet's forgiveness,

and his delirium was shortly at an end. At
another time Mr. Gallaudet, having entered a
patient's room and closed the door behind
him, found the man armed with a knife and
himself the subject of a wholly unexpected
attack. On the instant he drew a couple of
keys from his pocket and began twirling them
in a peculiar manner, saying with a smile:
" I don't believe you can do this." The patient's attention was diverted, and Mr. Gallaudet was able to call in assistance in time to
avoid all trouble.

It may have been inferred from the deeply
religious nature of many of the entries in Mr.
Gallaudet's diaries, that he was of a somber
disposition and habit. This was very far from
being the case. Though subject sometimes
to attacks of even extreme despondency,
owing wholly to physical causes, his external
manners were cheerful and often playful. No
man more thoroughly enjoyed a joke, and few
were able to tell an amusing story more enter-
tainingly.* It must not be supposed that in the

---

* Mr. Gallaudet was a good deal disappointed when his eldest son, after having been for some years a member of the same
religious society with his father, decided to become an Episco-
palian and study for the ministry in that branch of the church.
But he would not allow himself to take a gloomy view of the
event ; on the contrary, he was fond of telling the following

chaplain's visits to patients the talk was all of a pious nature. Far otherwise. In alluding to this jovial side of Mr. Gallaudet's nature Dr. Butler says: "It seemed when he died that sunlight went out of the house."*

Mr. Gallaudet's influence in the Retreat was felt in another important direction. He did much to maintain the authority of those who were called on to exercise it. Dr. E. K. Hunt, now residing in Hartford, was, as a very young man, called on unexpectedly to fill the office of superintendent of the Retreat

---

story in the presence of his son, which the writer has heard him do on several occasions:

A young Quaker loved a Baptist maiden. Their families looked with disfavor on the match. A grand council was held, at which each side hoped to gain a proselyte. But their efforts having continued for several hours fruitlessly, the young Quaker took his lady-love by the hand, and commanding attention, said a conclusion had been reached. "My family," said he, "have failed to make a Quakeress of Betsy, and her friends have not been able to make a Baptist of me, so we have decided to join the Episcopalians and go to the devil together."

*Judge Nathaniel Shipman, of Hartford, says of Mr. Gallaudet's conversational powers:

"I recollect most distinctly when I was but little more than a boy and used to see him in Prospect Street, and admired the way in which he punctuated Mr. Elizur Goodrich's theological talk with his own wit, in which Mrs. Goodrich delighted, and how he united philosophy and humor, and made conversation sparkle with quiet fun. People don't seem to talk now so well as those old gentlemen did."

temporarily, between the terms of Dr. Fuller and Dr. Brigham. He says that Mr. Gallaudet, though twice his age, treated him on all occasions with marked deference, thus greatly strengthening his hands in the difficult task of an *ad interim* administration.

Dr. Hunt paid a loving tribute to his friend, not long after his death, in a published letter, from which a few extracts may be taken :

" I remember well the first time I ever saw him, and the impression his manner and conversation then made upon my mind ; though I did not hear until afterwards that it was Mr. Gallaudet. It was on a pleasant morning in the fall of 1839 that, a stranger, I was standing in the hall of the Retreat for the Insane, waiting for an interview with the physician. Some of the more quiet of the male patients were also there, engaged in conversation, when a small man, of a quite unassuming, yet gentlemanly bearing, entered, and was cordially welcomed by the patients as a familiar acquaintance and friend.

" Of what transpired in particular I have no definite recollection, and only remember, as I do distinctly, that uncommon ease and kindness of manner ; a quiet yet animated and interesting address ; a quick, clear, and active,

as well as a highly cultivated mind, character-
ized the interview on the part of the gentleman in question.

"A feature of his character that a continued and close acquaintance brought prominently to my notice, was his ever-present
sense of accountability to God, as illustrated
by the scope and tenor of his conversation.
Though eminently cheerful, and appreciat-
ing the humorous and mirthful, perhaps even
more than a majority of people, still the
momentous thought, that 'for every idle
word that men shall speak, they shall give an
account thereof on the day of judgment,'
seemed to stand out as if written in letters of
light, continually before his mind. I know
not that I ever spent five minutes with him in
meaningless and unprofitable conversation.
It was one of his great excellences that he
both knew how and had the disposition always
to render an interview, however short, both
agreeable and useful.

" One of the subjects on which Mr. Gallaudet used often to speak, and dwell with special
interest—perhaps because he thought it would
be more acceptable to me as a physician than
most other topics—was that of the physical
training and education of the young. And on

this subject I am greatly mistaken if his views
were not profoundly philosophical and correct.
He highly esteemed—but to that degree only
which it justly merits—the vast importance of
physical culture, not as a mere political question,
but as it stands related to the intellectual and
moral part of our nature. And in his opinion
its importance related quite as much to the
female sex as our own.

"He understood better than most men the
laws which infinite wisdom has set over the
organization of man, and the mutual reactions
of its several parts; and was also keenly alive
to its clear and harmonious development. He
knew, indeed, no completeness, either moral
or intellectual, aside from a sound bodily constitution."

With a few extracts from the annual report
of Dr. Butler, written soon after Mr. Gallaudet's death, the record of his labors as chaplain among the insane must be closed.

"This field of labor was admirably adapted
to call into exercise the peculiar characteristics
of Mr. Gallaudet, and all these found ample
scope for their full development among the
ever-varying peculiarities of our family.

"His equanimity and calmness checked the
unduly excited; his suavity and quiet dignity

calmed the turbulent ; his kindness, cheerfulness, and wit, with his ready repartee, cheered and amused the desponding, while his rare conversational powers, and his fund of anecdote, and of general and useful knowledge, made him the welcome companion of all.

" His aptness of illustration, the happy manner in which he applied practical religious truth to the varying circumstances of the different patients, together with his quick perception of individual peculiarities, gave him ready access to every mind, especially to that class of religious monomaniacs who are difficult of approach, and whose minds appear most obstinately closed against right and natural views.

" The aim of his daily life was *to do good*. His whole warm heart was in his work, and he did that work well. He seemed to bring sunlight with him into our household, and he left its cheering influence in every heart."

CHAPTER X.

BEFORE speaking of the closing days of Mr. Gallaudet's life, which followed directly on the conclusion of his labors as chaplain of the Retreat, certain matters deserve a place in this narrative which could not, easily, have been related in chronological order.

Allusions have been made to a home school, organized for the purpose of educating his own children, but into which the children of his neighbors and friends were, to a limited extent, admitted. This school, though never large, held no insignificant place in Hartford, and not a few who began their education in it have risen to commanding positions in social life, in letters and in art.

One of the early pupils, now residing in Hartford, writes thus of her experience :

You have asked me to give you what facts I could recollect of the private school for the children of your father's family, which was taught by a teacher whom he selected for this purpose, a few of his chosen friends being kindly invited to send their children to profit by the same instruction.

I find that the well-worn little books, which I used then, and had so carefully kept for so long a time, have been lately destroyed or given away; thus one of the sources of information upon which I had relied has been lost.

I do not remember any school life previous to this time. This school I must have left when about ten or eleven years of age. It may seem strange to some, that a child so young should have been at all impressed with a sense of the peculiar powers with which your father was endowed. No especial reverence, beyond that of usual good behavior, was expected of the pupils when he made his accustomed visits to the school. Yet unconsciously to him, we were all, I am sure, more or less aware of a presence we could dimly feel was both noble and wise. Those visits never failed to be of lasting benefit by way of suggestion or incitement to some achievement on our part. Each thought was given to us in so clear, direct and original a way that youthful minds could not fail to absorb it. Perhaps in his methods of teaching the young there was an unfolding, thus

early, of the now popular Kinder Gärten system;
for in all his books which instruct the young in regard to the truths of natural science, there are such
full and apt illustrations and explanations, that it
might well be called object-teaching.

In comparing the past with the present, Dr. Gallaudet appears much in advance of his own times
in his views of education—in his estimate of what
is essential to health and vigor of both mind and
body. Only his genius, perhaps, could have led
even children themselves to feel that education is a
priceless thing; that the accepted means to that
end should be carefully considered by them even to
the care of their school-books!

I can see him now, as with a serious face, yet a
twinkle in his eye, he took up a hardly-used book
which some little hand had idly held, and turning
the pages slowly, shook his head, saying: "Children, do you know that these curling covers are
'dog's ears?' We can not have any of them in *our*
books." One of these same scholars remembers that
on coming into the school room he always noted
how the thermometer stood, and showed to us all
his appreciation of a thorough ventilation.

Of physical exercise he was as duly mindful. It
is much less of a surprise now than it was then, that
every day the children must have a share of exercise in the open air, whether they cared for it or
not.

In his visits to the school Dr. Gallaudet would
occasionally seek, in familiar conversations, to lead
our minds to worshipful and loving thoughts of our

Father in Heaven; and no one could be long under his influence and teaching without being led into some spiritual appreciation of the truths so dear and vital to him.

This home school was an important factor in the family. The spirit which governed the ' one was the same that controlled the other. Firm authority with love as the motive for every action, every rule, every restraint made the household of Mr. Gallaudet pre-eminently a happy one. His philanthropy was not of the Borrio-boola Gha order. In his labors for the good of mankind he never neglected his wife or his children. He was their companion and their sympathizing friend. Even the youngest child, fifty years his father's junior, remembers him as an eager comrade in many a sport, ready to stand as one of the chief mourners by the grave of such of his chickens or rabbits as came to untimely ends, or to write tear-drawing verses on the death of his sister's pet canary. He remembers journeys taken with his father, notably one that included the ascent of Mt. Holyoke on foot, in which the old man and the child were boys together. Mr. Gallaudet was a marvelous teacher in his family. He knew how to make instruction an entertainment. The

youngest son recalls a bright summer morning when he crept into his father's bed, and
how the father gave him his first insight into
geometry. The mysteries of planes and
angles, curves and straight lines, surfaces and
solids, were so magically unfolded, that ever
after "the science of quantity, extension or
magnitude, abstractly considered," was an
open book to the boy ; the passage of the
pons asinorum, when it came, a joyous and
victorious march.

Mr. Gallaudet's power in the discipline of
his children was as marked as his teaching
ability. The eldest son (Rev. Thomas Gallaudet, D. D., rector of St. Ann's Church for
Deaf-Mutes, New York), says: "When I
did wrong I would have rather taken a whip-
ping at his hands than to have him call me to
his study for a kind and serious talk, con-
vincing me of my fault, making me ashamed
of what I had done, and leading me to repentance and a better mind. He evidently·be-
lieved in training children to grow up as
Christians without passing through a sudden
process. Father took every opportunity to
drop seed-corns into my mind, giving me
hints on which I could not help meditating.
He was shaping my life and character without

seeming to interfere with my own gradually developing mental processes. He had a high idea of the purity and sacredness which should characterize the life of a Christian family, though smiling on all innocent recreations."

His second son (P. W. Gallaudet, a banker in Wall Street, New York), speaks of his "dread of a talk in the study," and "the power of his father's eye." He remembers a punishment, also, which he thinks was well deserved, though it may seem to some unduly severe. Wallace had given a terrible fright to a deaf-mute seamstress employed in the family, by putting an old shoe in her bed in a way to make her think it was a rat. For this his father kept him a week in his room on bread and water; allowing him to leave his room only to attend school, which was in the house. But the discipline of the family was not often secured through severe means.

One of the younger sons stayed out one summer evening far beyond his usual bed-time, which was eight o'clock. Coming in with dread at ten, the boy found his father lying on the sofa reading a newspaper. "Come," said the father as the boy entered, " I have been waiting for some one to play backgammon with me; let us have a few games." And the astonished boy was kept playing with his father until midnight, and then sent to bed without a word as to his having been out late. The discipline was effective.

Mr. Gallaudet believed that one of the most important elements in the education of a family was the making of the house a resort for interesting and entertaining people. And though he could never indulge in expensive hospitality, the number of guests who slept under his roof and ate at his table was legion. It was always spoken of with surprise among the children when the "spare room" was empty.

Mr. Gallaudet's fame as an educator, a philanthropist and an author, and his wide correspondence, brought to his home many guests whom it was an honor and a pleasure to entertain. His children were taught to show equal courtesy to the black missionary from Africa and the white diplomat from Europe.

Mr. Gallaudet loved a joke, even a practical one, when it did not bear too hard on the victim. On one occasion a distinguished missionary, the late Dr. Poor, was, with his wife, visiting Mr. Gallaudet during the month of May. The day was warm, but the good

Bushnell stove in the dining-room, though it had no fire in it, had not been taken down. Mrs. Poor sat with her back to the stove, and presently began to show signs of being uncomfortably warm. " Won't you change your seat to the other side of the table, Mrs. Poor ? " said the host ; " you seem to feel the stove somewhat." " Thank you," said Mrs. Poor, and one of the children changed places with her. Wiping the perspiration from her face, Mrs. Poor expressed satisfaction with her cooler place, and when Mr. Gallaudet, with a sly twinkle in his eye, said, " I am so glad, Mrs. Poor, though there was no fire in the stove," the titter which had been with difficulty suppressed by the children broke into a laugh, in which all were glad to join, none being more amused than the victim.

It would be impossible even to name these many visitors, much less to describe their visits. But the impressions of one whose presence with his friends excited unusual interest in the family, may be given a place. Dr. Yung Wing, well known as a distinguished graduate of Yale College, a mandarin of high rank in his own country, China, the promoter of the American education of Chinese youth, and for several years assistant Chinese minis-

ter at Washington, writes thus of a visit made
in his boyhood to the family of Mr. Gallaudet :

It was during the winter vacation of 1848 that
Dr. S. R. Brown* took Wong Shing, Wong Fün
and myself to Hartford from Munson, on a visit to
the Rev. Dr. Gallaudet. The visit, though a brief
one, made a lasting impression on my mind. Were
I an artist, I could reproduce on canvas the group
of that happy family, which appeared to me, even
then, like a little heaven on earth.

The entire domestic surroundings carried with
them a heavenly atmosphere; and no one who was
present in that home in Prospect Street, either
immediately after breakfast or after tea in the evening, when all the members met together, could have
failed to be charmed with the scene.

There was the doctor himself the central figure
of the group. In person he was of medium height.
He wore spectacles. He had a full, oval face, every
feature of which bore lines of thought, and beamed
with gentle cheerfulness. His uppermost thoughts
seemed to be of Christ and humanity; and his whole
appearance bespoke a soul well anchored in Christian trust and serenity.

Then came Mrs. Gallaudet. I remember she was
the last member of the family to whom I was introduced. I was not aware, at first, that she was a
mute; her face was full of healthful color, with large,
clear brown eyes that spoke volumes, though she

---

* The eminent missionary to China.

could not give her thoughts articulate expression. She had a dignified and queen-like air, softened with a sweet smile which seemed to be perennial.

Three sons, Thomas, William and Edward, the last the youngest member of the family, being about my own age, and two daughters, Kate and Alice, completed the group.* I remember their faces well. The two young ladies played on the flute, while one of the brothers played on the piano. The sight and sound were novel to me, but the music they made at evenings was symbolic of the gentleness and harmony that pervaded the family.

On the morning of my departure from Hartford the doctor handed me a hymn which he said he had composed in the silent watches of the night previous, during his wakeful hours. This hymn I have preserved for thirty-eight years. Inclosed herewith is a true copy of it.

YUNG WING.

HARTFORD, Conn., Dec. 1, 1885.

A Hymn, for A Wing, composed in the night watches, Feb. 1, 1848, from his friend, T. H. Gallaudet.

TO JESUS.

Ever near, oh! Jesus, be,
With thy grace to succor me,
Lest I stray away from thee ;
Leave, ah ! leave me not alone.

---

* Peter Wallace, the second son, and Sophia and Jane, the two elder daughters, were absent from home.

In temptation's fearful hour,
When the Evil One has power,
And his legions round me lower,
Leave, ah ! leave me not alone.

When the scenes of Earth delight,
With its pleasures fair and bright,
Falsely promising delight,
Leave, ah ! leave me not alone.

Should its gold allure my heart,
From thy service to depart,
Keep me from its wily art ;
Leave, ah ! leave me not alone.

When its glory cheats my eye,
Like a meteor in the sky,
Help me from its lure to fly ;
Leave, ah ! leave me not alone.

In my darkest, dreariest day,
Still thy grace to me convey,
Still thy power to save display ;
Leave, ah ! leave me not alone.

While thy goodness I adore,
May I love thee more and more ;
Till the conflict all is o'er,
Leave, ah ! leave me not alone.

Till the struggling race is run,
Till the fight of faith is won,
And the Crown of Victory won,
Leave, ah ! leave me not alone.

Dr. Wing speaks of the pleasant element of music in the family. This was keenly enjoyed and sedulously cultivated by Mr. Gallaudet. He had himself a fine ear and a sweet voice. In sacred music he never failed to take a part, and not infrequently he contributed to the entertainment of the home circle in a solo. One of his favorite songs was Dibdin's

> Here a sheer hulk lies poor Tom Bowling,
> The darling of our crew.

The feeling with which he rendered the lines :

> And though his body's under hatches
> His soul has gone aloft,

never failed to move deeply those who heard him.

Mr. Gallaudet had all his children taught to sing, most of them in a school conducted by Mr. S. T. Gordon, now the veteran music publisher of New York, and organist of the Jerry McAuley Mission ; and it was a source of as much delight to him as to the younger ones when, through the generosity of a friend, Alfred Smith, Esq., one of T. Gilbert & Son's pianos, with an organ attachment, came into

the house as a gift to the two younger daughters.   The one drawback to music in the
family was the fact that the dear wife and
mother could derive no enjoyment from it.
Her pathetic curiosity could only be met with
an assurance that she might look forward to a
day when the "ears of the deaf should be
unstopped, and the tongue of the dumb sing."

It was during the last year of Mr. Gallaudet's life that Jenny Lind made her memorable visit to the United States.   His interest
in her wonderful singing was so great that he
not only went himself to New York to hear
her, but felt justified, so keen was his pleasure,
in sending his three youngest children to New
York, though he could ill afford to do so, that
they might have the great treasure of a life-
long memory of the sweetest music that has
yet fallen from human lips.

Letter to Jenny Lind.

HARTFORD, CT., June 3d, 1851.
MLLE. LIND:—Will you do me the favor to
accept the accompanying reports of two of the
prominent benevolent institutions of our country.
You love to do good, and it may interest you to see
something of the good we are trying to do to such
classes of the unfortunate as the deaf-mutes and the

insane. It has been my lot to devote thirteen years of my life to the former and as many to the latter, among whom I am still engaged as their minister of the Gospel. .

Precious Gospel! whose benign influence, of late years, has been found to be adapted, with singular efficacy, to the relief of those who, although bereft of reason, have hearts to respond to its consolations and hopes. .

While devoutly praying that these consolations and hopes may richly abound to you through the grace which is in Jesus Christ, will you suffer me to append to these lines a few thoughts which occurred to me after reading, not long since, some lines which it was said, I do not know how truly, you had written in a lady's album, and to tell you what great gratification I enjoyed in listening to your inimitable voice at the concert in Tripler's Hall on Monday evening, the second of June.

Yours very respectfully,

T. H. GALLAUDET.

Written in the album :—

.

In vain I seek for rest
In all created good ;
It leaves me still unblest,
And makes me cry for God.
At rest, be sure, I shall not be,
Until my soul finds rest in thee.

How shall my soul find rest in thee,
Thou God of spotless purity,
   And I a sinner vile !
For Sinai thunders loud and clear
Its law-curse on my trembling ear,
   With awful note the while.

But a sweet voice from Calvary
Still bids my soul find rest in thee,
   Through Jesus' dying love;
I hear, I come; receive, forgive,
O Lord, and fit thy child to live
   In rest with thee above.

During the year 1850, the last full year of
Mr. Gallaudet's life, two events took place
which gave him great satisfaction. Late in
1849, the Leffingwell house on Prospect Street,
in which the family had lived for more than
eight years, was sold, and it became necessary
for Mr. Gallaudet to provide another home
by the following spring. He had long desired
to own a house, and for several years he had
felt the length of his daily walks to and from
the Retreat to be too great.

Very fortunately, or providentially, as he
would have been apt to say, an opportunity
occurred for him to purchase a pleasant home
in the southern part of the city, comparatively
near the Retreat, for two thousand five hun-

dred dollars, and he had a little more than that sum in the savings bank. The house was in Buckingham Street, and adjoined that of his old friend Seth Terry, who had been for many years connected with the management of the institution for deaf-mutes, and who was at that time commissioner of the fund of the institution.

No one knew better than Mr. Terry that Mr. Gallaudet's means were very limited, and no one more fully appreciated the value of Mr. Gallaudet's poorly requited services, even in a commercial sense, in the establishment and endowment of the school for the deaf. It was natural, therefore, that in view of Mr. Gallaudet's purchase of a house, Mr. Terry should have proposed to the directors of the institution the action recorded as follows :

At a meeting of the Board of Directors held February 22d, 1850, Hon. Thos. S. Williams, president, in the chair, the following was, on motion of Seth Terry, Esq., unanimously adopted :

Whereas, The Rev. Thomas H. Gallaudet has rendered many and great services for this institution, more particularly,

Whereas, Soon after he commenced his professional life, at the request of friends of the deaf and dumb he visited England, Scotland and France for

the purpose of obtaining information as to the best
mode of instructing deaf-mutes, and was absent on
this business fifteen months, and after many embarrassments finally returned with much valuable information upon this then new and interesting subject,
bringing with him at his own risk a distinguished
specimen of what had been accomplished by the instruction of this unfortunate class; thereby removing
the doubts which had paralyzed the exertions of
many, and laying the foundation of this institution
and of the funds with which it has since been endowed ; and

Whereas, No pecuniary recompense beyond his
actual expenses was ever made to him therefor; and

Whereas, Since his connection with this institution
as principal was dissolved, he has rendered valuable
services for which he has not been compensated ;
therefore,

Voted, That we believe it to be the duty of this
institution to make a reasonable compensation to
Mr. Gallaudet for the time and labor thus devoted to
this important work ;

Voted, That the sum of two thousand dollars be
appropriated for this purpose, and that the same be
paid to him by the order of the directing committee on the treasurer, one-half payable on the
15th day of April, and one-half on the 15th day of
July next.

In his journal Mr. Gallaudet writes under
date of March 1st, 1850:

I think it worthy of record that after having been searching for a house to rent, for two or three months, without success, and having once applied to Mr. E—— to hire his, he declining—some new arrangements of his led him to come to me with the offer of his house for sale. It was thus providentially and unexpectedly preserved to me, and my concluding to purchase it being soon known to my friends, I have no doubt led to the movement which will place two thousand dollars in my hands to help pay for it. In all this I see the hand of a kind Providence, locking up and reserving this sum for me till I most should need it, and when it would do me and my family the most good. O! Lord, lead me to be grateful and faithful. What shall I render unto thee for all thy benefits?

In addition to the sum voted Mr. Gallaudet, a purse of five hundred dollars was presented him on April 1st, the day he received the deed of his house, by Hon. Thos. S. Williams, David Watkinson, Elizur Goodrich, and James M. Bunce of Hartford, and Richard Bigelow of New York, thus providing for the full discharge of the purchase money. Of the donors of this last gift Mr. Gallaudet writes : "May the Lord reward them, and especially with spiritual blessings on themselves and theirs." On the 9th of April the family occupied the new house, which was to be Mr. Gallaudet's home for seventeen months only. But these were happy months, and Mr. Gallaudet took unalloyed pleasure in the little garden and orchard and vineyard which formed part of his new possession.

The second event of unusual interest, occurring in 1850, was the presentation of a testimonial of regard from his old pupils, of which Mr. Gallaudet speaks in his diary as follows :

"September 27th. — Yesterday a silver pitcher and salver, of beautifully exquisite workmanship, with appropriate devices and inscriptions, costing nearly three hundred dollars, were presented to me in the Center Church, by the hands of Mr. George H. Loring, one of my earliest pupils, in the presence of a very large assembly, appropriate addresses accompanying them, as a testimonial of the gratitude and affection of many of my old pupils, nearly two hundred of whom were present from various parts of the country, principally from New England. A similar pitcher and salver were presented to Mr. Clerc.

"Lord! give me grace to view this in its true light. Let not my pride in any degree be inflated by it. I feel humbled before thee for my many deficiencies in duty, while laboring in the education of deaf-mutes. I would feel that I was then but the very weak, imperfect and sinful instrument in thy hands of doing some good, and to thee be all the glory."

Mr. Luzerne Rae, an instructor in the school for the deaf at Hartford, and editor of the *American Annals* in 1850, writes thus of the origin of this testimonial :

The deaf and dumb were entirely self-moved in this matter. The idea originated with Mr. Thomas Brown, of New Hampshire, one of Mr. Gallaudet's earliest and most intelligent pupils. He said to me, in his graphic language of signs, that his spirit could find no rest until he had devised some method of giving expression to the grateful feeling which filled his heart, and which the lapse of years served only to increase. He had but to suggest the thought to others of his former associates, when it was eagerly seized and made the common property of them all. In the vivid simile of the orator of the day, the flame of love ran, like a prairie fire, through the hearts of the whole deaf-mute band, scattered as they were in various parts of the country ; and measures were immediately adopted for the further-ance of the object. In a very short time the hand-some sum of six hundred dollars was obtained ; wholly, let it be understood, from the deaf and dumb themselves.

Upon one side of the pitcher is an engraved scene, representing Mr. Gallaudet in France in 1816, with Mr. Clerc, who offers to accompany him to America, and a ship waiting to convey them. Across the sea appears the Hartford Institution. On the other side is seen a picture of a school-room, with teacher and pupils and apparatus. In front and between these scenes is a good likeness of the Abbe Sicard, Mr. Gallaudet's teacher in Paris. On the neck of the pitcher are chased the coats of arms of the New England States; and on the handles are representations of mute cupids, and also closed hands, indicating the sign of the mutes for the first letter of the alphabet.

The presentation of the pitchers took place in the Center Church, which was filled with deaf-mutes, the officers of the institution, and many interested citizens.

Prayer was offered by Rev. Joel Hawes, D. D., and addresses were made by Lewis Weld, principal of the Institution for Deaf-Mutes, Thomas Brown, of New Hampshire, Fisher Ames Spofford, of Ohio, and George H. Loring, of Boston, these three being early pupils of Mr. Gallaudet.

In responding to Mr. Loring, who made

the presentation address, Mr. Gallaudet said in closing :

I beg you to accept my cordial thanks for the part with which you indulge me, in the touching interest of the scene. I thank you all. I thank your committee individually. In him from whose hands I have just received this testimonial of your grateful regard, I recognize one of my very earliest and youngest pupils—one whom I taught for a long course of years, and who now, in the maturity of manhood, is reaping the rich reward of his faithful use of the means of improvement which he then enjoyed. This testimonial of your affection I shall ever cherish with emotions which I can not here express. As I look at it from time to time, should my life be spared for a few more years, I shall think of all the past in which you were concerned with a melancholy pleasure—of this day, as standing out with a strong and immovable prominence among the days of my earthly pilgrimage—and of you and your fellow-pupils with a father's love. I shall ever pray that God may shed down upon you His choicest blessings, and prepare you, by His grace in Christ Jesus, for the holiness and happiness of heaven."

Soon after the conclusion of the public exercises the deaf-mutes assembled within the walls of their *alma mater* for social intercourse, and to partake of the bountiful entertainment provided for them by the officers of the institution. They were met by the directors and instructors, with their families, together with a few invited guests, among whom, apparently not the least interested of the party, was the governor of the state.

It will be difficult to understand the peculiar pleasure afforded to Mr. Gallaudet by this notable assemblage of his old pupils. But it needed no close observer to discover that while he was gratified to be remembered *as he was*, his greatest satisfaction grew out of the impression made by the deaf-mutes as mature men and women, in the community which had before known them only as school children.

Their intelligence, dignity and courtesy elicited favorable comment from all observers, even in cultivated Hartford.

The memory of these days was a sunbeam to Mr. Gallaudet during the short year of life that remained to him, and it was his expressed wish that the plate should be carefully guarded as an heir-loom in the family.

The record of Mr. Gallaudet's life would be far from complete without definite mention of his labors as a preacher.

Though he was never settled as a pastor,

the number of his sermons was greater than
that of many a minister in a life-long pastorate.

His manuscripts and notes would furnish
material for a score of volumes.

His services were in constant request for
the supply of vacant pulpits, and he seldom
spent a Sabbath on a journey, even when
seeking rest, that he did not preach.

He often spoke from very brief notes, but
more frequently wrote his sermons. In his
delivery, however, he was never a slave to his
manuscript.

His relations with the clergy of his city and
state were intimate and cordial. He admired
Dr. Bushnell, and sympathized with him in
his difficulties. The two were often seen on
the streets of Hartford engaged in earnest
discussion.

A friend who knew both well relates that
on a certain Saturday they were walking
together, when Bushnell exclaimed : " I have
no sermon for to-morrow morning." " Come
with me to your study," said Gallaudet, " and
I will open the Bible and put my finger on a
text for you, without seeing it." Bushnell
laughingly led the way, and on reaching the
study handed a Bible to Gallaudet, who

opened it and rested his finger on a page, asking Bushnell to see what had come to him. Finding these words: "Who is made not after the law of a carnal commandment, but after the power of an endless life," he at once accepted them as his text for the next · day. Gallaudet left him, bidding him Godspeed, and he wrote, scarcely leaving his table, until the hour of service the following day, when he ascended his pulpit and delivered one of his finest discourses.

The same friend, long a parishioner of Bushnell's, says of the two as preachers:

"Bushnell influenced men through their reason, saying: 'My friends, here is this statement and the reasons for it; if you can not comprehend or accept it, so much the worse for you.' Gallaudet swayed his hearers and led them by his personal presence and sympathy—by a magnetism few could resist. None ever heard him without wanting to know him personally, and to come near to him."   .

Dr. Barnard in his eulogy speaks thus of Mr. Gallaudet's power as a speaker:

As a public speaker, in the pulpit or the lecturer's desk, soon after he entered the ministry and during his early work as a teacher, he was eminently popular. As a sermonizer he had but few equals.

His subject was distinctly set forth, the topics log-
ically arranged, his language polished, his imagination chaste, his manner earnest and his voice persuasive. The hearer was borne along by a constantly
swelling tide, rather than swept away by a sudden
billow.

Mr. Gallaudet was intimate with the ministers
of all denominations, not excluding Israelites
and Roman Catholics. Father Brady, a well-
known Catholic priest living in Hartford at
the time of his death, was so warmly attached
to him that he preferred to incur the censure
of his superior rather than forego the satisfaction of attending the funeral of his friend,
which was, naturally, in a Protestant church.

When the first Unitarian clergyman, Rev.
Joseph Harrington, came to settle in Hartford, he was coldly received by many of his
orthodox brethren. But Mr. Gallaudet's
charity was broader, and he made a friend
of him at once.

" He never took the freeman's oath nor
exercised the elective franchise until he
was sixty years of age. This was not because he had no settled opinions on political subjects or was indifferent to the welfare
of the country. He was conscientious in
thinking that he could do more good to his

fellow men by taking no part in such matters, as thus he could secure the co-operation of all parties in promoting his views and schemes." *
And his only vote for a President of the United States was cast in 1848, at the urgent instance of his youngest son, then eleven years of age, who was the zealous leader of a boys' Taylor and Fillmore club. .

Mr. Gallaudet's personal journals and diaries were fragmentary, but he commenced a little book on the day he was sixty years old, in which there are entries in each month from this date, Dec. 10, 1847, up to the time of his last illness in 1851.

In the first entry he recounts with grati-tude to God his many and great blessings, chief among which he mentions his dear wife and his eight children, all in health and vigor — the youngest ten years of age. Feeling even in his day the value of efficient domestic service, he speaks thus of one of his mercies: "We have a faithful and honest woman to do the kitchen work, who has been with us nearly four years, Sarah Grady, a Roman Catholic, devout in her religion." This estim-able woman, well deserving to be named in these pages, was a valued member of the fam-

---

* Sprague's Annals of the American Pulpit.

ily long after Mr. Gallaudet's death, and still lives at Hartford, almost a centenarian, having, apparently, no greater pleasure than to meet a friend or relative of her old employer, to whom she may open her heart in praise of him.

But in this birthday entry, as will seem natural, the burden of Mr. Gallaudet's prayer is that spiritual blessings may abound to all the members of his household.

Glancing through the pages of the journal one is made to think of the Good Samaritan, so constantly are visits to the sick and the afflicted noted.

Jan. 4th, 1848.—Yesterday forenoon I called to see Mrs. L., the wife of Mr. Henry L——, who mends our shoes, and their deaf-mute son. Both were on beds in the same room. I conversed and prayed with the son by signs, and also conversed and prayed with his mother.

Scores of visits are recorded to these two humble people, whose dying beds were by the loving ministrations of their faithful friend, "made soft as downy pillows are."

19th.—I found lately that Mr. S——, of whom I buy my meat, has not attended church for five years, and that he professes to be a Universalist. I have conversed with him and put several tracts in his hands, which he says he will read. I have also given him " The Child's Book on the Soul " for his children, and " The Christian Family Almanac " for his wife. Lord, open his heart, and the hearts of his wife and children, to receive and love the truth as it is in Jesus. Give me grace to pray for them.

Feb. 22d.—I called to see the wife of the French cook at the Retreat, who has a little son very sick with scarlet fever, and gave her a trifle of money, and some religious counsel.

May 15, 1849.—I called on Mrs. ———, whose husband was found dead in his office yesterday. I endeavored to direct her mind to the only true source of consolation, and begged her to accept a present of money for the children (for I thought in their circumstances they might need it), but she would not.

Mr. Gallaudet's diary shows that he was made the almoner of charity for others who knew how often he found his way into the homes of those needing help. Not infrequently, also, he records gifts made to himself by kind friends who wished to share with him of their abundance. Evidence appears of his unbounded hospitality. Friends came and went—as many as seven guests being lodged and fed at one time. And never does a word of complaint appear, though many of these visitors were evidently self-invited.

In dealing with his fellow-men, Mr. Gallaudet was seldom deceived as to the character of those who sought his aid. The writer, however, recalls one Jacob G——, claiming to be a broken-down pastor from Germany, who imposed on his father with signal success. This Jacob was always raising money to take him home, and as regularly failing to sail, coming back to Hartford with plausible stories of how he had to spend the money for sickness, or that he had been robbed, etc. Mr. Gallaudet's neighbor and pastor, Rev. Dr. Hawes, soon lost faith in Jacob, who came one day from the study of the latter to the former lamenting that "Minister Hawes, he very fine shpeakit, but his heart is stone." Mr. Gallaudet's faith in the poor German was overstrained at length, and he came no more.

Evidences abound in this journal that in the two closing years of his life Mr. Gallaudet's physical strength, never great, was failing. On his last birthday, when he was sixty-three, he writes : " Three peculiar bodily infirmities, one of them of only a few months' continuance, and another considerably aggravated for a few days past, remind me of my frailty and mortality. Am I to recover some strength, and have comfortable health during the coming year, or to find my infirmities increasing, and perhaps be removed to the spirit world ? Lord, thou knowest. Oh ! forsake me not. Give me a stronger faith in Christ, more fidelity in thy service, more power to subdue my sins, more meekness, more humility, and self-denying benevolence in my family and in all my intercourse with my fellow-men, and a calm, quiet, secure and hopeful submission to thy will."

Thus did the noble soul, conscious that the night was coming in which no man can work, pray for an increase of that self-forgetful spirit the brightness of which, like an aureole, had made his whole life radiant.

What wonder that it was said of him, " He could not walk the length of Main Street without doing some good, by word or act, to some being, young or old ;" and, " I presume it is safe to say, that Mr. Gallaudet never rose in the morning without having in his mind or on his hands some extra duty of philanthropy to perform—something beyond what attached to him from his official or regular engagements." During the winter of 1850–51, and the spring of the latter year, Mr. Gallaudet

discharged his ordinary duties with little interruption, and few of his friends were aware of
his gradually increasing feebleness. The
members of his family noticed that his step
was often languid and his spirits less buoyant
than was common. He was thinking of his
usual summer trip for rest and recuperation,
when the extreme heat of the first week of
July prostrated both him and his wife with
severe attacks of dysentery. Mrs. Gallaudet's natural vigor helped her to a speedy
recovery. But it was otherwise with him.
After some weeks the disease seemed to have
left him, but his strength did not revive. The
effect of stimulants was only temporary.

But in all his weakness Mr. Gallaudet did
not forget the causes he had labored for in
the days of his strength. On the 27th of
August, two weeks before his death, a convention of instructors of the deaf convened
in Hartford at the institution. It was a great
disappointment to Mr. Gallaudet that he
could not meet his professional brethren on
this occasion, and he expressed his regret in
the following note, dictated to his son Thomas :

HARTFORD, August 28, 1851.
To the President, Officers and Members of the
Convention of those Interested in the Cause of the

Instruction of Deaf-mutes, now in Session in this City :

GENTLEMEN:—With deep regret I perceive that the state of my health is such as to prevent my enjoying the pleasures and the privileges of participating with you in the objects of the convention. Look to God for His wisdom and grace, and may it be richly imparted to you. Accept the assurances of my personal regard, and best wishes for your success in your various operations.

Yours sincerely,

T. H. GALLAUDET.

Nor was he forgotten by his friends, for in the convention a paper was read by Rev. W. W. Turner, then a teacher in and afterwards principal of the school in Hartford, on the subject of a high school for the deaf, which did not then exist, which closed as follows :

" Who will undertake this enterprise ? This is a difficult question, and one which we are not prepared to answer. If the educated mutes of our country were called upon to make the selection, their eyes would turn to him whom they have been accustomed to regard in a peculiar sense as their father, and the founder of institutions for their benefit in this country. In confirmation of their choice our eyes turn involuntarily to the chair which

he should have occupied on this occasion. To
this election of grateful hearts there comes
back no response. Our father, our teacher,
our guide, lies low and helpless upon the bed
of sickness, it may be upon the bed of death.
If his work is done, it has been well done;
and the name of Gallaudet will stand conspic-
uous and high upon the roll of fame among the
names of those who have been public benefac-
tors and friends of suffering humanity."

Mr. Gallaudet had the gratification of knowing that he had been thus spoken of in the
house of his friends.

Another mark of appreciation came to him
not many days before his death, with which he
was pleased, though he had never sought or
even cared for such honors. The Western
Reserve College, in Ohio, recognizing his
important work as a promoter of education in
many forms, conferred on him the degree
of Doctor of Laws, and as the parchment lay
in his emaciated hand he remarked with an
amused twinkle in his eye : " It has come just
in time not to be too late."

Through all his illness he was cheerful and
often jocose. He saw many of his friends—
too many, perhaps—but he could not bear to
have them refused admission. He was anx-

ious to recover, and expected to, up to within a few days of his death. He had no fear of what was to come after death, but he dreaded the act of dying and often prayed that he might pass off unconsciously. This prayer was granted. On Sunday, the 7th of September, he felt the heat extremely, and during the two following days he lay much of the time in an unconscious state. About noon on Wednesday, the 10th, he told one of his daughters, who was sitting by his bed, that he felt better. Taking her hand he turned himself over and said, ." I will go to sleep." In the quiet and peaceful slumber which followed they

"Thought him sleeping when he died."

CHAPTER XI.

Funeral, Tributes of Respect, Public Meeting and Eulogy by
Hon. Henry Barnard, LL. D.—Action of the Directors of
the Institution for the Deaf—Monument Erected by the
Deaf of the United States—A Bronze Statue of Dr. Gallau-
det to be Erected at Washington by the Deaf of the Whole.
Country in 1888.

IT is not necessary to say that Dr. Gallaudet's death cast a gloom over the community where he had so long lived.

His house was thronged by those who came
to proffer their sympathy to his wife and children. Many stood at his gate weeping who
felt they had no right to intrude on the grief
of his family.

To his funeral, held in the South Congregational Church,* there came a multitude of
loving mourners, from all ranks of society.

Appreciative mention was made of him in

---

*His own church, the Center, was at the time closed for
repairs.

most of the churches of the city on the following Sabbath.

A few days after his death a public meeting was held at the suggestion of thirty of the principal citizens of Hartford, with a view of devising measures for some public tribute of respect to his memory.

This meeting was called to order by His Excellency Thomas H. Seymour, then governor of the state, and organized by the appointment of Hon. Thomas Day, chairman, and Luzerne Rae (a teacher in the school for the deaf), secretary.

The following preamble and resolutions were presented by the Rev. William W. Turner, which, after brief remarks by the mover, the Hon. Seth Terry, the Rev. Dr. Bushnell, and others, were unanimously adopted :

Whereas, It having pleased Almighty God to remove by death the Rev. Thomas H. Gallaudet, LL. D., a resident of Hartford for half a century, universally known and not less universally beloved and honored, both as a private citizen and public benefactor ;

Resolved, That, in the view of this meeting, the occasion is one which demands a more public and particular recognition than properly belongs to the demise of an ordinary citizen.

Resolved, That the whole character of the eminent and excellent man whose death we mourn, commanding, as it did, our reverence and admiration while he lived among us, will be long remembered now that he is dead, as a happy union of various and often disunited qualities; of Christian faith and philanthropic works; of liberality without laxity; of firmness without bigotry; of sympathy with the vicious and criminal in their sufferings, without undue tenderness toward vice and crime; and as furnishing in its whole development a beautiful proof of the possibility of uniting the most vigorous demands of conscience and of God, and of securing, at the same time, the love and respect of all classes and conditions of men.

Resolved, That, by the death of Dr. Gallaudet, society has lost one of its brightest ornaments; the cause of education a most able and faithful advocate; religion a shining example of daily devotion to its principles; the young a kind and judicious counselor; and the unfortunate of every class a self-denying and never wearying friend.

Resolved, That the noblest monuments of the deceased are already erected; and that his name will never be forgotten, so long as the two benevolent institutions, one of which received its existence from the labor of his early manhood, while the other enjoyed the devoted services of his later years, remain to crown the beautiful hills in the neighborhood of our city.

Resolved, That a committee of five be appointed by this meeting, to devise such measures as may seem expedient, in further tribute to the memory of Dr. Gallaudet; and to make all ·the arrangements necessary to carry these measures into effect.

The committee, consisting of Governor Seymour, B. Hudson, James H. Wells, Philip Ripley, and Dr. John S. Butler, planned a public meeting to be held in the South Congregational Church on the evening of January 7th, 1852, the chief feature of which was a eulogy by Hon. Henry Barnard, LL.D.

The meeting was largely attended, and original hymns were sung from the pens of Mrs. Lydia Huntley Sigourney, Luzerne Rae, and Dr. Gallaudet.

Mrs. Sigourney and Mr. Rae pay tribute to Dr. Gallaudet's two great labors as follows :—

We mourn his loss . .

Who strove through nature's prisoning shades
　　The hermit heart to reach,
And with philosophy divine
　　To give the silent, speech.

Who 'mid the cells of dire disease
　　In prayerful patience wrought,
And stricken and bewildered souls
　　To a Great Healer brought .

He dies, and still around his grave,
The silent sons of sorrow bend,
With tears for him they could not save,
Their guide—their father—and their friend;
And minds in ruin ask for him,
With wondering woe that he is gone;
And cheeks are pale, and eyes are dim
Among the outcast and forlorn.

The dirge had been written many years before by Dr. Gallaudet, with no thought of its
being sung in his own honor.

A paraphrase of Collins' " How Sleep the Brave."

How sleep the good ! who sink to rest,
With their Redeemer's favor blest:
When dawns the day, by seers of old,
In sacred prophecy foretold,
Then they shall burst their humble sod,
And rise to meet their Saviuor—God.

To seats of bliss by angel tongue,
With rapture is their welcome sung ;
And at their tomb when evening gray
Hallows the hour of closing day,
Shall Faith and Hope awhile repair,
To dwell with weeping Friendship there.

Dr. Barnard's eulogy was the tribute of a
loving friend, who had walked for many years
by the side of Dr. Gallaudet as a trusted
younger brother, and yet he spoke nothing

more than was in the heart of every one who heard him.

In forming, says Dr. Barnard, any just estimate or analysis of Dr. Gallaudet's character, we
must assign the first and prominent place to his religious views and habits. In his love to God and
love to man we are to find the hiding of his power
as a practical philanthropist.

The greatest service rendered by him as an educator and teacher—his highest claim to the gratitude
of all who are laboring to advance the cause of education in any grade or class of schools, is to be
found in his practical acknowledgment and able ad-
vocacy of the great fundamental truth, of the necessity of special training, even for minds of the
highest order, as a pre-requisite of success in the
art of teaching. In view of this truth, he traversed
the ocean to make himself practically acquainted
with the principles and art of instructing the deaf
and dumb; to this end, he became a normal pupil
under the great normal teacher Sicard, in the great
normal school of deaf-mute instruction in Paris.
And still distrusting his own attainments, he thought
himself peculiarly fortunate in bringing back with
him to this country a teacher of still larger experience
than himself, and of an already acquired reputation.
He was ever the earnest advocate for training, under
able master-workmen in the business of education,
all who aspired to teach the young in any grade of
.schools.-

His conversational powers were remarkable, and he never failed to interest all who came into his society. To a command of language, at once simple and felicitous, he added a stock of personal reminiscences drawn from a large acquaintance with the best society in this country and in Europe—a quick sense of the beautiful in nature, art, literature and morals, a liveliness of manner, a ready use of all that he had read or seen, and a real desire to make others happy, which made his conversation always entertaining and instructive. He was, besides, a good listener, always deferential to old and young, and could have patience even with the dull and rude. With children he was eminently successful, winning their confidence by his kind and benevolent manner, and gaining their attention by the simplicity and pertinency of his remarks. He seemed in society, as in the world, to make it a matter of principle " to remember the forgotten," and thus to draw the old and the retiring into the circle of the regards and attention of others.

He never spoke ill of any man, and could not listen, without exhibiting his impatience, to such speaking in others, and never without suggesting a charitable construction of motives, or the extenuating circumstances of ignorance, or the force of temptation. His sympathy and charity for the erring, whether in conduct or opinion, were peculiar.

He was emphatically the friend of the poor and the distressed. He did not muse on human misery, but sought out its victims and did something for their relief. There was a womanly tenderness in his nature, which was touched by the voice of sorrow, whether it came from the hovel of the poor, or the mansion of the rich.   His benevolence was displayed not simply in bestowing alms, although his own contributions were neither few nor small according to his means—not simply as the judicious almoner of the bounty of others—not simply by prayers earnest and appropriate in the hour of mourning—but by the *mode* and the *spirit* in which he discharged these several duties.

The least we can do to prove ourselves worthy of possessing his name and example among the moral treasures of our city and state, is to cherish the family—the objects of his tenderest solicitude and care—which he has left behind him ; and by some fit memorial to hold in fresh and everlasting remembrance his deeds of beneficence to us and our posterity forever.   The ashes of such a man, in whose character the sublimest Christian virtues ceased to be abstractions, if his memory is properly cherished, will, like the bones of the prophet, impart life to all who come in contact therewith.   The youth of our city should be led, by some memorial of our gratitude for his services, to study his life till its beauty and spirit shall pass into their own souls, and flow out afresh in their own acts of self-denying beneficence.

These pages would be unduly burdened by an attempt even to name the tributes of respect which were shown to Dr. Gallaudet's

memory in the journals of the day, by the
·institutions and societies with which he had
been connected, and by personal friends in
many lands. For a very few only, can space
be taken.

Dr. Gallaudet's associates in the management of the institution for deaf-mutes speak
thus of him in the annual report issued a few
months after his death :

The society and its representatives, the members
of this board, the subscribers to our funds, the
parents and friends of deaf-mutes, the deaf
and dumb themselves, as they came to us, indeed
the community around us and individuals in all
parts of the country, regarded him as the central
power in a movement destined to effect great
good in the world; and which did, in fact, during
the remainder of his life, continue to increase in
magnitude and usefulness. · As the institution
went forward and began to exhibit its appropriate
results, Dr. Gallaudet still occupied the central
position in its sphere of operations, and many
hearts were turned to him as in truth its animat-
ing principle, the chief source of its actual and
prospective prosperity. But when, after two or
three years, he became associated with us in a new
relation, as a member of this board, we too learned
to regard his views of education with even a
higher interest than ever before, and so have con-

tinued to look to him chiefly as the embodiment of those views which ought to influence us in. directing the instruction, the government and general internal affairs of the establishment, as well as its relations with other institutions, with legislative bodies and the cause of benevolence.

Dr. Harvey P. Peet, President of the New York Institution for the Deaf and Dumb at the time of Dr. Gallaudet's death, and who began a long life of efficient labor for the deaf at his side in the Hartford institution, speaks thus of his early preceptor's power as an instructor :

As a teacher Dr. Gallaudet was mainly distinguished for the clearness and perspicacity with which he could unfold even complex and elevated ideas in pantomime, intelligible to the youngest and dullest of his pupils. Even the particles, and grammatical inflections of language, which so much embarrass an ordinary teacher, acquired clearness and significance in his signs; and this facility led him to disregard regularity of method in introducing the difficulties of language to a greater degree than less gifted teachers would find safe. But it was in his religious lessons that his power was most manifested. First of all teachers of the deaf and dumb, he established for his pupils the regular worship of God, including prayer, praise, instruction, exhortation, in the only language which can be made intelligible to the mass of an assembly

of deaf-mutes; the only language, also, which even
with well-educated deaf-mutes, goes most directly
to the understanding, the conscience, and the heart.
And the greatest triumph of his method was the
clearness with which he could unfold, to pupils of a
few weeks' standing, the new and startling ideas of
immaterial existence, God and immortality.

A discriminating analysis of Dr Gallaudet's
character and life-work appeared in *The Christian Examiner*, of July, 1852, from the pen of
the Rev. Joseph Harrington. A brief extract
only can be taken from this tribute :

We can not but feel, if our estimate thus far of the
character of this remarkable person be true, that in
him the spirit of the two commandments on which
Christ " hung all the law and the prophets" found
a beautiful realization.

We suppose the world would withhold from the
subject of these remarks the position of a "great
man." Yet to be classed with Oberlin, and Vincent
de Paul, and Clarkson, and Howard, and Tuckerman,
is a distinction of which few, certainly, are worthy.
In that company, however, is Dr. Gallaudet's place.
In certain qualities of intellect he had no superior.
His judgment in practical affairs possessed the
accuracy of almost supernatural insight. When he
had once investigated a subject of this character,
little more remained to be discovered on the same
side. This sagacity was the result of his candor,

which enabled him to do justice to the objector's
position; of his fidelity, which permitted him to
slight no work when once before him to be done;
of his power of continuous attention, which pre-
cluded the possibility of any part of the subject,
whether in its present relations or its probable issues,
eluding his scrutiny; and of his habit of applying
to these examinations the systematized fruits of his
experience.   We regard his style in writing as almost
faultless.   It possessed the high charm of showing
itself the instrument of truth, not of him who held
the pen.   What he wrote answered its end, in arrest-
ing attention and producing conviction.

The rich and the poor mourned his departure.
All sects rendered to his mortal remains the tribute
of their grief, and to his memory they render the
tribute of their reverence.

While many voices joined to honor Dr.
Gallaudet in eloquent words, the most touching and effective tribute of respect came from
those who were without voice among their
fellow-men, but whose minds had been set
free from the bondage of ignorance by him
who was now no more.

Republics may be ungrateful; men with all
their faculties may be slow to do honor to
those by whom they have been blessed; but
not so were those whom "the finger of God
had touched."

Hardly had the remains of Dr. Gallaudet been laid in the grave before the children of silence, his grateful pupils, stirred in the matter of a permanent memorial of his philanthropy.

An association was formed with Mr. Clerc as its president. Agents were appointed in the several states of the Union to solicit subscriptions, which were to come only from deaf-mutes. An eminent deaf-mute artist of Philadelphia, Mr. Albert Newsam, prepared the design which was adopted. Another distinguished artist, Mr. John Carlin of New York, also a deaf-mute, designed a sculptured group for one of the panels.

The amount needed for the construction of the monument was raised within two years, and in September, 1854, just three years from the date of Dr. Gallaudet's death, the monument was unveiled with appropriate ceremonies, on the grounds of the institution for deaf-mutes in Hartford, in· the presence of a large concourse of citizens of Hartford, and deaf-mutes from all parts of the United States, Mr. Carlin, above referred to, being the orator of the day.

The monument, resting on a base of Quincy granite, is of marble, and a little more than twenty feet high. The die consists of four panels, one of which is the bas-relief designed by Mr. Carlin, representing Dr. Gallaudet in his school-room in the act of teaching, with three pupils around him. The likeness of the teacher is excellent. The opposite panel contains the name Gallaudet in letters of the manual alphabet, represented by sculptured hands. On the other panels are inscriptions, one giving the dates of Dr. Gallaudet's birth and death, the other being as follows:

ERECTED TO THE MEMORY OF
REV. THOMAS HOPKINS GALLAUDET, LL.D.
BY THE DEAF AND DUMB
OF THE UNITED STATES,
AS A TESTIMONIAL
OF PROFOUND GRATITUDE
TO THEIR
EARLIEST AND BEST FRIEND
AND BENEFACTOR.

On the south side of the column, surrounded by *radii*, is the Syriac word *Ephphatha*, spoken by our Saviour when he caused the dumb man to speak.

One who, though never a pupil of Dr. Gallaudet's, was one of the many who contributed to rear the monument, added a personal tribute which will interest those who

have followed this narrative thus far. It was
published in the American Annals of the
Deaf in January, 1885.

THE GALLAUDET MONUMENT.

BY MARY TOLES PEET.

Raise we the marble here,
Where many a silent tear
Has dropped unbidden from the swimming eye ;
Join here in voiceless prayer,
And through the stilly air
Let our mute orisons ascend on high.

Here for long years he trod,
Leading-our hearts to God,
A lowly, silent, and neglected band —
Here opened to our sight
The glories of that light,
Which streams from the blest star of Bethlehem.

No flaunting banners wave,
No pomp surrounds his grave,
No arch triumphal blazons forth his name ;
More fitting pile we raise
For one whose brightest days
Were given to deeds worth a far nobler fame.

Plain monumental stone!
Whereon the summer's sun
And autumn moonbeams silently will lie.
O'er thee soft gales of spring
May float with unseen wing,
And mingle here with the mute pilgrim's sigh.

And while we linger round
This consecrated ground,
Perchance, as star-beams mirrored in the wave,
His spirit lingering near,
May be reflected here,
In silent hearts, inspiring works of love.

It would be natural to suppose that the deaf-mutes of America, having thus promptly erected a permanent memorial, in the form of a monument to their benefactor, might consider their duty discharged in such a direction. This, however, has not been the case, and in a national convention of deaf-mutes held in New York city in 1884, it was urged that a national memorial, to be erected at the capital city, was due to a man whose life had blessed the people of the whole country in so many ways. It was accordingly resolved that funds should be raised to provide for a bronze statue of Dr. Gallaudet, to be placed on the grounds of the National Deaf-Mute College at Washington in the summer of 1888 — a few months after the completion of one hundred years since his birth. More than eight thousand dollars have been already secured for this object, and it is probable the statue will be unveiled at the time named.*

* A commission for the statue of Dr. Gallaudet has been given to Daniel C. French of Concord, Mass.

He whose hand has written the foregoing pages finds it difficult to bring his labor of love to a close, and especially to lay down his pen without opening his heart in that dutiful homage which filial affection for such a father would naturally call forth. But since this privilege is denied him, it is with especial pleasure that he can draw once more, as he has several times done, on the work of his father's college classmate and life-long friend, Rev. Dr. Humphrey, for fitting words with which to close this little volume.

"Whether Dr. Gallaudet should be regarded as a great man, as well as one of the most distinguished philanthropists, depends upon the question in what true greatness consists. The term admits of more than one meaning. The deepest channel is not the greatest river. There may be as much water, or more, in one that spreads itself out over a wide surface, and laves the shores of many beautiful islands, and irrigates all the meadows in its leisurely overflowings, as in the deep, impetuous torrent, that struggles and foams in the rapids, and shakes the earth with its muffled thunder as it leaps headlong over the precipice. So there may be as much talent in a man who spreads himself out over a wide surface, and cheers and refreshes suffering humanity by his personal ministrations, and puts in motion a thousand springs of benevolent enterprise, as in a man who concentrates the powers of his mind upon one object, moves on in one beaten path, and reaches any of the high pinnacles of human renown. Because he excels all his contemporaries in that one thing, the popular notion and verdict is, that he is the greatest man; when those whom he looks down upon might, perhaps, even have eclipsed him by a like concentration of their powers, but, by throwing themselves into the wide current of human sufferings to be mitigated, and human interests to be promoted, have done infinitely more good.

"We are not anxious to enroll the name of Gallaudet with those whom the world delights to honor. It would be a low ambition in his friends, and the thousands who have been blessed by his philanthropic labors, his wise counsels, and the ripe fruits of the talents and attainments which he has bequeathed to the young in his writings. In the best sense of the term he was a great man. He had talents of a high order. He could have placed himself in the first rank of living mathematicians; he could have made himself a renowned linguist; he could have taken a high rank with the best preachers of his day. In other departments of the higher calendars of human attainments, he might have distinguished himself had he chosen. But his mission was to the sons and daughters of affliction; to the deaf and the dumb; to the insane; and to the children of every class, who have been charmed, and will be charmed and instructed by his juvenile publications. If to be an eminent benefactor of the most unfortunate and neglected of his race is to be great, then was Thomas H. Gallaudet a great man. But no matter. He was a *good* man, with a great, overflowing heart. His philanthropy was no spring freshet, to be dried up in the summer, but a perennial fountain, always refreshing whenever the stream flowed. He was a good man—full of faith, abounding in charity and good works, and his record is on high."

THE END.